Anton Chekhov – An Incident & Other Short Stories

The short story is often viewed as an inferior relation to the Novel. But it is an art in itself. To take a story and distil its essence into fewer pages while keeping character and plot rounded and driven is not an easy task. Many try and many fail.

In this series we look at short stories from many of our most accomplished writers. Miniature masterpieces with a lot to say. In this volume we examine some of the short stories of Anton Chekhov.

Russian Literature is probably more known for the sheer length, scope and breadth of its novels. Chekhov was no exception to this with such masterpieces as War And Peace. But he also wrote such plays such as Uncle Vanya, The Cherry Orchard and The Seagull. But he also sits atop most literary critics as one of the greatest short story writers ever.

Born in 1860 Anton Chekhov was born on 29 January 1860, the third of six surviving children, in Taganrog, a port in the south of Russia.

Chekhov attended a school for Greek boys, followed by the Taganrog gymnasium, where he was kept down for a year at fifteen for failing a Greek exam. Despite having a religious background and education, he later on became an atheist.

In 1876, Chekhov's father was declared bankrupt after over-extending his finances building a new house. To avoid the debtor's prison he fled to Moscow, where his two eldest sons, Alexander and Nikolay, were attending university. The family lived in poverty in Moscow, Chekhov's mother physically and emotionally broken. Chekhov was left behind to sell the family possessions and finish his education.

In 1879, Chekhov completed his schooling and joined his family in Moscow, having gained admission to the medical school at Moscow University

Chekhov now assumed responsibility for the whole family. To support them and to pay his tuition fees, he wrote daily short, humorous sketches and vignettes of contemporary Russian life, many under pseudonyms. His prodigious output earned him a reputation as a satirical chronicler of Russian street life, and by 1882 he was writing for Oskolki (Fragments), owned by Nikolai Leykin, one of the leading publishers of the time.

In 1884, Chekhov qualified as a physician, which he considered his principal profession though he made little money from it and treated the poor free of charge.

In 1884 and 1885, Chekhov found himself coughing blood, and in 1886 the attacks worsened; but he would not admit tuberculosis to his family and friends

In the next twenty years his writing was to elevate him to that of a literary giant though he continued to practice medicine "Medicine is my lawful wife", he once said, "and literature is my mistress. When I get tired of one, I spend the night with the other"

One of the first to use the stream-of-consciousness technique, later adopted by the modernists, combined with a disavowal of the moral finality of traditional story structure. He made no apologies for the difficulties this posed to readers, insisting that the role of an artist was to ask questions, not to answer them.

But his health continued to deteriorate; he moved on doctors advice to a warmer climate at Yalta but yearned for Moscow and travel. Though the tuberculosis was to gradually worsen he kept working, his output prodigious but exemplary. But by May 1904, the outlook was terminal. Mikhail Chekhov recalled that "everyone who saw him secretly thought the end was not far off, but the nearer he was to the end, the less he seemed to realise it."

In 1908, Olga wrote this account of her husband's last moments: Anton sat up unusually straight and said loudly and clearly in German): Ich sterbe ("I'm dying"). The doctor calmed him, took a syringe, gave him an injection of camphor, and ordered champagne. Anton took a full glass, examined it, smiled at me and said: "It's a long time since I drank champagne." He drank it, lay quietly on his left side and died.

Chekhov's body was transported to Moscow in a refrigerated railway car for fresh oysters. Some of the thousands of mourners followed the funeral procession of a General Keller by mistake, to the accompaniment of a military band.

Chekhov was buried next to his father at the Novodevichy Cemetery.

Some of these stories are also available as an audiobook from our sister company Word Of Mouth. Many samples are at our youtube channel http://www.youtube.com/user/PortablePoetry?feature=mhee The full volume can be purchased from iTunes, Amazon and other digital stores.

Index Of Stories

THE COOK'S WEDDING
SLEEPY
CHILDREN
THE RUNAWAY
GRISHA
OYSTERS
HOME
A CLASSICAL STUDENT
VANKA
AN INCIDENT
A DAY IN THE COUNTRY
BOYS
SHROVE TUESDAY
THE OLD HOUSE
IN PASSION WEEK
WHITEBROW
KASHTANKA
A CHAMELEON
THE DEPENDENTS

WHO WAS TO BLAME?
THE BIRD MARKET
AN ADVENTURE
THE FISH
ART
THE SWEDISH MATCH
ANTON CHEKHOV – A BIOGRAPHY
GREATEST QUOTES

THE COOK'S WEDDING

GRISHA, a fat, solemn little person of seven, was standing by the kitchen door listening and peeping through the keyhole. In the kitchen something extraordinary, and in his opinion never seen before, was taking place. A big, thick-set, red-haired peasant, with a beard, and a drop of perspiration on his nose, wearing a cabman's full coat, was sitting at the kitchen table on which they chopped the meat and sliced the onions. He was balancing a saucer on the five fingers of his right hand and drinking tea out of it, and crunching sugar so loudly that it sent a shiver down Grisha's back. Aksinya Stepanovna, the old nurse, was sitting on the dirty stool facing him, and she, too, was drinking tea. Her face was grave, though at the same time it beamed with a kind of triumph. Pelageya, the cook, was busy at the stove, and was apparently trying to hide her face. And on her face Grisha saw a regular illumination: it was burning and shifting through every shade of colour, beginning with a crimson purple and ending with a deathly white. She was continually catching hold of knives, forks, bits of wood, and rags with trembling hands, moving, grumbling to herself, making a clatter, but in reality doing nothing. She did not once glance at the table at which they were drinking tea, and to the questions put to her by the nurse she gave jerky, sullen answers without turning her face.

"Help yourself, Danilo Semyonitch," the nurse urged him hospitably. "Why do you keep on with tea and nothing but tea? You should have a drop of vodka!"

And nurse put before the visitor a bottle of vodka and a wine-glass, while her face wore a very wily expression.

"I never touch it. . . . No . . ." said the cabman, declining.

"Don't press me, Aksinya Stepanovna."

"What a man! . . . A cabman and not drink! . . . A bachelor can't get on without drinking. Help yourself!"

The cabman looked askance at the bottle, then at nurse's wily face, and his own face assumed an expression no less cunning, as much as to say, "You won't catch me, you old witch!"

"I don't drink; please excuse me. Such a weakness does not do in our calling. A man who works at a trade may drink, for he sits at home, but we cabmen are always in view of the public. Aren't we? If one goes into a pothouse one finds one's horse gone; if one takes a drop too much it is worse still; before you know where you are you will fall asleep or slip off the box. That's where it is."

"And how much do you make a day, Danilo Semyonitch?"

"That's according. One day you will have a fare for three roubles, and another day you will come back to the yard without a farthing. The days are very different. Nowadays our business is no good. There are lots and lots of cabmen as you know, hay is dear, and folks are paltry nowadays and always contriving to go by tram. And yet, thank God, I have nothing to complain of. I have plenty to eat and good clothes to wear, and . . . we could even provide well for another. . ." (the cabman stole a glance at Pelageya) "if it were to their liking. . . ."

Grisha did not hear what was said further. His mamma came to the door and sent him to the nursery to learn his lessons.

"Go and learn your lesson. It's not your business to listen here!"

When Grisha reached the nursery, he put "My Own Book" in front of him, but he did not get on with his reading. All that he had just seen and heard aroused a multitude of questions in his mind.

"The cook's going to be married," he thought. "Strange—I don't understand what people get married for. Mamma was married to papa, Cousin Verotchka to Pavel Andreyitch. But one might be married to papa and Pavel Andreyitch after all: they have gold watch-chains and nice suits, their boots are always polished; but to marry that dreadful cabman with a red nose and felt boots. . . . Fi! And why is it nurse wants poor Pelageya to be married?"

When the visitor had gone out of the kitchen, Pelageya appeared and began clearing away. Her agitation still persisted. Her face was red and looked scared. She scarcely touched the floor with the broom, and swept every corner five times over. She lingered for a long time in the room where mamma was sitting. She was evidently oppressed by her isolation, and she was longing to express herself, to share her impressions with some one, to open her heart.

"He's gone," she muttered, seeing that mamma would not begin the conversation.

"One can see he is a good man," said mamma, not taking her eyes off her sewing. "Sober and steady."

"I declare I won't marry him, mistress!" Pelageya cried suddenly, flushing crimson. "I declare I won't!"

"Don't be silly; you are not a child. It's a serious step; you must think it over thoroughly, it's no use talking nonsense. Do you like him?"

"What an idea, mistress!" cried Pelageya, abashed. "They say such things that . . . my goodness. . . ."

"She should say she doesn't like him!" thought Grisha.

"What an affected creature you are. . . . Do you like him?"

"But he is old, mistress!"

"Think of something else," nurse flew out at her from the next room. "He has not reached his fortieth year; and what do you want a young man for? Handsome is as handsome does. . . . Marry him and that's all about it!"

"I swear I won't," squealed Pelageya.

"You are talking nonsense. What sort of rascal do you want? Anyone else would have bowed down to his feet, and you declare you won't marry him. You want to be always winking at the postmen and tutors. That tutor that used to come to Grishenka, mistress . . . she was never tired of making eyes at him. O-o, the shameless hussy!"

"Have you seen this Danilo before?" mamma asked Pelageya.

"How could I have seen him? I set eyes on him to-day for the first time. Aksinya picked him up and brought him along . . . the accursed devil. . . . And where has he come from for my undoing!"

At dinner, when Pelageya was handing the dishes, everyone looked into her face and teased her about the cabman. She turned fearfully red, and went off into a forced giggle.

"It must be shameful to get married," thought Grisha. "Terribly shameful."

All the dishes were too salt, and blood oozed from the half-raw chickens, and, to cap it all, plates and knives kept dropping out of Pelageya's hands during dinner, as though from a shelf that had given way; but no one said a word of blame to her, as they all understood the state of her feelings. Only once papa flicked his table-napkin angrily and said to mamma:

"What do you want to be getting them all married for? What business is it of yours? Let them get married of themselves if they want to."

After dinner, neighbouring cooks and maidservants kept flitting into the kitchen, and there was the sound of whispering till late evening. How they had scented out the matchmaking, God knows. When Grisha woke in the night he heard his nurse and the cook whispering together in the nursery. Nurse was talking persuasively, while the cook alternately sobbed and giggled. When he fell asleep after this, Grisha dreamed of Pelageya being carried off by Tchernomor and a witch.

Next day there was a calm. The life of the kitchen went on its accustomed way as though the cabman did not exist. Only from time to time nurse put on her new shawl, assumed a solemn and austere air, and went off somewhere for an hour or two, obviously to conduct negotiations. . . . Pelageya did not see the cabman, and when his name was mentioned she flushed up and cried:

"May he be thrice damned! As though I should be thinking of him! Tfoo!"

In the evening mamma went into the kitchen, while nurse and Pelageya were zealously mincing something, and said:

"You can marry him, of course—that's your business—but I must tell you, Pelageya, that he cannot live here. . . . You know I don't like to have anyone sitting in the kitchen. Mind now, remember . . . . And I can't let you sleep out."

"Goodness knows! What an idea, mistress!" shrieked the cook. "Why do you keep throwing him up at me? Plague take him! He's a regular curse, confound him! . . ."

Glancing one Sunday morning into the kitchen, Grisha was struck dumb with amazement. The kitchen was crammed full of people. Here were cooks from the whole courtyard, the porter, two policemen, a non-commissioned officer with good-conduct stripes, and the boy Filka. . . . This Filka was generally hanging about the laundry playing with the dogs; now he was combed and washed, and was holding an ikon in a tinfoil setting. Pelageya was standing in the middle of the kitchen in a new cotton dress, with a flower on her head. Beside her stood the cabman. The happy pair were red in the face and perspiring and blinking with embarrassment.

"Well . . . I fancy it is time," said the non-commissioned officer, after a prolonged silence.

Pelageya's face worked all over and she began blubbering. . . .

The soldier took a big loaf from the table, stood beside nurse, and began blessing the couple. The cabman went up to the soldier, flopped down on his knees, and gave a smacking kiss on his hand. He did the same before nurse. Pelageya followed him mechanically, and she too bowed down to the ground. At last the outer door was opened, there was a whiff of white mist, and the whole party flocked noisily out of the kitchen into the yard.

"Poor thing, poor thing," thought Grisha, hearing the sobs of the cook. "Where have they taken her? Why don't papa and mamma protect her?"

After the wedding there was singing and concertina-playing in the laundry till late evening. Mamma was cross all the evening because nurse smelt of vodka, and owing to the wedding there was no one to heat the samovar. Pelageya had not come back by the time Grisha went to bed.

"The poor thing is crying somewhere in the dark!" he thought. "While the cabman is saying to her 'shut up!'"

Next morning the cook was in the kitchen again. The cabman came in for a minute. He thanked mamma, and glancing sternly at Pelageya, said:

"Will you look after her, madam? Be a father and a mother to her. And you, too, Aksinya Stepanovna, do not forsake her, see that everything is as it should be . . . without any nonsense. . . . And also, madam, if you would kindly advance me five roubles of her wages. I have got to buy a new horse-collar."

Again a problem for Grisha: Pelageya was living in freedom, doing as she liked, and not having to account to anyone for her actions, and all at once, for no sort of reason, a stranger turns up, who has somehow acquired rights over her conduct and her property! Grisha was distressed. He longed passionately, almost to tears, to comfort this victim, as he supposed, of man's injustice. Picking out the very biggest apple in the store-room he stole into the kitchen, slipped it into Pelageya's hand, and darted headlong away.

SLEEPY

NIGHT. Varka, the little nurse, a girl of thirteen, is rocking the cradle in which the baby is lying, and humming hardly audibly:

"Hush-a-bye, my baby wee,
While I sing a song for thee."

A little green lamp is burning before the ikon; there is a string stretched from one end of the room to the other, on which baby-clothes and a pair of big black trousers are hanging. There is a big patch of green on the ceiling from the ikon lamp, and the baby-clothes and the trousers throw long shadows on the stove, on the cradle, and on Varka. . . . When the lamp begins to flicker, the green patch and the shadows come to life, and are set in motion, as though by the wind. It is stuffy. There is a smell of cabbage soup, and of the inside of a boot-shop.

The baby's crying. For a long while he has been hoarse and exhausted with crying; but he still goes on screaming, and there is no knowing when he will stop. And Varka is sleepy. Her eyes are glued together, her head droops, her neck aches. She cannot move her eyelids or her lips, and she feels as though her face is dried and wooden, as though her head has become as small as the head of a pin.

"Hush-a-bye, my baby wee," she hums, "while I cook the groats for thee. . . ."

A cricket is churring in the stove. Through the door in the next room the master and the apprentice Afanasy are snoring. . . . The cradle creaks plaintively, Varka murmurs—and it all blends into that soothing music of the night to which it is so sweet to listen, when one is lying in bed. Now that music is merely irritating and oppressive, because it goads her to sleep, and she must not sleep; if Varka—God forbid!--should fall asleep, her master and mistress would beat her.

The lamp flickers. The patch of green and the shadows are set in motion, forcing themselves on Varka's fixed, half-open eyes, and in her half slumbering brain are fashioned into misty visions. She sees dark clouds chasing one another over the sky, and screaming like the baby. But then the wind blows, the clouds are gone, and Varka sees a broad high road covered with liquid mud; along the high road stretch files of wagons, while people with wallets on their backs are trudging along and shadows flit backwards and forwards; on both sides she can see forests through the cold harsh mist. All at once the people with their wallets and their shadows fall on the ground in the liquid mud. "What is that for?" Varka asks. "To sleep, to sleep!" they answer her. And they fall sound asleep, and sleep sweetly, while crows and magpies sit on the telegraph wires, scream like the baby, and try to wake them.

"Hush-a-bye, my baby wee, and I will sing a song to thee," murmurs Varka, and now she sees herself in a dark stuffy hut.

Her dead father, Yefim Stepanov, is tossing from side to side on the floor. She does not see him, but she hears him moaning and rolling on the floor from pain. "His guts have burst," as he says; the pain is so violent that he cannot utter a single word, and can only draw in his breath and clack his teeth like the rattling of a drum:

"Boo—boo—boo—boo. . . ."

Her mother, Pelageya, has run to the master's house to say that Yefim is dying. She has been gone a long time, and ought to be back. Varka lies awake on the stove, and hears her father's "boo—boo—boo." And then she hears someone has driven up to the hut. It is a young doctor from the town, who has been sent from the big house where he is staying on a visit. The doctor comes into the hut; he cannot be seen in the darkness, but he can be heard coughing and rattling the door.

"Light a candle," he says.

"Boo—boo—boo," answers Yefim.

Pelageya rushes to the stove and begins looking for the broken pot with the matches. A minute passes in silence. The doctor, feeling in his pocket, lights a match.

"In a minute, sir, in a minute," says Pelageya. She rushes out of the hut, and soon afterwards comes back with a bit of candle.

Yefim's cheeks are rosy and his eyes are shining, and there is a peculiar keenness in his glance, as though he were seeing right through the hut and the doctor.

"Come, what is it? What are you thinking about?" says the doctor, bending down to him. "Aha! have you had this long?"

"What? Dying, your honour, my hour has come. . . . I am not to stay among the living."

"Don't talk nonsense! We will cure you!"

"That's as you please, your honour, we humbly thank you, only we understand. . . . Since death has come, there it is."

The doctor spends a quarter of an hour over Yefim, then he gets up and says:

"I can do nothing. You must go into the hospital, there they will operate on you. Go at once . . . You must go! It's rather late, they will all be asleep in the hospital, but that doesn't matter, I will give you a note. Do you hear?"

"Kind sir, but what can he go in?" says Pelageya. "We have no horse."

"Never mind. I'll ask your master, he'll let you have a horse."

The doctor goes away, the candle goes out, and again there is the sound of "boo— boo—boo." Half an hour later someone drives up to the hut. A cart has been sent to take Yefim to the hospital. He gets ready and goes. . . .

But now it is a clear bright morning. Pelageya is not at home; she has gone to the hospital to find what is being done to Yefim. Somewhere there is a baby crying, and Varka hears someone singing with her own voice:

"Hush-a-bye, my baby wee, I will sing a song to thee."

Pelageya comes back; she crosses herself and whispers:

"They put him to rights in the night, but towards morning he gave up his soul to God. . . . The Kingdom of Heaven be his and peace everlasting. . . . They say he was taken too late. . . . He ought to have gone sooner. . . ."

Varka goes out into the road and cries there, but all at once someone hits her on the back of her head so hard that her forehead knocks against a birch tree. She raises her eyes, and sees facing her, her master, the shoemaker.

"What are you about, you scabby slut?" he says. "The child is crying, and you are asleep!"

He gives her a sharp slap behind the ear, and she shakes her head, rocks the cradle, and murmurs her song. The green patch and the shadows from the trousers and the baby-clothes move up and down, nod to her, and soon take possession of her brain again. Again she sees the high road covered with liquid mud. The people with wallets on their backs and the shadows have lain down and are fast asleep. Looking at them, Varka has a passionate longing for sleep; she would lie down with enjoyment, but her mother Pelageya is walking beside her, hurrying her on. They are hastening together to the town to find situations.

"Give alms, for Christ's sake!" her mother begs of the people they meet. "Show us the Divine Mercy, kind-hearted gentlefolk!"

"Give the baby here!" a familiar voice answers. "Give the baby here!" the same voice repeats, this time harshly and angrily. "Are you asleep, you wretched girl?"

Varka jumps up, and looking round grasps what is the matter: there is no high road, no Pelageya, no people meeting them, there is only her mistress, who has come to feed the baby, and is standing in the middle of the room. While the stout, broad-shouldered woman nurses the child and soothes it, Varka stands looking at her and waiting till she has done. And outside the windows the air is already turning blue, the shadows and the green patch on the ceiling are visibly growing pale, it will soon be morning.

"Take him," says her mistress, buttoning up her chemise over her bosom; "he is crying. He must be bewitched."

Varka takes the baby, puts him in the cradle and begins rocking it again. The green patch and the shadows gradually disappear, and now there is nothing to force itself on her eyes and cloud her brain. But she is as sleepy as before, fearfully sleepy! Varka lays her head on the edge of the cradle, and rocks her whole body to overcome her sleepiness, but yet her eyes are glued together, and her head is heavy.

"Varka, heat the stove!" she hears the master's voice through the door.

So it is time to get up and set to work. Varka leaves the cradle, and runs to the shed for firewood. She is glad. When one moves and runs about, one is not so sleepy as when one is sitting down. She brings the wood, heats the stove, and feels that her wooden face is getting supple again, and that her thoughts are growing clearer.

"Varka, set the samovar!" shouts her mistress.

Varka splits a piece of wood, but has scarcely time to light the splinters and put them in the samovar, when she hears a fresh order:

"Varka, clean the master's goloshes!"

She sits down on the floor, cleans the goloshes, and thinks how nice it would be to put her head into a big deep golosh, and have a little nap in it. . . . And all at once the golosh grows, swells, fills up the whole room. Varka drops the brush, but at once shakes her head, opens her eyes wide, and tries to look at things so that they may not grow big and move before her eyes.

"Varka, wash the steps outside; I am ashamed for the customers to see them!"

Varka washes the steps, sweeps and dusts the rooms, then heats another stove and runs to the shop. There is a great deal of work: she hasn't one minute free.

But nothing is so hard as standing in the same place at the kitchen table peeling potatoes. Her head droops over the table, the potatoes dance before her eyes, the knife tumbles out of her hand while her fat, angry mistress is moving about near her with her sleeves tucked up, talking so loud that it makes a ringing in Varka's ears. It is agonising, too, to wait at dinner, to wash, to sew, there are minutes when she longs to flop on to the floor regardless of everything, and to sleep.

The day passes. Seeing the windows getting dark, Varka presses her temples that feel as though they were made of wood, and smiles, though she does not know why. The dusk of evening caresses her eyes that will hardly keep open, and promises her sound sleep soon. In the evening visitors come.

"Varka, set the samovar!" shouts her mistress. The samovar is a little one, and before the visitors have drunk all the tea they want, she has to heat it five times. After tea Varka stands for a whole hour on the same spot, looking at the visitors, and waiting for orders.

"Varka, run and buy three bottles of beer!"

She starts off, and tries to run as quickly as she can, to drive away sleep.

"Varka, fetch some vodka! Varka, where's the corkscrew? Varka, clean a herring!"

But now, at last, the visitors have gone; the lights are put out, the master and mistress go to bed.

"Varka, rock the baby!" she hears the last order.

The cricket churrs in the stove; the green patch on the ceiling and the shadows from the trousers and the baby-clothes force themselves on Varka's half-opened eyes again, wink at her and cloud her mind.

"Hush-a-bye, my baby wee," she murmurs, "and I will sing a song to thee."

And the baby screams, and is worn out with screaming. Again Varka sees the muddy high road, the people with wallets, her mother Pelageya, her father Yefim. She understands everything, she recognises everyone, but through her half sleep she cannot understand the force which binds her, hand and foot, weighs upon her, and prevents her from living. She looks round, searches for that force that she may escape from it, but she cannot find it. At last, tired to death, she does her very utmost, strains her eyes, looks up at the flickering green patch, and listening to the screaming, finds the foe who will not let her live.

That foe is the baby.

She laughs. It seems strange to her that she has failed to grasp such a simple thing before. The green patch, the shadows, and the cricket seem to laugh and wonder too.

The hallucination takes possession of Varka. She gets up from her stool, and with a broad smile on her face and wide unblinking eyes, she walks up and down the room. She feels pleased and tickled at the thought that she will be rid directly of the baby that binds her hand and foot. . . . Kill the baby and then sleep, sleep, sleep. . . .

Laughing and winking and shaking her fingers at the green patch, Varka steals up to the cradle and bends over the baby. When she has strangled him, she quickly lies down on the floor, laughs with delight that she can sleep, and in a minute is sleeping as sound as the dead.

CHILDREN

PAPA and mamma and Aunt Nadya are not at home. They have gone to a christening party at the house of that old officer who rides on a little grey horse. While waiting for them to come home, Grisha, Anya, Alyosha, Sonya, and the cook's son, Andrey, are sitting at the table in the dining-room, playing at loto. To tell the truth, it is bedtime, but how can one go to sleep without hearing from mamma what the baby was like at the christening, and what they had for supper? The table, lighted by a hanging lamp, is dotted with numbers, nutshells, scraps of paper, and little bits of glass. Two cards lie in front of each player, and a heap of bits of glass for covering the numbers. In the middle of the table is a white saucer with five kopecks in it. Beside the saucer, a half-eaten apple, a pair of scissors, and a plate on which they have been told to put their nutshells. The children are playing for money. The stake is a kopeck. The rule is: if anyone cheats, he is turned out at once. There is no one in the dining-room but the players, and nurse, Agafya Ivanovna, is in the kitchen, showing the cook how to cut a pattern, while their elder brother, Vasya, a schoolboy in the fifth class, is lying on the sofa in the drawing-room, feeling bored.

They are playing with zest. The greatest excitement is expressed on the face of Grisha. He is a small boy of nine, with a head cropped so that the bare skin shows through, chubby cheeks, and thick lips like a negro's. He is already in the preparatory class, and so is regarded as grown up, and the cleverest. He is playing entirely for the sake of the money. If there had been no kopecks in the saucer, he would have been asleep long ago. His brown eyes stray uneasily and jealously over the other players' cards. The fear that he may not win, envy, and the financial combinations of which his cropped head is full, will not let him sit still and concentrate his mind. He fidgets as though he were sitting on thorns. When he wins, he snatches up the money greedily, and instantly puts it in his pocket. His sister, Anya, a girl of eight, with a sharp chin and clever shining eyes, is also afraid that someone else may win. She flushes and turns pale, and watches the players keenly. The kopecks do not interest her. Success in the game is for her a question of vanity. The other sister, Sonya, a child of six with a curly head, and a complexion such as is seen only in very healthy children, expensive dolls, and the faces on bonbon boxes, is playing loto for the process of the game itself. There is bliss all over her face. Whoever wins, she laughs and claps her hands. Alyosha, a chubby, spherical little figure, gasps, breathes hard through his nose, and stares open-eyed at the cards. He is moved neither by covetousness nor vanity. So long as he is not driven out of the room, or sent to bed, he is thankful. He looks phlegmatic, but at heart he is rather a little beast. He is not there so much for the sake of the loto, as for the sake of the misunderstandings which are inevitable in the game. He is greatly delighted if one hits another, or calls him names. He ought to have run off somewhere long ago, but he won't leave the table for a minute, for fear they should steal his counters or his kopecks. As he can only count the units and numbers which end in nought, Anya covers his numbers for him. The fifth player, the cook's son, Andrey, a dark-skinned and sickly looking boy in a cotton shirt, with a copper cross on his breast, stands motionless, looking dreamily at the numbers. He takes no interest in winning, or in the success of the others, because he is entirely engrossed by the arithmetic of the game, and its far from complex theory;

"How many numbers there are in the world," he is thinking, "and how is it they don't get mixed up?"

They all shout out the numbers in turn, except Sonya and Alyosha. To vary the monotony, they have invented in the course of time a number of synonyms and comic nicknames. Seven, for instance, is called the "ovenrake," eleven the "sticks," seventy-seven "Semyon Semyonitch," ninety "grandfather," and so on. The game is going merrily.

"Thirty-two," cries Grisha, drawing the little yellow cylinders out of his father's cap. "Seventeen! Ovenrake! Twenty-eight! Lay them straight. . . ."

Anya sees that Andrey has let twenty-eight slip. At any other time she would have pointed it out to him, but now when her vanity lies in the saucer with the kopecks, she is triumphant.

"Twenty-three!" Grisha goes on, "Semyon Semyonitch! Nine!"

"A beetle, a beetle," cries Sonya, pointing to a beetle running across the table. "Aie!"

"Don't kill it," says Alyosha, in his deep bass, "perhaps it's got children . . . ."

Sonya follows the black beetle with her eyes and wonders about its children: what tiny little beetles they must be!

"Forty-three! One!" Grisha goes on, unhappy at the thought that Anya has already made two fours. "Six!"

"Game! I have got the game!" cries Sonya, rolling her eyes coquettishly and giggling.

The players' countenances lengthen.

"Must make sure!" says Grisha, looking with hatred at Sonya.

Exercising his rights as a big boy, and the cleverest, Grisha takes upon himself to decide. What he wants, that they do. Sonya's reckoning is slowly and carefully verified, and to the great regret of her fellow players, it appears that she has not cheated. Another game is begun.

"I did see something yesterday!" says Anya, as though to herself. "Filipp Filippitch turned his eyelids inside out somehow and his eyes looked red and dreadful, like an evil spirit's."

"I saw it too," says Grisha. "Eight! And a boy at our school can move his ears. Twenty-seven!"

Andrey looks up at Grisha, meditates, and says:

"I can move my ears too. . . ."

"Well then, move them."

Andrey moves his eyes, his lips, and his fingers, and fancies that his ears are moving too. Everyone laughs.

"He is a horrid man, that Filipp Filippitch," sighs Sonya. "He came into our nursery yesterday, and I had nothing on but my chemise . . . And I felt so improper!"

"Game!" Grisha cries suddenly, snatching the money from the saucer.

"I've got the game! You can look and see if you like."

The cook's son looks up and turns pale.

"Then I can't go on playing any more," he whispers.

"Why not?"

"Because . . . because I have got no more money."

"You can't play without money," says Grisha.

Andrey ransacks his pockets once more to make sure. Finding nothing in them but crumbs and a bitten pencil, he drops the corners of his mouth and begins blinking miserably. He is on the point of crying. . . .

"I'll put it down for you!" says Sonya, unable to endure his look of agony. "Only mind you must pay me back afterwards."

The money is brought and the game goes on.

"I believe they are ringing somewhere," says Anya, opening her eyes wide.

They all leave off playing and gaze open-mouthed at the dark window.

The reflection of the lamp glimmers in the darkness.

"It was your fancy."

"At night they only ring in the cemetery," says Andrey.

"And what do they ring there for?"

"To prevent robbers from breaking into the church. They are afraid of the bells."

"And what do robbers break into the church for?" asks Sonya.

"Everyone knows what for: to kill the watchmen."

A minute passes in silence. They all look at one another, shudder, and go on playing. This time Andrey wins.

"He has cheated," Alyosha booms out, apropos of nothing.

"What a lie, I haven't cheated."

Andrey turns pale, his mouth works, and he gives Alyosha a slap on the head! Alyosha glares angrily, jumps up, and with one knee on the table, slaps Andrey on the cheek! Each gives the other a second blow, and both howl. Sonya, feeling such horrors too much for her, begins crying too, and the dining-room resounds with lamentations on various notes. But do not imagine that that is the end of the game. Before five minutes are over, the children are laughing and talking peaceably again. Their faces are tear-stained, but that does not prevent them from smiling; Alyosha is positively blissful, there has been a squabble!

Vasya, the fifth form schoolboy, walks into the dining-room. He looks sleepy and disillusioned.

"This is revolting!" he thinks, seeing Grisha feel in his pockets in which the kopecks are jingling. "How can they give children money? And how can they let them play games of chance? A nice way to bring them up, I must say! It's revolting!"

But the children's play is so tempting that he feels an inclination to join them and to try his luck.

"Wait a minute and I'll sit down to a game," he says.

"Put down a kopeck!"

"In a minute," he says, fumbling in his pockets. "I haven't a kopeck, but here is a rouble. I'll stake a rouble."

"No, no, no. . . . You must put down a kopeck."

"You stupids. A rouble is worth more than a kopeck anyway," the schoolboy explains. "Whoever wins can give me change."

"No, please! Go away!"

The fifth form schoolboy shrugs his shoulders, and goes into the kitchen to get change from the servants. It appears there is not a single kopeck in the kitchen.

"In that case, you give me change," he urges Grisha, coming back from the kitchen. "I'll pay you for the change. Won't you? Come, give me ten kopecks for a rouble."

Grisha looks suspiciously at Vasya, wondering whether it isn't some trick, a swindle.

"I won't," he says, holding his pockets.

Vasya begins to get cross, and abuses them, calling them idiots and blockheads.

"I'll put down a stake for you, Vasya!" says Sonya. "Sit down." He sits down and lays two cards before him. Anya begins counting the numbers.

"I've dropped a kopeck!" Grisha announces suddenly, in an agitated voice. "Wait!"

He takes the lamp, and creeps under the table to look for the kopeck. They clutch at nutshells and all sorts of nastiness, knock their heads together, but do not find the kopeck. They begin looking again, and look till Vasya takes the lamp out of Grisha's hands and puts it in its place. Grisha goes on looking in the dark. But at last the kopeck is found. The players sit down at the table and mean to go on playing.

"Sonya is asleep!" Alyosha announces.

Sonya, with her curly head lying on her arms, is in a sweet, sound, tranquil sleep, as though she had been asleep for an hour. She has fallen asleep by accident, while the others were looking for the kopeck.

"Come along, lie on mamma's bed!" says Anya, leading her away from the table. "Come along!"

They all troop out with her, and five minutes later mamma's bed presents a curious spectacle. Sonya is asleep. Alyosha is snoring beside her. With their heads to the others' feet, sleep Grisha and Anya. The cook's son, Andrey too, has managed to snuggle in beside them. Near them lie the kopecks, that have lost their power till the next game. Good-night!

THE RUNAWAY

IT had been a long business. At first Pashka had walked with his mother in the rain, at one time across a mown field, then by forest paths, where the yellow leaves stuck to his boots; he had walked until it was daylight. Then he had stood for two hours in the dark passage, waiting for the door to open. It was not so cold and damp in the passage as in the yard, but with the high wind spurts of rain flew in even there. When the passage gradually became packed with people Pashka, squeezed among them, leaned his face against somebody's sheepskin which smelt strongly of salt fish, and sank into a doze. But at last the bolt clicked, the door flew open, and Pashka and his mother went into the waiting-room. All the patients sat on benches without stirring or speaking. Pashka looked round at them, and he too was silent, though he was seeing a great deal that was strange and funny. Only once, when a lad came into the waiting-room hopping on one leg, Pashka longed to hop too; he nudged his mother's elbow, giggled in his sleeve, and said: "Look, mammy, a sparrow."

"Hush, child, hush!" said his mother.

A sleepy-looking hospital assistant appeared at the little window.

"Come and be registered!" he boomed out.

All of them, including the funny lad who hopped, filed up to the window. The assistant asked each one his name, and his father's name, where he lived, how long he had been ill, and so on. From his mother's answers, Pashka learned that his name was not Pashka, but Pavel Galaktionov, that he was seven years old, that he could not read or write, and that he had been ill ever since Easter.

Soon after the registration, he had to stand up for a little while; the doctor in a white apron, with a towel round his waist, walked across the waiting-room. As he passed by the boy who hopped, he shrugged his shoulders, and said in a sing-song tenor:

"Well, you are an idiot! Aren't you an idiot? I told you to come on Monday, and you come on Friday. It's nothing to me if you don't come at all, but you know, you idiot, your leg will be done for!"

The lad made a pitiful face, as though he were going to beg for alms, blinked, and said:

"Kindly do something for me, Ivan Mikolaitch!"

"It's no use saying 'Ivan Mikolaitch,'" the doctor mimicked him. "You were told to come on Monday, and you ought to obey. You are an idiot, and that is all about it."

The doctor began seeing the patients. He sat in his little room, and called up the patients in turn. Sounds were continually coming from the little room, piercing wails, a child's crying, or the doctor's angry words:

"Come, why are you bawling? Am I murdering you, or what? Sit quiet!"

Pashka's turn came.

"Pavel Galaktionov!" shouted the doctor.

His mother was aghast, as though she had not expected this summons, and taking Pashka by the hand, she led him into the room.

The doctor was sitting at the table, mechanically tapping on a thick book with a little hammer.

"What's wrong?" he asked, without looking at them.

"The little lad has an ulcer on his elbow, sir," answered his mother, and her face assumed an expression as though she really were terribly grieved at Pashka's ulcer.

"Undress him!"

Pashka, panting, unwound the kerchief from his neck, then wiped his nose on his sleeve, and began deliberately pulling off his sheepskin.

"Woman, you have not come here on a visit!" said the doctor angrily.

"Why are you dawdling? You are not the only one here."

Pashka hurriedly flung the sheepskin on the floor, and with his mother's help took off his shirt. . . The doctor looked at him lazily, and patted him on his bare stomach.

"You have grown quite a respectable corporation, brother Pashka," he said, and heaved a sigh. "Come, show me your elbow."

Pashka looked sideways at the basin full of bloodstained slops, looked at the doctor's apron, and began to cry.

"May-ay!" the doctor mimicked him. "Nearly old enough to be married, spoilt boy, and here he is blubbering! For shame!"

Pashka, trying not to cry, looked at his mother, and in that look could be read the entreaty: "Don't tell them at home that I cried at the hospital."

The doctor examined his elbow, pressed it, heaved a sigh, clicked with his lips, then pressed it again.

"You ought to be beaten, woman, but there is no one to do it," he said. "Why didn't you bring him before? Why, the whole arm is done for. Look, foolish woman. You see, the joint is diseased!"

"You know best, kind sir . . ." sighed the woman.

"Kind sir. . . . She's let the boy's arm rot, and now it is 'kind sir.' What kind of workman will he be without an arm? You'll be nursing him and looking after him for ages. I bet if you had had a pimple on your nose, you'd have run to the hospital quick enough, but you have left your boy to rot for six months. You are all like that."

The doctor lighted a cigarette. While the cigarette smoked, he scolded the woman, and shook his head in time to the song he was humming inwardly, while he thought of something else. Pashka stood naked before him, listening and looking at the smoke. When the cigarette went out, the doctor started, and said in a lower tone:

"Well, listen, woman. You can do nothing with ointments and drops in this case. You must leave him in the hospital."

"If necessary, sir, why not?"

"We must operate on him. You stop with me, Pashka," said the doctor, slapping Pashka on the shoulder. "Let mother go home, and you and I will stop here, old man. It's nice with me, old boy, it's first-rate here. I'll tell you what we'll do, Pashka, we will go catching finches together. I will show you a fox! We will go visiting together! Shall we? And mother will come for you tomorrow! Eh?"

Pashka looked inquiringly at his mother.

"You stay, child!" she said.

"He'll stay, he'll stay!" cried the doctor gleefully. "And there is no need to discuss it. I'll show him a live fox! We will go to the fair together to buy candy! Marya Denisovna, take him upstairs!"

The doctor, apparently a light-hearted and friendly fellow, seemed glad to have company; Pashka wanted to oblige him, especially as he had never in his life been to a fair, and would have been glad to have a look at a live fox, but how could he do without his mother?

After a little reflection he decided to ask the doctor to let his mother stay in the hospital too, but before he had time to open his mouth the lady assistant was already taking him upstairs. He walked up and looked about him with his mouth open. The staircase, the floors, and the doorposts—everything huge, straight, and bright-were painted a splendid yellow colour, and had a delicious smell of Lenten oil. On all sides lamps were hanging, strips of carpet stretched along the floor, copper taps stuck out on the walls. But best of all Pashka liked the bedstead upon which he was made to sit down, and the grey woollen coverlet. He touched the pillows and the coverlet with his hands, looked round the ward, and made up his mind that it was very nice at the doctor's.

The ward was not a large one, it consisted of only three beds. One bed stood empty, the second was occupied by Pashka, and on the third sat an old man with sour eyes, who kept coughing and spitting into a mug. From Pashka's bed part of another ward could be seen with two beds; on one a very pale wasted-looking man with an india-rubber bottle on his head was asleep; on the other a peasant with his head tied up, looking very like a woman, was sitting with his arms spread out.

After making Pashka sit down, the assistant went out and came back a little later with a bundle of clothes under her arm.

"These are for you," she said, "put them on."

Pashka undressed and, not without satisfaction began attiring himself in his new array. When he had put on the shirt, the drawers, and the little grey dressing-gown, he looked at himself complacently, and thought that it would not be bad to walk through the village in that costume. His imagination pictured his mother's sending him to the kitchen garden by the river to gather cabbage leaves for the little pig; he saw himself walking along, while the boys and girls surrounded him and looked with envy at his little dressing-gown.

A nurse came into the ward, bringing two tin bowls, two spoons, and two pieces of bread. One bowl she set before the old man, the other before Pashka.

"Eat!" she said.

Looking into his bowl, Pashka saw some rich cabbage soup, and in the soup a piece of meat, and thought again that it was very nice at the doctor's, and that the doctor was not nearly so cross as he had seemed at first. He spent a long time swallowing the soup, licking the spoon after each mouthful, then when there was nothing left in the bowl but the meat he stole a look at the old man, and felt envious that he was still eating the soup. With a sigh Pashka attacked the meat, trying to make it last as long as possible, but his efforts were fruitless; the meat, too, quickly vanished. There was nothing left but the piece of bread. Plain bread without anything on it was not appetising, but there was no help for it. Pashka thought a little, and ate the bread. At that moment the nurse came in with another bowl. This time there was roast meat with potatoes in the bowl.

"And where is the bread?" asked the nurse.

Instead of answering, Pashka puffed out his cheeks, and blew out the air.

"Why did you gobble it all up?" said the nurse reproachfully. "What are you going to eat your meat with?"

She went and fetched another piece of bread. Pashka had never eaten roast meat in his life, and trying it now found it very nice. It vanished quickly, and then he had a piece of bread left bigger than the first. When the old man had finished his dinner, he put away the remains of his bread in a little table. Pashka meant to do the same, but on second thoughts ate his piece.

When he had finished he went for a walk. In the next ward, besides the two he had seen from the door, there were four other people. Of these only one drew his attention. This was a tall, extremely emaciated peasant with a morose-looking, hairy face. He was sitting on the bed, nodding his head and swinging his right arm all the time like a pendulum. Pashka could not take his eyes off him for a long time. At first the man's regular pendulum-like movements seemed to him curious, and he thought they were done for the general amusement, but when he looked into the man's face he felt frightened, and realised that he was terribly ill. Going into a third ward he saw two peasants with dark red faces as though they were smeared with clay. They were sitting motionless on their beds, and with their strange faces, in which it was hard to distinguish their features, they looked like heathen idols.

"Auntie, why do they look like that?" Pashka asked the nurse.

"They have got smallpox, little lad."

Going back to his own ward, Pashka sat down on his bed and began waiting for the doctor to come and take him to catch finches, or to go to the fair. But the doctor did not come. He got a passing glimpse of a hospital assistant at the door of the next ward. He bent over the patient on whose head lay a bag of ice, and cried:

"Mihailo!"

But the sleeping man did not stir. The assistant made a gesture and went away. Pashka scrutinised the old man, his next neighbour. The old man coughed without ceasing and spat into a mug. His cough had a long-drawn-out, creaking sound.

Pashka liked one peculiarity about him; when he drew the air in as he coughed, something in his chest whistled and sang on different notes.

"Grandfather, what is it whistles in you?" Pashka asked.

The old man made no answer. Pashka waited a little and asked:

"Grandfather, where is the fox?"

"What fox?"

"The live one."

"Where should it be? In the forest!"

A long time passed, but the doctor still did not appear. The nurse brought in tea, and scolded Pashka for not having saved any bread for his tea; the assistant came once more and set to work to wake Mihailo. It turned blue outside the windows, the wards were lighted up, but the doctor did not appear. It was too late now to go to the fair and catch finches; Pashka stretched himself on his bed and began thinking. He remembered the candy promised him by the doctor, the face and voice of his mother, the darkness in his hut at home, the stove, peevish granny Yegorovna . . . and he suddenly felt sad and dreary. He remembered that his mother was coming for him next day, smiled, and shut his eyes.

He was awakened by a rustling. In the next ward someone was stepping about and speaking in a whisper. Three figures were moving about Mihailo's bed in the dim light of the night-light and the ikon lamp.

"Shall we take him, bed and all, or without?" asked one of them.

"Without. You won't get through the door with the bed."

"He's died at the wrong time, the Kingdom of Heaven be his!"

One took Mihailo by his shoulders, another by his legs and lifted him up: Mihailo's arms and the skirt of his dressing-gown hung limply to the ground. A third—it was the peasant who looked like a woman—crossed himself, and all three tramping clumsily with their feet and stepping on Mihailo's skirts, went out of the ward.

There came the whistle and humming on different notes from the chest of the old man who was asleep. Pashka listened, peeped at the dark windows, and jumped out of bed in terror.

"Ma-a-mka!" he moaned in a deep bass.

And without waiting for an answer, he rushed into the next ward. There the darkness was dimly lighted up by a night-light and the ikon lamp; the patients, upset by the death of Mihailo, were sitting on their bedsteads: their dishevelled figures, mixed up with the shadows, looked broader, taller, and seemed to be growing bigger and bigger; on the furthest bedstead in the corner, where it was darkest, there sat the peasant moving his head and his hand.

Pashka, without noticing the doors, rushed into the smallpox ward, from there into the corridor, from the corridor he flew into a big room where monsters, with long hair and the faces of old women, were lying and sitting on the beds. Running through the women's wing he found himself again in the corridor, saw the banisters of the staircase he knew already, and ran downstairs. There he recognised the waiting-room in which he had sat that morning, and began looking for the door into the open air.

The latch creaked, there was a whiff of cold wind, and Pashka, stumbling, ran out into the yard. He had only one thought—to run, to run! He did not know the way, but felt convinced that if he ran he would be sure to find himself at home with his mother. The sky was overcast, but there was a moon behind the clouds. Pashka ran from the steps straight forward, went round the barn and stumbled into some thick bushes; after stopping for a minute and thinking, he dashed back again to the hospital, ran round it, and stopped again undecided; behind the hospital there were white crosses.

"Ma-a-mka!" he cried, and dashed back.

Running by the dark sinister buildings, he saw one lighted window.

The bright red patch looked dreadful in the darkness, but Pashka, frantic with terror, not knowing where to run, turned towards it. Beside the window was a porch with steps, and a front door with a white board on it; Pashka ran up the steps, looked in at the window, and was at once possessed by intense overwhelming joy. Through the window he saw the merry affable doctor sitting at the table reading a book. Laughing with happiness, Pashka stretched out his hands to the person he knew and tried to call out, but some unseen force choked him and struck at his legs; he staggered and fell down on the steps unconscious.

When he came to himself it was daylight, and a voice he knew very well, that had promised him a fair, finches, and a fox, was saying beside him:

"Well, you are an idiot, Pashka! Aren't you an idiot? You ought to be beaten, but there's no one to do it."

GRISHA

GRISHA, a chubby little boy, born two years and eight months ago, is walking on the boulevard with his nurse. He is wearing a long, wadded pelisse, a scarf, a big cap with a fluffy pom-pom, and warm over-boots. He feels hot and stifled, and now, too, the rollicking April sunshine is beating straight in his face, and making his eyelids tingle.

The whole of his clumsy, timidly and uncertainly stepping little figure expresses the utmost bewilderment.

Hitherto Grisha has known only a rectangular world, where in one corner stands his bed, in the other nurse's trunk, in the third a chair, while in the fourth there is a little lamp burning. If one looks under the bed, one sees a doll with a broken arm and a drum; and behind nurse's trunk, there are a great many things of all sorts: cotton reels, boxes without lids, and a broken Jack-a-dandy. In that world, besides nurse and Grisha, there are often mamma and the cat. Mamma is like a doll, and puss is like papa's fur-coat, only the coat hasn't got eyes and a tail. From the world which is called the nursery a door leads to a great expanse where they have dinner and tea. There stands Grisha's chair on high legs, and on the wall hangs a clock which exists to swing its pendulum and chime. From the dining-room, one can go into a room where there are red arm-chairs. Here, there is a dark patch on the carpet, concerning which fingers are still shaken at Grisha. Beyond that room is still another, to which one is not admitted, and where one sees glimpses of papa—an extremely enigmatical person! Nurse and mamma are comprehensible: they dress Grisha, feed him, and put him to bed, but what papa exists for is unknown. There is another enigmatical person, auntie, who presented Grisha with a drum. She appears and disappears. Where does she disappear to? Grisha has more than once looked under the bed, behind the trunk, and under the sofa, but she was not there.

In this new world, where the sun hurts one's eyes, there are so many papas and mammas and aunties, that there is no knowing to whom to run. But what is stranger and more absurd than anything is the horses. Grisha gazes at their moving legs, and can make nothing of it. He looks at his nurse for her to solve the mystery, but she does not speak.

All at once he hears a fearful tramping. . . . A crowd of soldiers, with red faces and bath brooms under their arms, move in step along the boulevard straight upon him. Grisha turns cold all over with terror, and looks inquiringly at nurse to know whether it is dangerous. But nurse neither weeps nor runs away, so there is no danger. Grisha looks after the soldiers, and begins to move his feet in step with them himself.

Two big cats with long faces run after each other across the boulevard, with their tongues out, and their tails in the air. Grisha thinks that he must run too, and runs after the cats.

"Stop!" cries nurse, seizing him roughly by the shoulder. "Where are you off to? Haven't you been told not to be naughty?"

Here there is a nurse sitting holding a tray of oranges. Grisha passes by her, and, without saying anything, takes an orange.

"What are you doing that for?" cries the companion of his travels, slapping his hand and snatching away the orange. "Silly!"

Now Grisha would have liked to pick up a bit of glass that was lying at his feet and gleaming like a lamp, but he is afraid that his hand will be slapped again.

"My respects to you!" Grisha hears suddenly, almost above his ear, a loud thick voice, and he sees a tall man with bright buttons.

To his great delight, this man gives nurse his hand, stops, and begins talking to her. The brightness of the sun, the noise of the carriages, the horses, the bright buttons are all so impressively new and not dreadful, that Grisha's soul is filled with a feeling of enjoyment and he begins to laugh.

"Come along! Come along!" he cries to the man with the bright buttons, tugging at his coattails.

"Come along where?" asks the man.

"Come along!" Grisha insists.

He wants to say that it would be just as well to take with them papa, mamma, and the cat, but his tongue does not say what he wants to.

A little later, nurse turns out of the boulevard, and leads Grisha into a big courtyard where there is still snow; and the man with the bright buttons comes with them too. They carefully avoid the lumps of snow and the puddles, then, by a dark and dirty staircase, they go into a room. Here there is a great deal of smoke, there is a smell of roast meat, and a woman is standing by the stove frying cutlets. The cook and the nurse kiss each other, and sit down on the bench together with the man, and begin talking in a low voice. Grisha, wrapped up as he is, feels insufferably hot and stifled.

"Why is this?" he wonders, looking about him.

He sees the dark ceiling, the oven fork with two horns, the stove which looks like a great black hole.

"Mam-ma," he drawls.

"Come, come, come!" cries the nurse. "Wait a bit!"

The cook puts a bottle on the table, two wine-glasses, and a pie. The two women and the man with the bright buttons clink glasses and empty them several times, and, the man puts his arm round first the cook and then the nurse. And then all three begin singing in an undertone.

Grisha stretches out his hand towards the pie, and they give him a piece of it. He eats it and watches nurse drinking. . . . He wants to drink too.

"Give me some, nurse!" he begs.

The cook gives him a sip out of her glass. He rolls his eyes, blinks, coughs, and waves his hands for a long time afterwards, while the cook looks at him and laughs.

When he gets home Grisha begins to tell mamma, the walls, and the bed where he has been, and what he has seen. He talks not so much with his tongue, as with his face and his hands. He shows how the sun shines, how the horses run, how the terrible stove looks, and how the cook drinks. . . .

In the evening he cannot get to sleep. The soldiers with the brooms, the big cats, the horses, the bit of glass, the tray of oranges, the bright buttons, all gathered together, weigh on his brain. He tosses from side to side, babbles, and, at last, unable to endure his excitement, begins crying.

"You are feverish," says mamma, putting her open hand on his forehead.

"What can have caused it?

"Stove!" wails Grisha. "Go away, stove!"

"He must have eaten too much . . ." mamma decides.

And Grisha, shattered by the impressions of the new life he has just experienced, receives a spoonful of castor-oil from mamma.

OYSTERS

I NEED no great effort of memory to recall, in every detail, the rainy autumn evening when I stood with my father in one of the more frequented streets of Moscow, and felt that I was gradually being overcome by a strange illness. I had no pain at all, but my legs were giving way under me, the words stuck in my throat, my head slipped weakly on one side . . . It seemed as though, in a moment, I must fall down and lose consciousness.

If I had been taken into a hospital at that minute, the doctors would have had to write over my bed: *Fames*, a disease which is not in the manuals of medicine.

Beside me on the pavement stood my father in a shabby summer overcoat and a serge cap, from which a bit of white wadding was sticking out. On his feet he had big heavy goloshes. Afraid, vain man, that people would see that his feet were bare under his goloshes, he had drawn the tops of some old boots up round the calves of his legs.

This poor, foolish, queer creature, whom I loved the more warmly the more ragged and dirty his smart summer overcoat became, had come to Moscow, five months before, to look for a job as copying-clerk. For those five months he had been trudging about Moscow looking for work, and it was only on that day that he had brought himself to go into the street to beg for alms.

Before us was a big house of three storeys, adorned with a blue signboard with the word "Restaurant" on it. My head was drooping feebly backwards and on one side, and I could not help looking upwards at the lighted windows of the restaurant. Human figures were flitting about at the windows. I could see the right side of the orchestrion, two oleographs, hanging lamps . . . . Staring into one window, I saw a patch of white. The patch was motionless, and its rectangular outlines stood out sharply against the dark, brown background. I looked intently and made out of the patch a white placard on the wall. Something was written on it, but what it was, I could not see. . .

For half an hour I kept my eyes on the placard. Its white attracted my eyes, and, as it were, hypnotised my brain. I tried to read it, but my efforts were in vain.

At last the strange disease got the upper hand.

The rumble of the carriages began to seem like thunder, in the stench of the street I distinguished a thousand smells. The restaurant lights and the lamps dazzled my eyes like lightning. My five senses were overstrained and sensitive beyond the normal. I began to see what I had not seen before.

"Oysters . . ." I made out on the placard.

A strange word! I had lived in the world eight years and three months, but had never come across that word. What did it mean? Surely it was not the name of the restaurant-keeper? But signboards with names on them always hang outside, not on the walls indoors!

"Papa, what does 'oysters' mean?" I asked in a husky voice, making an effort to turn my face towards my father.

My father did not hear. He was keeping a watch on the movements of the crowd, and following every passer-by with his eyes. . . . From his eyes I saw that he wanted to say something to the passers-by, but the fatal word hung like a heavy weight on his trembling lips and could not be flung off. He even took a step after one passer-by and touched him on the sleeve, but when he turned round, he said, "I beg your pardon," was overcome with confusion, and staggered back.

"Papa, what does 'oysters' mean?" I repeated.

"It is an animal . . . that lives in the sea."

I instantly pictured to myself this unknown marine animal. . . . I thought it must be something midway between a fish and a crab. As it was from the sea they made of it, of course, a very nice hot fish soup with savoury pepper and laurel leaves, or broth with vinegar and fricassee of fish and cabbage, or crayfish sauce, or served it cold with horse-radish. . . . I vividly imagined it being brought from the market, quickly cleaned, quickly put in the pot, quickly, quickly, for everyone was hungry . . . awfully hungry! From the kitchen rose the smell of hot fish and crayfish soup.

I felt that this smell was tickling my palate and nostrils, that it was gradually taking possession of my whole body. . . . The restaurant, my father, the white placard, my sleeves were all smelling of it, smelling so strongly that I began to chew. I moved my jaws and swallowed as though I really had a piece of this marine animal in my mouth.

My legs gave way from the blissful sensation I was feeling, and I clutched at my father's arm to keep myself from falling, and leant against his wet summer overcoat. My father was trembling and shivering. He was cold . . .

"Papa, are oysters a Lenten dish?" I asked.

"They are eaten alive . . ." said my father. "They are in shells like tortoises, but . . . in two halves."

The delicious smell instantly left off affecting me, and the illusion vanished. . . . Now I understood it all!

"How nasty," I whispered, "how nasty!"

So that's what "oysters" meant! I imagined to myself a creature like a frog. A frog sitting in a shell, peeping out from it with big, glittering eyes, and moving its revolting jaws. I imagined this creature in a shell with claws, glittering eyes, and a slimy skin, being brought from the market. . . . The children would all hide while the cook, frowning with an air of disgust, would take the creature by its claw, put it on a plate, and carry it into the dining-room. The grown-ups would take it and eat it, eat it alive with its eyes, its teeth, its legs! While it squeaked and tried to bite their lips. . . .

I frowned, but . . . but why did my teeth move as though I were munching? The creature was loathsome, disgusting, terrible, but I ate it, ate it greedily, afraid of distinguishing its taste or smell. As soon as I had eaten one, I saw the glittering eyes of a second, a third . . . I ate them too. . . . At last I ate the table-napkin, the plate, my father's goloshes, the white placard . . . I ate everything that caught my eye, because I felt that nothing but eating would take away my illness. The oysters had a terrible look in their eyes and were loathsome. I shuddered at the thought of them, but I wanted to eat! To eat!

"Oysters! Give me some oysters!" was the cry that broke from me and I stretched out my hand.

"Help us, gentlemen!" I heard at that moment my father say, in a hollow and shaking voice. "I am ashamed to ask but—my God!--I can bear no more!"

"Oysters!" I cried, pulling my father by the skirts of his coat.

"Do you mean to say you eat oysters? A little chap like you!" I heard laughter close to me.

Two gentlemen in top hats were standing before us, looking into my face and laughing.

"Do you really eat oysters, youngster? That's interesting! How do you eat them?"

I remember that a strong hand dragged me into the lighted restaurant. A minute later there was a crowd round me, watching me with curiosity and amusement. I sat at a table and ate something slimy, salt with a flavour of dampness and mouldiness. I ate greedily without chewing, without looking and trying to discover what I was eating. I fancied that if I opened my eyes I should see glittering eyes, claws, and sharp teeth.

All at once I began biting something hard, there was a sound of a scrunching.

"Ha, ha! He is eating the shells," laughed the crowd. "Little silly, do you suppose you can eat that?"

After that I remember a terrible thirst. I was lying in my bed, and could not sleep for heartburn and the strange taste in my parched mouth. My father was walking up and down, gesticulating with his hands.

"I believe I have caught cold," he was muttering. "I've a feeling in my head as though someone were sitting on it. . . . Perhaps it is because I have not . . . er . . . eaten anything to-day. . . . I really am a queer, stupid creature. . . . I saw those gentlemen pay ten roubles for the oysters. Why didn't I go up to them and ask them . . . to lend me something? They would have given something."

Towards morning, I fell asleep and dreamt of a frog sitting in a shell, moving its eyes. At midday I was awakened by thirst, and looked for my father: he was still walking up and down and gesticulating.

HOME

"SOMEONE came from the Grigoryevs' to fetch a book, but I said you were not at home. The postman brought the newspaper and two letters. By the way, Yevgeny Petrovitch, I should like to ask you to speak to Seryozha. To-day, and the day before yesterday, I have noticed that he is smoking. When I began to expostulate with him, he put his fingers in his ears as usual, and sang loudly to drown my voice."

Yevgeny Petrovitch Bykovsky, the prosecutor of the circuit court, who had just come back from a session and was taking off his gloves in his study, looked at the governess as she made her report, and laughed.

"Seryozha smoking . . ." he said, shrugging his shoulders. "I can picture the little cherub with a cigarette in his mouth! Why, how old is he?"

"Seven. You think it is not important, but at his age smoking is a bad and pernicious habit, and bad habits ought to be eradicated in the beginning."

"Perfectly true. And where does he get the tobacco?"

"He takes it from the drawer in your table."

"Yes? In that case, send him to me."

When the governess had gone out, Bykovsky sat down in an arm-chair before his writing-table, shut his eyes, and fell to thinking. He pictured his Seryozha with a huge cigar, a yard long, in the midst of clouds of tobacco smoke, and this caricature made him smile; at the same time, the grave, troubled face of the governess called up memories of the long past, half-forgotten time when smoking aroused in his teachers and parents a strange, not quite intelligible horror. It really was horror. Children were mercilessly flogged and expelled from school, and their lives were made a misery on account of smoking, though not a single teacher or father knew exactly what was the harm or sinfulness of smoking. Even very intelligent people did not scruple to wage war on a vice which they did not understand. Yevgeny Petrovitch remembered the head-master of the high school, a very cultured and good-natured old man, who was so appalled when he found a high-school boy with a cigarette in his mouth that he turned pale, immediately summoned an emergency committee of the teachers, and sentenced the sinner to expulsion. This was probably a law of social life: the less an evil was understood, the more fiercely and coarsely it was attacked.

The prosecutor remembered two or three boys who had been expelled and their subsequent life, and could not help thinking that very often the punishment did a great deal more harm than the crime itself. The living organism has the power of rapidly adapting itself, growing accustomed and inured to any atmosphere whatever, otherwise man would be bound to feel at every moment what an irrational basis there often is underlying his rational activity, and how little of established truth and certainty there is even in work so responsible and so terrible in its effects as that of the teacher, of the lawyer, of the writer. . . .

And such light and discursive thoughts as visit the brain only when it is weary and resting began straying through Yevgeny Petrovitch's head; there is no telling whence and why they come, they do not remain long in the mind, but seem to glide over its surface without sinking deeply into it. For people who are forced for whole hours, and even days, to think by routine in one direction, such free private thinking affords a kind of comfort, an agreeable solace.

It was between eight and nine o'clock in the evening. Overhead, on the second storey, someone was walking up and down, and on the floor above that four hands were playing scales. The pacing of the man overhead who, to judge from his nervous step, was thinking of something harassing, or was suffering from toothache, and the monotonous scales gave the stillness of the evening a drowsiness that disposed to lazy reveries. In the nursery, two rooms away, the governess and Seryozha were talking.

"Pa-pa has come!" carolled the child. "Papa has co-ome. Pa! Pa!

Pa!"

"Votre pere vous appelle, allez vite!" cried the governess, shrill as a frightened bird. "I am speaking to you!"

"What am I to say to him, though?" Yevgeny Petrovitch wondered.

But before he had time to think of anything whatever his son Seryozha, a boy of seven, walked into the study.

He was a child whose sex could only have been guessed from his dress: weakly, white-faced, and fragile. He was limp like a hot-house plant, and everything about him seemed extraordinarily soft and tender: his movements, his curly hair, the look in his eyes, his velvet jacket.

"Good evening, papa!" he said, in a soft voice, clambering on to his father's knee and giving him a rapid kiss on his neck. "Did you send for me?"

"Excuse me, Sergey Yevgenitch," answered the prosecutor, removing him from his knee. "Before kissing we must have a talk, and a serious talk . . . I am angry with you, and don't love you any more. I tell you, my boy, I don't love you, and you are no son of mine. . . ."

Seryozha looked intently at his father, then shifted his eyes to the table, and shrugged his shoulders.

"What have I done to you?" he asked in perplexity, blinking. "I haven't been in your study all day, and I haven't touched anything."

"Natalya Semyonovna has just been complaining to me that you have been smoking. . . . Is it true? Have you been smoking?"

"Yes, I did smoke once. . . . That's true. . . ."

"Now you see you are lying as well," said the prosecutor, frowning to disguise a smile. "Natalya Semyonovna has seen you smoking twice. So you see you have been detected in three misdeeds: smoking, taking someone else's tobacco, and lying. Three faults."

"Oh yes," Seryozha recollected, and his eyes smiled. "That's true, that's true; I smoked twice: to-day and before."

"So you see it was not once, but twice. . . . I am very, very much displeased with you! You used to be a good boy, but now I see you are spoilt and have become a bad one."

Yevgeny Petrovitch smoothed down Seryozha's collar and thought:

"What more am I to say to him!"

"Yes, it's not right," he continued. "I did not expect it of you. In the first place, you ought not to take tobacco that does not belong to you. Every person has only the right to make use of his own property; if he takes anyone else's . . . he is a bad man!" ("I am not saying the right thing!" thought Yevgeny Petrovitch.) "For instance, Natalya Semyonovna has a box with her clothes in it. That's her box, and we—that is, you and I—dare not touch it, as it is not ours. That's right, isn't it? You've got toy horses and pictures. . . . I don't take them, do I? Perhaps I might like to take them, but . . . they are not mine, but yours!"

"Take them if you like!" said Seryozha, raising his eyebrows. "Please don't hesitate, papa, take them! That yellow dog on your table is mine, but I don't mind. . . . Let it stay."

"You don't understand me," said Bykovsky. "You have given me the dog, it is mine now and I can do what I like with it; but I didn't give you the tobacco! The tobacco is mine." ("I am not explaining properly!" thought the prosecutor. "It's wrong! Quite wrong!") "If I want to smoke someone else's tobacco, I must first of all ask his permission. . . ."

Languidly linking one phrase on to another and imitating the language of the nursery, Bykovsky tried to explain to his son the meaning of property. Seryozha gazed at his chest and listened attentively (he liked talking to his father in the evening), then he leaned his elbow on the edge of the table and began screwing up his short-sighted eyes at the papers and the inkstand. His eyes strayed over the table and rested on the gum-bottle.

"Papa, what is gum made of?" he asked suddenly, putting the bottle to his eyes.

Bykovsky took the bottle out of his hands and set it in its place and went on:

"Secondly, you smoke. . . . That's very bad. Though I smoke it does not follow that you may. I smoke and know that it is stupid, I blame myself and don't like myself for it." ("A clever teacher, I am!" he thought.) "Tobacco is very bad for the health, and anyone who smokes dies earlier than he should. It's particularly bad for boys like you to smoke. Your chest is weak, you haven't reached your full strength yet, and smoking leads to consumption and other illness in weak people. Uncle Ignat died of consumption, you know. If he hadn't smoked, perhaps he would have lived till now."

Seryozha looked pensively at the lamp, touched the lamp-shade with his finger, and heaved a sigh.

"Uncle Ignat played the violin splendidly!" he said. "His violin is at the Grigoryevs' now."

Seryozha leaned his elbows on the edge of the table again, and sank into thought. His white face wore a fixed expression, as though he were listening or following a train of thought of his own; distress and something like fear came into his big staring eyes. He was most likely thinking now of death, which had so lately carried off his mother and Uncle Ignat. Death carries mothers and uncles off to the other world, while their children and violins remain upon the earth. The dead live somewhere in the sky beside the stars, and look down from there upon the earth. Can they endure the parting?

"What am I to say to him?" thought Yevgeny Petrovitch. "He's not listening to me. Obviously he does not regard either his misdoings or my arguments as serious. How am I to drive it home?"

The prosecutor got up and walked about the study.

"Formerly, in my time, these questions were very simply settled," he reflected. "Every urchin who was caught smoking was thrashed. The cowardly and faint-hearted did actually give up smoking, any who were somewhat more plucky and intelligent, after the thrashing took to carrying tobacco in the legs of their boots, and smoking in the barn. When they were caught in the barn and thrashed again, they would go away to smoke by the river . . . and so on, till the boy grew up. My mother used to give me money and sweets not to smoke. Now that method is looked upon as worthless and immoral. The modern teacher, taking his stand on logic, tries to make the child form good principles, not from fear, nor from desire for distinction or reward, but consciously."

While he was walking about, thinking, Seryozha climbed up with his legs on a chair sideways to the table, and began drawing. That he might not spoil official paper nor touch the ink, a heap of half-sheets, cut on purpose for him, lay on the table together with a blue pencil.

"Cook was chopping up cabbage to-day and she cut her finger," he said, drawing a little house and moving his eyebrows. "She gave such a scream that we were all frightened and ran into the kitchen. Stupid thing! Natalya Semyonovna told her to dip her finger in cold water, but she sucked it . . . And how could she put a dirty finger in her mouth! That's not proper, you know, papa!"

Then he went on to describe how, while they were having dinner, a man with a hurdy-gurdy had come into the yard with a little girl, who had danced and sung to the music.

"He has his own train of thought!" thought the prosecutor. "He has a little world of his own in his head, and he has his own ideas of what is important and unimportant. To gain possession of his attention, it's not enough to imitate his language, one must also be able to think in the way he does. He would understand me perfectly if I really were sorry for the loss of the tobacco, if I felt injured and cried. . . . That's why no one can take the place of a mother in bringing up a child, because she can feel, cry, and laugh together with the child. One can do nothing by logic and morality. What more shall I say to him? What?"

And it struck Yevgeny Petrovitch as strange and absurd that he, an experienced advocate, who spent half his life in the practice of reducing people to silence, forestalling what they had to say, and punishing them, was completely at a loss and did not know what to say to the boy.

"I say, give me your word of honour that you won't smoke again," he said.

"Word of hon-nour!" carolled Seryozha, pressing hard on the pencil and bending over the drawing. "Word of hon-nour!"

"Does he know what is meant by word of honour?" Bykovsky asked himself. "No, I am a poor teacher of morality! If some schoolmaster or one of our legal fellows could peep into my brain at this moment he would call me a poor stick, and would very likely suspect me of unnecessary subtlety. . . . But in school and in court, of course, all these wretched questions are far more simply settled than at home; here one has to do with people whom one loves beyond everything, and love is exacting and complicates the question. If this boy were not my son, but my pupil, or a prisoner on his trial, I should not be so cowardly, and my thoughts would not be racing all over the place!"

Yevgeny Petrovitch sat down to the table and pulled one of Seryozha's drawings to him. In it there was a house with a crooked roof, and smoke which came out of the chimney like a flash of lightning in zigzags up to the very edge of the paper; beside the house stood a soldier with dots for eyes and a bayonet that looked like the figure 4.

"A man can't be taller than a house," said the prosecutor.

Seryozha got on his knee, and moved about for some time to get comfortably settled there.

"No, papa!" he said, looking at his drawing. "If you were to draw the soldier small you would not see his eyes."

Ought he to argue with him? From daily observation of his son the prosecutor had become convinced that children, like savages, have their own artistic standpoints and requirements peculiar to them, beyond the grasp of grown-up people. Had he been attentively observed, Seryozha might have struck a grown-up person as abnormal. He thought it possible and reasonable to draw men taller than houses, and to represent in pencil, not only objects, but even his sensations. Thus he would depict the sounds of an orchestra in the form of smoke like spherical blurs, a whistle in the form of a spiral thread. . . . To his mind sound was closely connected with form and colour, so that when he painted letters he invariably painted the letter L yellow, M red, A black, and so on.

Abandoning his drawing, Seryozha shifted about once more, got into a comfortable attitude, and busied himself with his father's beard. First he carefully smoothed it, then he parted it and began combing it into the shape of whiskers.

"Now you are like Ivan Stepanovitch," he said, "and in a minute you will be like our porter. Papa, why is it porters stand by doors? Is it to prevent thieves getting in?"

The prosecutor felt the child's breathing on his face, he was continually touching his hair with his cheek, and there was a warm soft feeling in his soul, as soft as though not only his hands but his whole soul were lying on the velvet of Seryozha's jacket.

He looked at the boy's big dark eyes, and it seemed to him as though from those wide pupils there looked out at him his mother and his wife and everything that he had ever loved.

"To think of thrashing him . . ." he mused. "A nice task to devise a punishment for him! How can we undertake to bring up the young? In old days people were simpler and thought less, and so settled problems boldly. But we think too much, we are eaten up by logic . . . . The more developed a man is, the more he reflects and gives himself up to subtleties, the more undecided and scrupulous he becomes, and the more timidity he shows in taking action. How much courage and self-confidence it needs, when one comes to look into it closely, to undertake to teach, to judge, to write a thick book. . . ."

It struck ten.

"Come, boy, it's bedtime," said the prosecutor. "Say good-night and go."

"No, papa," said Seryozha, "I will stay a little longer. Tell me something! Tell me a story. . . ."

"Very well, only after the story you must go to bed at once."

Yevgeny Petrovitch on his free evenings was in the habit of telling Seryozha stories. Like most people engaged in practical affairs, he did not know a single poem by heart, and could not remember a single fairy tale, so he had to improvise. As a rule he began with the stereotyped: "In a certain country, in a certain kingdom," then he heaped up all kinds of innocent nonsense and had no notion as he told the beginning how the story would go on, and how it would end. Scenes, characters, and situations were taken at random, impromptu, and the plot and the moral came of itself as it were, with no plan on the part of the story-teller. Seryozha was very fond of this improvisation, and the prosecutor noticed that the simpler and the less ingenious the plot, the stronger the impression it made on the child.

"Listen," he said, raising his eyes to the ceiling. "Once upon a time, in a certain country, in a certain kingdom, there lived an old, very old emperor with a long grey beard, and . . . and with great grey moustaches like this. Well, he lived in a glass palace which sparkled and glittered in the sun, like a great piece of clear ice. The palace, my boy, stood in a huge garden, in which there grew oranges, you know . . . bergamots, cherries . . . tulips, roses, and lilies-of-the-valley were in flower in it, and birds of different colours sang there. . . . Yes. . . . On the trees there hung little glass bells, and, when the wind blew, they rang so sweetly that one was never tired of hearing them. Glass gives a softer, tenderer note than metals. . . . Well, what next? There were fountains in the garden. . . . Do you remember you saw a fountain at Auntie Sonya's summer villa? Well, there were fountains just like that in the emperor's garden, only ever so much bigger, and the jets of water reached to the top of the highest poplar."

Yevgeny Petrovitch thought a moment, and went on:

"The old emperor had an only son and heir of his kingdom—a boy as little as you. He was a good boy. He was never naughty, he went to bed early, he never touched anything on the table, and altogether he was a sensible boy. He had only one fault, he used to smoke. . . ."

Seryozha listened attentively, and looked into his father's eyes without blinking. The prosecutor went on, thinking: "What next?"

He spun out a long rigmarole, and ended like this:

"The emperor's son fell ill with consumption through smoking, and died when he was twenty. His infirm and sick old father was left without anyone to help him. There was no one to govern the kingdom and defend the palace. Enemies came, killed the old man, and destroyed the palace, and now there are neither cherries, nor birds, nor little bells in the garden. . . . That's what happened."

This ending struck Yevgeny Petrovitch as absurd and naive, but the whole story made an intense impression on Seryozha. Again his eyes were clouded by mournfulness and something like fear; for a minute he looked pensively at the dark window, shuddered, and said, in a sinking voice:

"I am not going to smoke any more. . . ."

When he had said good-night and gone away his father walked up and down the room and smiled to himself.

"They would tell me it was the influence of beauty, artistic form," he meditated. "It may be so, but that's no comfort. It's not the right way, all the same. . . . Why must morality and truth never be offered in their crude form, but only with embellishments, sweetened and gilded like pills? It's not normal. . . . It's falsification . . . deception . . . tricks . . . ."

He thought of the jurymen to whom it was absolutely necessary to make a "speech," of the general public who absorb history only from legends and historical novels, and of himself and how he had gathered an understanding of life not from sermons and laws, but from fables, novels, poems.

"Medicine should be sweet, truth beautiful, and man has had this foolish habit since the days of Adam . . . though, indeed, perhaps it is all natural, and ought to be so. . . . There are many deceptions and delusions in nature that serve a purpose."

He set to work, but lazy, intimate thoughts still strayed through his mind for a good while. Overhead the scales could no longer be heard, but the inhabitant of the second storey was still pacing from one end of the room to another.

A CLASSICAL STUDENT

BEFORE setting off for his examination in Greek, Vanya kissed all the holy images. His stomach felt as though it were upside down; there was a chill at his heart, while the heart itself throbbed and stood still with terror before the unknown. What would he get that day? A three or a two? Six times he went to his mother for her blessing, and, as he went out, asked his aunt to pray for him. On the way to school he gave a beggar two kopecks, in the hope that those two kopecks would atone for his ignorance, and that, please God, he would not get the numerals with those awful forties and eighties.

He came back from the high school late, between four and five. He came in, and noiselessly lay down on his bed. His thin face was pale. There were dark rings round his red eyes.

"Well, how did you get on? How were you marked?" asked his mother, going to his bedside.

Vanya blinked, twisted his mouth, and burst into tears. His mother turned pale, let her mouth fall open, and clasped her hands. The breeches she was mending dropped out of her hands.

"What are you crying for? You've failed, then?" she asked.

"I am plucked. . . . I got a two."

"I knew it would be so! I had a presentiment of it," said his mother. "Merciful God! How is it you have not passed? What is the reason of it? What subject have you failed in?"

"In Greek. . . . Mother, I . . . They asked me the future of *phero*, and I . . . instead of saying *oisomai* said *opsomai*. Then . . . then there isn't an accent, if the last syllable is long, and I . . . I got flustered. . . . I forgot that the alpha was long in it . . . . I went and put in the accent. Then Artaxerxov told me to give the list of the enclitic particles. . . . I did, and I accidentally mixed in a pronoun . . . and made a mistake . . . and so he gave me a two. . . . I am a miserable person. . . . I was working all night. . . I've been getting up at four o'clock all this week . . . ."

"No, it's not you but I who am miserable, you wretched boy! It's I that am miserable! You've worn me to a threadpaper, you Herod, you torment, you bane of my life! I pay for you, you good-for-nothing rubbish; I've bent my back toiling for you, I'm worried to death, and, I may say, I am unhappy, and what do you care? How do you work?"

"I . . . I do work. All night. . . . You've seen it yourself."

"I prayed to God to take me, but He won't take me, a sinful woman . . . . You torment! Other people have children like everyone else, and I've one only and no sense, no comfort out of him. Beat you? I'd beat you, but where am I to find the strength? Mother of God, where am I to find the strength?"

The mamma hid her face in the folds of her blouse and broke into sobs. Vanya wriggled with anguish and pressed his forehead against the wall. The aunt came in.

"So that's how it is. . . . Just what I expected," she said, at once guessing what was wrong, turning pale and clasping her hands. "I've been depressed all the morning. . . . There's trouble coming, I thought . . . and here it's come. . . ."

"The villain, the torment!"

"Why are you swearing at him?" cried the aunt, nervously pulling her coffee-coloured kerchief off her head and turning upon the mother. "It's not his fault! It's your fault! You are to blame! Why did you send him to that high school? You are a fine lady! You want to be a lady? A-a-ah! I dare say, as though you'll turn into gentry! But if you had sent him, as I told you, into business . . . to an office, like my Kuzya . . . here is Kuzya getting five hundred a year. . . . Five hundred roubles is worth having, isn't it? And you are wearing yourself out, and wearing the boy out with this studying, plague take it! He is thin, he coughs . . . just look at him! He's thirteen, and he looks no more than ten."

"No, Nastenka, no, my dear! I haven't thrashed him enough, the torment! He ought to have been thrashed, that's what it is! Ugh . . . Jesuit, Mahomet, torment!" she shook her fist at her son. "You want a flogging, but I haven't the strength. They told me years ago when he was little, 'Whip him, whip him!' I didn't heed them, sinful woman as I am. And now I am suffering for it. You wait a bit! I'll flay you! Wait a bit . . . ."

The mamma shook her wet fist, and went weeping into her lodger's room. The lodger, Yevtihy Kuzmitch Kuporossov, was sitting at his table, reading "Dancing Self-taught." Yevtihy Kuzmitch was a man of intelligence and education. He spoke through his nose, washed with a soap the smell of which made everyone in the house sneeze, ate meat on fast days, and was on the look-out for a bride of refined education, and so was considered the cleverest of the lodgers. He sang tenor.

"My good friend," began the mamma, dissolving into tears. "If you would have the generosity—thrash my boy for me. . . . Do me the favour! He's failed in his examination, the nuisance of a boy! Would you believe it, he's failed! I can't punish him, through the weakness of my ill-health. . . . Thrash him for me, if you would be so obliging and considerate, Yevtihy Kuzmitch! Have regard for a sick woman!"

Kuporossov frowned and heaved a deep sigh through his nose. He thought a little, drummed on the table with his fingers, and sighing once more, went to Vanya.

"You are being taught, so to say," he began, "being educated, being given a chance, you revolting young person! Why have you done it?"

He talked for a long time, made a regular speech. He alluded to science, to light, and to darkness.

"Yes, young person."

When he had finished his speech, he took off his belt and took Vanya by the hand.

"It's the only way to deal with you," he said. Vanya knelt down submissively and thrust his head between the lodger's knees. His prominent pink ears moved up and down against the lodger's new serge trousers, with brown stripes on the outer seams.

Vanya did not utter a single sound. At the family council in the evening, it was decided to send him into business.

VANKA

VANKA ZHUKOV, a boy of nine, who had been for three months apprenticed to Alyahin the shoemaker, was sitting up on Christmas Eve. Waiting till his master and mistress and their workmen had gone to the midnight service, he took out of his master's cupboard a bottle of ink and a pen with a rusty nib, and, spreading out a crumpled sheet of paper in front of him, began writing. Before forming the first letter he several times looked round fearfully at the door and the windows, stole a glance at the dark ikon, on both sides of which stretched shelves full of lasts, and heaved a broken sigh. The paper lay on the bench while he knelt before it.

"Dear grandfather, Konstantin Makaritch," he wrote, "I am writing you a letter. I wish you a happy Christmas, and all blessings from God Almighty. I have neither father nor mother, you are the only one left me."

Vanka raised his eyes to the dark ikon on which the light of his candle was reflected, and vividly recalled his grandfather, Konstantin Makaritch, who was night watchman to a family called Zhivarev. He was a thin but extraordinarily nimble and lively little old man of sixty-five, with an everlastingly laughing face and drunken eyes. By day he slept in the servants' kitchen, or made jokes with the cooks; at night, wrapped in an ample sheepskin, he walked round the grounds and tapped with his little mallet. Old Kashtanka and Eel, so-called on account of his dark colour and his long body like a weasel's, followed him with hanging heads. This Eel was exceptionally polite and affectionate, and looked with equal kindness on strangers and his own masters, but had not a very good reputation. Under his politeness and meekness was hidden the most Jesuitical cunning. No one knew better how to creep up on occasion and snap at one's legs, to slip into the store-room, or steal a hen from a peasant. His hind legs had been nearly pulled off more than once, twice he had been hanged, every week he was thrashed till he was half dead, but he always revived.

At this moment grandfather was, no doubt, standing at the gate, screwing up his eyes at the red windows of the church, stamping with his high felt boots, and joking with the servants. His little mallet was hanging on his belt. He was clasping his hands, shrugging with the cold, and, with an aged chuckle, pinching first the housemaid, then the cook.

"How about a pinch of snuff?" he was saying, offering the women his snuff-box.

The women would take a sniff and sneeze. Grandfather would be indescribably delighted, go off into a merry chuckle, and cry:

"Tear it off, it has frozen on!"

They give the dogs a sniff of snuff too. Kashtanka sneezes, wriggles her head, and walks away offended. Eel does not sneeze, from politeness, but wags his tail. And the weather is glorious. The air is still, fresh, and transparent. The night is dark, but one can see the whole village with its white roofs and coils of smoke coming from the chimneys, the trees silvered with hoar frost, the snowdrifts. The whole sky spangled with gay twinkling stars, and the Milky Way is as distinct as though it had been washed and rubbed with snow for a holiday. . . .

Vanka sighed, dipped his pen, and went on writing:

"And yesterday I had a wigging. The master pulled me out into the yard by my hair, and whacked me with a boot-stretcher because I accidentally fell asleep while I was rocking their brat in the cradle. And a week ago the mistress told me to clean a herring, and I began from the tail end, and she took the herring and thrust its head in my face. The workmen laugh at me and send me to the tavern for vodka, and tell me to steal the master's cucumbers for them, and the master beats me with anything that comes to hand. And there is nothing to eat. In the morning they give me bread, for dinner, porridge, and in the evening, bread again; but as for tea, or soup, the master and mistress gobble it all up themselves. And I am put to sleep in the passage, and when their wretched brat cries I get no sleep at all, but have to rock the cradle. Dear grandfather, show the divine mercy, take me away from here, home to the village. It's more than I can bear. I bow down to your feet, and will pray to God for you for ever, take me away from here or I shall die."

Vanka's mouth worked, he rubbed his eyes with his black fist, and gave a sob.

"I will powder your snuff for you," he went on. "I will pray for you, and if I do anything you can thrash me like Sidor's goat. And if you think I've no job, then I will beg the steward for Christ's sake to let me clean his boots, or I'll go for a shepherd-boy instead of Fedka. Dear grandfather, it is more than I can bear, it's simply no life at all. I wanted to run away to the village, but I have no boots, and I am afraid of the frost. When I grow up big I will take care of you for this, and not let anyone annoy you, and when you die I will pray for the rest of your soul, just as for my mammy's."

"Moscow is a big town. It's all gentlemen's houses, and there are lots of horses, but there are no sheep, and the dogs are not spiteful. The lads here don't go out with the star, and they don't let anyone go into the choir, and once I saw in a shop window fishing-hooks for sale, fitted ready with the line and for all sorts of fish, awfully good ones, there was even one hook that would hold a forty-pound sheat-fish. And I have seen shops where there are guns of all sorts, after the pattern of the master's guns at home, so that I shouldn't wonder if they are a hundred roubles each. . . . And in the butchers' shops there are grouse and woodcocks and fish and hares, but the shopmen don't say where they shoot them."

"Dear grandfather, when they have the Christmas tree at the big house, get me a gilt walnut, and put it away in the green trunk. Ask the young lady Olga Ignatyevna, say it's for Vanka."

Vanka gave a tremulous sigh, and again stared at the window. He remembered how his grandfather always went into the forest to get the Christmas tree for his master's family, and took his grandson with him. It was a merry time! Grandfather made a noise in his throat, the forest crackled with the frost, and looking at them Vanka chortled too. Before chopping down the Christmas tree, grandfather would smoke a pipe, slowly take a pinch of snuff, and laugh at frozen Vanka. . . . The young fir trees, covered with hoar frost, stood motionless, waiting to see which of them was to die. Wherever one looked, a hare flew like an arrow over the snowdrifts . . . . Grandfather could not refrain from shouting: "Hold him, hold him . . . hold him! Ah, the bob-tailed devil!"

When he had cut down the Christmas tree, grandfather used to drag it to the big house, and there set to work to decorate it. . . . The young lady, who was Vanka's favourite, Olga Ignatyevna, was the busiest of all. When Vanka's mother Pelageya was alive, and a servant in the big house, Olga Ignatyevna used to give him goodies, and having nothing better to do, taught him to read and write, to count up to a hundred, and even to dance a quadrille. When Pelageya died, Vanka had been transferred to the servants' kitchen to be with his grandfather, and from the kitchen to the shoemaker's in Moscow.

"Do come, dear grandfather," Vanka went on with his letter. "For Christ's sake, I beg you, take me away. Have pity on an unhappy orphan like me; here everyone knocks me about, and I am fearfully hungry; I can't tell you what misery it is, I am always crying. And the other day the master hit me on the head with a last, so that I fell down. My life is wretched, worse than any dog's. . . . I send greetings to Alyona, one-eyed Yegorka, and the coachman, and don't give my concertina to anyone. I remain, your grandson, Ivan Zhukov. Dear grandfather, do come."

Vanka folded the sheet of writing-paper twice, and put it into an envelope he had bought the day before for a kopeck. . . . After thinking a little, he dipped the pen and wrote the address:

> To grandfather in the village.

Then he scratched his head, thought a little, and added: Konstantin Makaritch. Glad that he had not been prevented from writing, he put on his cap and, without putting on his little greatcoat, ran out into the street as he was in his shirt. . . .

The shopmen at the butcher's, whom he had questioned the day before, told him that letters were put in post-boxes, and from the boxes were carried about all over the earth in mailcarts with drunken drivers and ringing bells. Vanka ran to the nearest post-box, and thrust the precious letter in the slit. . . .

An hour later, lulled by sweet hopes, he was sound asleep. . . . He dreamed of the stove. On the stove was sitting his grandfather, swinging his bare legs, and reading the letter to the cooks. . . .

By the stove was Eel, wagging his tail.

AN INCIDENT

MORNING. Brilliant sunshine is piercing through the frozen lacework on the window-panes into the nursery. Vanya, a boy of six, with a cropped head and a nose like a button, and his sister Nina, a short, chubby, curly-headed girl of four, wake up and look crossly at each other through the bars of their cots.

"Oo-oo-oo! naughty children!" grumbles their nurse. "Good people have had their breakfast already, while you can't get your eyes open."

The sunbeams frolic over the rugs, the walls, and nurse's skirts, and seem inviting the children to join in their play, but they take no notice. They have woken up in a bad humour. Nina pouts, makes a grimace, and begins to whine:

"Brea-eakfast, nurse, breakfast!"

Vanya knits his brows and ponders what to pitch upon to howl over. He has already begun screwing up his eyes and opening his mouth, but at that instant the voice of mamma reaches them from the drawing-room, saying: "Don't forget to give the cat her milk, she has a family now!"

The children's puckered countenances grow smooth again as they look at each other in astonishment. Then both at once begin shouting, jump out of their cots, and filling the air with piercing shrieks, run barefoot, in their nightgowns, to the kitchen.

"The cat has puppies!" they cry. "The cat has got puppies!"

Under the bench in the kitchen there stands a small box, the one in which Stepan brings coal when he lights the fire. The cat is peeping out of the box. There is an expression of extreme exhaustion on her grey face; her green eyes, with their narrow black pupils, have a languid, sentimental look. From her face it is clear that the only thing lacking to complete her happiness is the presence in the box of "him," the father of her children, to whom she had abandoned herself so recklessly! She wants to mew, and opens her mouth wide, but nothing but a hiss comes from her throat; the squealing of the kittens is audible.

The children squat on their heels before the box, and, motionless, holding their breath, gaze at the cat. . . . They are surprised, impressed, and do not hear nurse grumbling as she pursues them. The most genuine delight shines in the eyes of both.

Domestic animals play a scarcely noticed but undoubtedly beneficial part in the education and life of children. Which of us does not remember powerful but magnanimous dogs, lazy lapdogs, birds dying in captivity, dull-witted but haughty turkeys, mild old tabby cats, who forgave us when we trod on their tails for fun and caused them agonising pain? I even fancy, sometimes, that the patience, the fidelity, the readiness to forgive, and the sincerity which are characteristic of our domestic animals have a far stronger and more definite effect on the mind of a child than the long exhortations of some dry, pale Karl Karlovitch, or the misty expositions of a governess, trying to prove to children that water is made up of hydrogen and oxygen.

"What little things!" says Nina, opening her eyes wide and going off into a joyous laugh. "They are like mice!"

"One, two, three," Vanya counts. "Three kittens. So there is one for you, one for me, and one for somebody else, too."

"Murrm . . . murrm . . ." purrs the mother, flattered by their attention. "Murrm."

After gazing at the kittens, the children take them from under the cat, and begin squeezing them in their hands, then, not satisfied with this, they put them in the skirts of their nightgowns, and run into the other rooms.

"Mamma, the cat has got pups!" they shout.

Mamma is sitting in the drawing-room with some unknown gentleman. Seeing the children unwashed, undressed, with their nightgowns held up high, she is embarrassed, and looks at them severely.

"Let your nightgowns down, disgraceful children," she says. "Go out of the room, or I will punish you."

But the children do not notice either mamma's threats or the presence of a stranger. They put the kittens down on the carpet, and go off into deafening squeals. The mother walks round them, mewing imploringly. When, a little afterwards, the children are dragged off to the nursery, dressed, made to say their prayers, and given their breakfast, they are full of a passionate desire to get away from these prosaic duties as quickly as possible, and to run to the kitchen again.

Their habitual pursuits and games are thrown completely into the background.

The kittens throw everything into the shade by making their appearance in the world, and supply the great sensation of the day. If Nina or Vanya had been offered forty pounds of sweets or ten thousand kopecks for each kitten, they would have rejected such a barter without the slightest hesitation. In spite of the heated protests of the nurse and the cook, the children persist in sitting by the cat's box in the kitchen, busy with the kittens till dinner-time. Their faces are earnest and concentrated and express anxiety. They are worried not so much by the present as by the future of the kittens. They decide that one kitten shall remain at home with the old cat to be a comfort to her mother, while the second shall go to their summer villa, and the third shall live in the cellar, where there are ever so many rats.

"But why don't they look at us?" Nina wondered. "Their eyes are blind like the beggars'."

Vanya, too, is perturbed by this question. He tries to open one kitten's eyes, and spends a long time puffing and breathing hard over it, but his operation is unsuccessful. They are a good deal troubled, too, by the circumstance that the kittens obstinately refuse the milk and the meat that is offered to them. Everything that is put before their little noses is eaten by their grey mamma.

"Let's build the kittens little houses," Vanya suggests. "They shall live in different houses, and the cat shall come and pay them visits. . . ."

Cardboard hat-boxes are put in the different corners of the kitchen and the kittens are installed in them. But this division turns out to be premature; the cat, still wearing an imploring and sentimental expression on her face, goes the round of all the hat-boxes, and carries off her children to their original position.

"The cat's their mother," observed Vanya, "but who is their father?"

"Yes, who is their father?" repeats Nina.

"They must have a father."

Vanya and Nina are a long time deciding who is to be the kittens' father, and, in the end, their choice falls on a big dark-red horse without a tail, which is lying in the store-cupboard under the stairs, together with other relics of toys that have outlived their day. They drag him up out of the store-cupboard and stand him by the box.

"Mind now!" they admonish him, "stand here and see they behave themselves properly."

All this is said and done in the gravest way, with an expression of anxiety on their faces. Vanya and Nina refuse to recognise the existence of any world but the box of kittens. Their joy knows no bounds. But they have to pass through bitter, agonising moments, too.

Just before dinner, Vanya is sitting in his father's study, gazing dreamily at the table. A kitten is moving about by the lamp, on stamped note paper. Vanya is watching its movements, and thrusting first a pencil, then a match into its little mouth. . . . All at once, as though he has sprung out of the floor, his father is beside the table.

"What's this?" Vanya hears, in an angry voice.

"It's . . . it's the kitty, papa. . . ."

"I'll give it you; look what you have done, you naughty boy! You've dirtied all my paper!"

To Vanya's great surprise his papa does not share his partiality for the kittens, and, instead of being moved to enthusiasm and delight, he pulls Vanya's ear and shouts:

"Stepan, take away this horrid thing."

At dinner, too, there is a scene. . . . During the second course there is suddenly the sound of a shrill mew. They begin to investigate its origin, and discover a kitten under Nina's pinafore.

"Nina, leave the table!" cries her father angrily. "Throw the kittens in the cesspool! I won't have the nasty things in the house! . . ."

Vanya and Nina are horrified. Death in the cesspool, apart from its cruelty, threatens to rob the cat and the wooden horse of their children, to lay waste the cat's box, to destroy their plans for the future, that fair future in which one cat will be a comfort to its old mother, another will live in the country, while the third will catch rats in the cellar. The children begin to cry and entreat that the kittens may be spared. Their father consents, but on the condition that the children do not go into the kitchen and touch the kittens.

After dinner, Vanya and Nina slouch about the rooms, feeling depressed. The prohibition of visits to the kitchen has reduced them to dejection. They refuse sweets, are naughty, and are rude to their mother. When their uncle Petrusha comes in the evening, they draw him aside, and complain to him of their father, who wanted to throw the kittens into the cesspool.

"Uncle Petrusha, tell mamma to have the kittens taken to the nursery," the children beg their uncle, "do-o tell her."

"There, there . . . very well," says their uncle, waving them off.

"All right."

Uncle Petrusha does not usually come alone. He is accompanied by Nero, a big black dog of Danish breed, with drooping ears, and a tail as hard as a stick. The dog is silent, morose, and full of a sense of his own dignity. He takes not the slightest notice of the children, and when he passes them hits them with his tail as though they were chairs. The children hate him from the bottom of their hearts, but on this occasion, practical considerations override sentiment.

"I say, Nina," says Vanya, opening his eyes wide. "Let Nero be their father, instead of the horse! The horse is dead and he is alive, you see."

They are waiting the whole evening for the moment when papa will sit down to his cards and it will be possible to take Nero to the kitchen without being observed. . . . At last, papa sits down to cards, mamma is busy with the samovar and not noticing the children. . . .

The happy moment arrives.

"Come along!" Vanya whispers to his sister.

But, at that moment, Stepan comes in and, with a snigger, announces:

"Nero has eaten the kittens, madam."

Nina and Vanya turn pale and look at Stepan with horror.

"He really has . . ." laughs the footman, "he went to the box and gobbled them up."

The children expect that all the people in the house will be aghast and fall upon the miscreant Nero. But they all sit calmly in their seats, and only express surprise at the appetite of the huge dog. Papa and mamma laugh. Nero walks about by the table, wags his tail, and licks his lips complacently . . . the cat is the only one who is uneasy. With her tail in the air she walks about the rooms, looking suspiciously at people and mewing plaintively.

"Children, it's past nine," cries mamma, "it's bedtime."

Vanya and Nina go to bed, shed tears, and spend a long time thinking about the injured cat, and the cruel, insolent, and unpunished Nero.

A DAY IN THE COUNTRY

BETWEEN eight and nine o'clock in the morning.

A dark leaden-coloured mass is creeping over the sky towards the sun. Red zigzags of lightning gleam here and there across it. There is a sound of far-away rumbling. A warm wind frolics over the grass, bends the trees, and stirs up the dust. In a minute there will be a spurt of May rain and a real storm will begin.

Fyokla, a little beggar-girl of six, is running through the village, looking for Terenty the cobbler. The white-haired, barefoot child is pale. Her eyes are wide-open, her lips are trembling.

"Uncle, where is Terenty?" she asks every one she meets. No one answers. They are all preoccupied with the approaching storm and take refuge in their huts. At last she meets Silanty Silitch, the sacristan, Terenty's bosom friend. He is coming along, staggering from the wind.

"Uncle, where is Terenty?"

"At the kitchen-gardens," answers Silanty.

The beggar-girl runs behind the huts to the kitchen-gardens and there finds Terenty; the tall old man with a thin, pock-marked face, very long legs, and bare feet, dressed in a woman's tattered jacket, is standing near the vegetable plots, looking with drowsy, drunken eyes at the dark storm-cloud. On his long crane-like legs he sways in the wind like a starling-cote.

"Uncle Terenty!" the white-headed beggar-girl addresses him. "Uncle, darling!"

Terenty bends down to Fyokla, and his grim, drunken face is overspread with a smile, such as come into people's faces when they look at something little, foolish, and absurd, but warmly loved.

"Ah! servant of God, Fyokia," he says, lisping tenderly, "where have you come from?"

"Uncle Terenty," says Fyokia, with a sob, tugging at the lapel of the cobbler's coat. "Brother Danilka has had an accident! Come along!"

"What sort of accident? Ough, what thunder! Holy, holy, holy. . . .

What sort of accident?"

"In the count's copse Danilka stuck his hand into a hole in a tree, and he can't get it out. Come along, uncle, do be kind and pull his hand out!"

"How was it he put his hand in? What for?"

"He wanted to get a cuckoo's egg out of the hole for me."

"The day has hardly begun and already you are in trouble. . . ." Terenty shook his head and spat deliberately. "Well, what am I to do with you now? I must come . . . I must, may the wolf gobble you up, you naughty children! Come, little orphan!"

Terenty comes out of the kitchen-garden and, lifting high his long legs, begins striding down the village street. He walks quickly without stopping or looking from side to side, as though he were shoved from behind or afraid of pursuit. Fyokla can hardly keep up with him.

They come out of the village and turn along the dusty road towards the count's copse that lies dark blue in the distance. It is about a mile and a half away. The clouds have by now covered the sun, and soon afterwards there is not a speck of blue left in the sky. It grows dark.

"Holy, holy, holy . . ." whispers Fyokla, hurrying after Terenty. The first rain-drops, big and heavy, lie, dark dots on the dusty road. A big drop falls on Fyokla's cheek and glides like a tear down her chin.

"The rain has begun," mutters the cobbler, kicking up the dust with his bare, bony feet. "That's fine, Fyokla, old girl. The grass and the trees are fed by the rain, as we are by bread. And as for the thunder, don't you be frightened, little orphan. Why should it kill a little thing like you?"

As soon as the rain begins, the wind drops. The only sound is the patter of rain dropping like fine shot on the young rye and the parched road.

"We shall get soaked, Fyolka," mutters Terenty. "There won't be a dry spot left on us. . . . Ho-ho, my girl! It's run down my neck! But don't be frightened, silly. . . . The grass will be dry again, the earth will be dry again, and we shall be dry again. There is the same sun for us all."

A flash of lightning, some fourteen feet long, gleams above their heads. There is a loud peal of thunder, and it seems to Fyokla that something big, heavy, and round is rolling over the sky and tearing it open, exactly over her head.

"Holy, holy, holy . . ." says Terenty, crossing himself. "Don't be afraid, little orphan! It is not from spite that it thunders."

Terenty's and Fyokla's feet are covered with lumps of heavy, wet clay. It is slippery and difficult to walk, but Terenty strides on more and more rapidly. The weak little beggar-girl is breathless and ready to drop.

But at last they go into the count's copse. The washed trees, stirred by a gust of wind, drop a perfect waterfall upon them. Terenty stumbles over stumps and begins to slacken his pace.

"Whereabouts is Danilka?" he asks. "Lead me to him."

Fyokla leads him into a thicket, and, after going a quarter of a mile, points to Danilka. Her brother, a little fellow of eight, with hair as red as ochre and a pale sickly face, stands leaning against a tree, and, with his head on one side, looking sideways at the sky. In one hand he holds his shabby old cap, the other is hidden in an old lime tree.

The boy is gazing at the stormy sky, and apparently not thinking of his trouble. Hearing footsteps and seeing the cobbler he gives a sickly smile and says:

"A terrible lot of thunder, Terenty. . . . I've never heard so much thunder in all my life."

"And where is your hand?"

"In the hole. . . . Pull it out, please, Terenty!"

The wood had broken at the edge of the hole and jammed Danilka's hand: he could push it farther in, but could not pull it out. Terenty snaps off the broken piece, and the boy's hand, red and crushed, is released.

"It's terrible how it's thundering," the boy says again, rubbing his hand. "What makes it thunder, Terenty?"

"One cloud runs against the other," answers the cobbler. The party come out of the copse, and walk along the edge of it towards the darkened road. The thunder gradually abates, and its rumbling is heard far away beyond the village.

"The ducks flew by here the other day, Terenty," says Danilka, still rubbing his hand. "They must be nesting in the Gniliya Zaimishtcha marshes. . . . Fyolka, would you like me to show you a nightingale's nest?"

"Don't touch it, you might disturb them," says Terenty, wringing the water out of his cap. "The nightingale is a singing-bird, without sin. He has had a voice given him in his throat, to praise God and gladden the heart of man. It's a sin to disturb him."

"What about the sparrow?"

"The sparrow doesn't matter, he's a bad, spiteful bird. He is like a pickpocket in his ways. He doesn't like man to be happy. When Christ was crucified it was the sparrow brought nails to the Jews, and called 'alive! alive!'"

A bright patch of blue appears in the sky.

"Look!" says Terenty. "An ant-heap burst open by the rain! They've been flooded, the rogues!"

They bend over the ant-heap. The downpour has damaged it; the insects are scurrying to and fro in the mud, agitated, and busily trying to carry away their drowned companions.

"You needn't be in such a taking, you won't die of it!" says Terenty, grinning. "As soon as the sun warms you, you'll come to your senses again. . . . It's a lesson to you, you stupids. You won't settle on low ground another time."

They go on.

"And here are some bees," cries Danilka, pointing to the branch of a young oak tree.

The drenched and chilled bees are huddled together on the branch.
There are so many of them that neither bark nor leaf can be seen.
Many of them are settled on one another.
"That's a swarm of bees," Terenty informs them. "They were flying looking for a home, and when the rain came down upon them they settled. If a swarm is flying, you need only sprinkle water on them to make them settle. Now if, say, you wanted to take the swarm, you would bend the branch with them into a sack and shake it, and they all fall in."

Little Fyokla suddenly frowns and rubs her neck vigorously. Her brother looks at her neck, and sees a big swelling on it.

"Hey-hey!" laughs the cobbler. "Do you know where you got that from, Fyokla, old girl? There are Spanish flies on some tree in the wood.

The rain has trickled off them, and a drop has fallen on your neck that's what has made the swelling."

The sun appears from behind the clouds and floods the wood, the fields, and the three friends with its warm light. The dark menacing cloud has gone far away and taken the storm with it. The air is warm and fragrant. There is a scent of bird-cherry, meadowsweet, and lilies-of-the-valley.

"That herb is given when your nose bleeds," says Terenty, pointing to a woolly-looking flower. "It does good."

They hear a whistle and a rumble, but not such a rumble as the storm-clouds carried away. A goods train races by before the eyes of Terenty, Danilka, and Fyokla. The engine, panting and puffing out black smoke, drags more than twenty vans after it. Its power is tremendous. The children are interested to know how an engine, not alive and without the help of horses, can move and drag such weights, and Terenty undertakes to explain it to them:

"It's all the steam's doing, children. . . . The steam does the work. . . . You see, it shoves under that thing near the wheels, and it . . . you see . . . it works. . . ."

They cross the railway line, and, going down from the embankment, walk towards the river. They walk not with any object, but just at random, and talk all the way. . . . Danilka asks questions, Terenty answers them. . . .

Terenty answers all his questions, and there is no secret in Nature which baffles him. He knows everything. Thus, for example, he knows the names of all the wild flowers, animals, and stones. He knows what herbs cure diseases, he has no difficulty in telling the age of a horse or a cow. Looking at the sunset, at the moon, or the birds, he can tell what sort of weather it will be next day. And indeed, it is not only Terenty who is so wise. Silanty Silitch, the innkeeper, the market-gardener, the shepherd, and all the villagers, generally speaking, know as much as he does. These people have learned not from books, but in the fields, in the wood, on the river bank. Their teachers have been the birds themselves, when they sang to them, the sun when it left a glow of crimson behind it at setting, the very trees, and wild herbs.

Danilka looks at Terenty and greedily drinks in every word. In spring, before one is weary of the warmth and the monotonous green of the fields, when everything is fresh and full of fragrance, who would not want to hear about the golden may-beetles, about the cranes, about the gurgling streams, and the corn mounting into ear?

The two of them, the cobbler and the orphan, walk about the fields, talk unceasingly, and are not weary. They could wander about the world endlessly. They walk, and in their talk of the beauty of the earth do not notice the frail little beggar-girl tripping after them. She is breathless and moves with a lagging step. There are tears in her eyes; she would be glad to stop these inexhaustible wanderers, but to whom and where can she go? She has no home or people of her own; whether she likes it or not, she must walk and listen to their talk.

Towards midday, all three sit down on the river bank. Danilka takes out of his bag a piece of bread, soaked and reduced to a mash, and they begin to eat. Terenty says a prayer when he has eaten the bread, then stretches himself on the sandy bank and falls asleep. While he is asleep, the boy gazes at the water, pondering. He has many different things to think of. He has just seen the storm, the bees, the ants, the train. Now, before his eyes, fishes are whisking about. Some are two inches long and more, others are no bigger than one's nail. A viper, with its head held high, is swimming from one bank to the other.

Only towards the evening our wanderers return to the village. The children go for the night to a deserted barn, where the corn of the commune used to be kept, while Terenty, leaving them, goes to the tavern. The children lie huddled together on the straw, dozing.

The boy does not sleep. He gazes into the darkness, and it seems to him that he is seeing all that he has seen in the day: the storm-clouds, the bright sunshine, the birds, the fish, lanky Terenty. The number of his impressions, together with exhaustion and hunger, are too much for him; he is as hot as though he were on fire, and tosses from, side to side. He longs to tell someone all that is haunting him now in the darkness and agitating his soul, but there is no one to tell. Fyokla is too little and could not understand.

"I'll tell Terenty to-morrow," thinks the boy.

The children fall asleep thinking of the homeless cobbler, and, in the night, Terenty comes to them, makes the sign of the cross over them, and puts bread under their heads. And no one sees his love. It is seen only by the moon which floats in the sky and peeps caressingly through the holes in the wall of the deserted barn.

BOYS

"VOLODYA'S come!" someone shouted in the yard.

"Master Volodya's here!" bawled Natalya the cook, running into the dining-room. "Oh, my goodness!"

The whole Korolyov family, who had been expecting their Volodya from hour to hour, rushed to the windows. At the front door stood a wide sledge, with three white horses in a cloud of steam. The sledge was empty, for Volodya was already in the hall, untying his hood with red and chilly fingers. His school overcoat, his cap, his snowboots, and the hair on his temples were all white with frost, and his whole figure from head to foot diffused such a pleasant, fresh smell of the snow that the very sight of him made one want to shiver and say "brrr!"

His mother and aunt ran to kiss and hug him. Natalya plumped down at his feet and began pulling off his snowboots, his sisters shrieked with delight, the doors creaked and banged, and Volodya's father, in his waistcoat and shirt-sleeves, ran out into the hall with scissors in his hand, and cried out in alarm:

"We were expecting you all yesterday? Did you come all right? Had a good journey? Mercy on us! you might let him say 'how do you do' to his father! I am his father after all!"

"Bow-wow!" barked the huge black dog, Milord, in a deep bass, tapping with his tail on the walls and furniture.

For two minutes there was nothing but a general hubbub of joy. After the first outburst of delight was over the Korolyovs noticed that there was, besides their Volodya, another small person in the hall, wrapped up in scarves and shawls and white with frost. He was standing perfectly still in a corner, in the shadow of a big fox-lined overcoat.

"Volodya darling, who is it?" asked his mother, in a whisper.

"Oh!" cried Volodya. "This is—let me introduce my friend Lentilov, a schoolfellow in the second class. . . . I have brought him to stay with us."

"Delighted to hear it! You are very welcome," the father said cordially. "Excuse me, I've been at work without my coat. . . . Please come in! Natalya, help Mr. Lentilov off with his things.

Mercy on us, do turn that dog out! He is unendurable!"

A few minutes later, Volodya and his friend Lentilov, somewhat dazed by their noisy welcome, and still red from the outside cold, were sitting down to tea. The winter sun, making its way through the snow and the frozen tracery on the window-panes, gleamed on the samovar, and plunged its pure rays in the tea-basin. The room was warm, and the boys felt as though the warmth and the frost were struggling together with a tingling sensation in their bodies.

"Well, Christmas will soon be here," the father said in a pleasant sing-song voice, rolling a cigarette of dark reddish tobacco. "It doesn't seem long since the summer, when mamma was crying at your going . . . and here you are back again. . . . Time flies, my boy. Before you have time to cry out, old age is upon you. Mr. Lentilov, take some more, please help yourself! We don't stand on ceremony!"

Volodya's three sisters, Katya, Sonya, and Masha (the eldest was eleven), sat at the table and never took their eyes off the newcomer.

Lentilov was of the same height and age as Volodya, but not as round-faced and fair-skinned. He was thin, dark, and freckled; his hair stood up like a brush, his eyes were small, and his lips were thick. He was, in fact, distinctly ugly, and if he had not been wearing the school uniform, he might have been taken for the son of a cook. He seemed morose, did not speak, and never once smiled. The little girls, staring at him, immediately came to the conclusion that he must be a very clever and learned person. He seemed to be thinking about something all the time, and was so absorbed in his own thoughts, that, whenever he was spoken to, he started, threw his head back, and asked to have the question repeated.

The little girls noticed that Volodya, who had always been so merry and talkative, also said very little, did not smile at all, and hardly seemed to be glad to be home. All the time they were at tea he only once addressed his sisters, and then he said something so strange. He pointed to the samovar and said:

"In California they don't drink tea, but gin."

He, too, seemed absorbed in his own thoughts, and, to judge by the looks that passed between him and his friend Lentilov, their thoughts were the same.

After tea, they all went into the nursery. The girls and their father took up the work that had been interrupted by the arrival of the boys. They were making flowers and frills for the Christmas tree out of paper of different colours. It was an attractive and noisy occupation. Every fresh flower was greeted by the little girls with shrieks of delight, even of awe, as though the flower had dropped straight from heaven; their father was in ecstasies too, and every now and then he threw the scissors on the floor, in vexation at their bluntness. Their mother kept running into the nursery with an anxious face, asking:

"Who has taken my scissors? Ivan Nikolaitch, have you taken my scissors again?"

"Mercy on us! I'm not even allowed a pair of scissors!" their father would respond in a lachrymose voice, and, flinging himself back in his chair, he would pretend to be a deeply injured man; but a minute later, he would be in ecstasies again.

On his former holidays Volodya, too, had taken part in the preparations for the Christmas tree, or had been running in the yard to look at the snow mountain that the watchman and the shepherd were building. But this time Volodya and Lentilov took no notice whatever of the coloured paper, and did not once go into the stable. They sat in the window and began whispering to one another; then they opened an atlas and looked carefully at a map.

"First to Perm . . ." Lentilov said, in an undertone, "from there to Tiumen, then Tomsk . . . then . . . then . . . Kamchatka. There the Samoyedes take one over Behring's Straits in boats . . . . And then we are in America. . . . There are lots of furry animals there. . . ."

"And California?" asked Volodya.

"California is lower down. . . . We've only to get to America and California is not far off. . . . And one can get a living by hunting and plunder."

All day long Lentilov avoided the little girls, and seemed to look at them with suspicion. In the evening he happened to be left alone with them for five minutes or so. It was awkward to be silent.

He cleared his throat morosely, rubbed his left hand against his right, looked sullenly at Katya and asked:

"Have you read Mayne Reid?"

"No, I haven't. . . . I say, can you skate?"

Absorbed in his own reflections, Lentilov made no reply to this question; he simply puffed out his cheeks, and gave a long sigh as though he were very hot. He looked up at Katya once more and said:

"When a herd of bisons stampedes across the prairie the earth trembles, and the frightened mustangs kick and neigh."

He smiled impressively and added:

"And the Indians attack the trains, too. But worst of all are the mosquitoes and the termites."

"Why, what's that?"

"They're something like ants, but with wings. They bite fearfully.

Do you know who I am?"

"Mr. Lentilov."

"No, I am Montehomo, the Hawk's Claw, Chief of the Ever Victorious."

Masha, the youngest, looked at him, then into the darkness out of window and said, wondering:

"And we had lentils for supper yesterday."

Lentilov's incomprehensible utterances, and the way he was always whispering with Volodya, and the way Volodya seemed now to be always thinking about something instead of playing . . . all this was strange and mysterious. And the two elder girls, Katya and Sonya, began to keep a sharp look-out on the boys. At night, when the boys had gone to bed, the girls crept to their bedroom door, and listened to what they were saying. Ah, what they discovered! The boys were planning to run away to America to dig for gold: they had everything ready for the journey, a pistol, two knives, biscuits, a burning glass to serve instead of matches, a compass, and four roubles in cash. They learned that the boys would have to walk some thousands of miles, and would have to fight tigers and savages on the road: then they would get gold and ivory, slay their enemies, become pirates, drink gin, and finally marry beautiful maidens, and make a plantation.

The boys interrupted each other in their excitement. Throughout the conversation, Lentilov called himself "Montehomo, the Hawk's Claw," and Volodya was "my pale-face brother!"

"Mind you don't tell mamma," said Katya, as they went back to bed. "Volodya will bring us gold and ivory from America, but if you tell mamma he won't be allowed to go."

The day before Christmas Eve, Lentilov spent the whole day poring over the map of Asia and making notes, while Volodya, with a languid and swollen face that looked as though it had been stung by a bee, walked about the rooms and ate nothing. And once he stood still before the holy image in the nursery, crossed himself, and said:

"Lord, forgive me a sinner; Lord, have pity on my poor unhappy mamma!"

In the evening he burst out crying. On saying good-night he gave his father a long hug, and then hugged his mother and sisters. Katya and Sonya knew what was the matter, but little Masha was puzzled, completely puzzled. Every time she looked at Lentilov she grew thoughtful and said with a sigh:

"When Lent comes, nurse says we shall have to eat peas and lentils."

Early in the morning of Christmas Eve, Katya and Sonya slipped quietly out of bed, and went to find out how the boys meant to run away to America. They crept to their door.

"Then you don't mean to go?" Lentilov was saying angrily. "Speak out: aren't you going?"

"Oh dear," Volodya wept softly. "How can I go? I feel so unhappy about mamma."

"My pale-face brother, I pray you, let us set off. You declared you were going, you egged me on, and now the time comes, you funk it!"

"I . . . I . . . I'm not funking it, but I . . . I . . . I'm sorry for mamma."

"Say once and for all, are you going or are you not?"

"I am going, only . . . wait a little . . . I want to be at home a little."

"In that case I will go by myself," Lentilov declared. "I can get on without you. And you wanted to hunt tigers and fight! Since that's how it is, give me back my cartridges!"

At this Volodya cried so bitterly that his sisters could not help crying too. Silence followed.

"So you are not coming?" Lentilov began again.

"I . . . I . . . I am coming!"

"Well, put on your things, then."

And Lentilov tried to cheer Volodya up by singing the praises of America, growling like a tiger, pretending to be a steamer, scolding him, and promising to give him all the ivory and lions' and tigers' skins.

And this thin, dark boy, with his freckles and his bristling shock of hair, impressed the little girls as an extraordinary remarkable person. He was a hero, a determined character, who knew no fear, and he growled so ferociously, that, standing at the door, they really might imagine there was a tiger or lion inside. When the little girls went back to their room and dressed, Katya's eyes were full of tears, and she said:

"Oh, I feel so frightened!"

Everything was as usual till two o'clock, when they sat down to dinner. Then it appeared that the boys were not in the house. They sent to the servants' quarters, to the stables, to the bailiff's cottage. They were not to be found. They sent into the village— they were not there.

At tea, too, the boys were still absent, and by supper-time Volodya's mother was dreadfully uneasy, and even shed tears.

Late in the evening they sent again to the village, they searched everywhere, and walked along the river bank with lanterns. Heavens! what a fuss there was!

Next day the police officer came, and a paper of some sort was written out in the dining-room. Their mother cried. . . .

All of a sudden a sledge stopped at the door, with three white horses in a cloud of steam.

"Volodya's come," someone shouted in the yard.

"Master Volodya's here!" bawled Natalya, running into the dining-room.

And Milord barked his deep bass, "bow-wow."

It seemed that the boys had been stopped in the Arcade, where they had gone from shop to shop asking where they could get gunpowder.

Volodya burst into sobs as soon as he came into the hall, and flung himself on his mother's neck. The little girls, trembling, wondered with terror what would happen next. They saw their father take Volodya and Lentilov into his study, and there he talked to them a long while.

"Is this a proper thing to do?" their father said to them. "I only pray they won't hear of it at school, you would both be expelled. You ought to be ashamed, Mr. Lentilov, really. It's not at all the thing to do! You began it, and I hope you will be punished by your parents. How could you? Where did you spend the night?"

"At the station," Lentilov answered proudly.

Then Volodya went to bed, and had a compress, steeped in vinegar, on his forehead.

A telegram was sent off, and next day a lady, Lentilov's mother, made her appearance and bore off her son.

Lentilov looked morose and haughty to the end, and he did not utter a single word at taking leave of the little girls. But he took Katya's book and wrote in it as a souvenir: "Montehomo, the Hawk's Claw, Chief of the Ever Victorious."

SHROVE TUESDAY

"PAVEL VASSILITCH!" cries Pelageya Ivanovna, waking her husband. "Pavel Vassilitch! You might go and help Styopa with his lessons, he is sitting crying over his book. He can't understand something again!"

Pavel Vassilitch gets up, makes the sign of the cross over his mouth as he yawns, and says softly: "In a minute, my love!"

The cat who has been asleep beside him gets up too, straightens out its tail, arches its spine, and half-shuts its eyes. There is stillness. . . . Mice can be heard scurrying behind the wall-paper. Putting on his boots and his dressing-gown, Pavel Vassilitch, crumpled and frowning from sleepiness, comes out of his bedroom into the dining-room; on his entrance another cat, engaged in sniffing a marinade of fish in the window, jumps down to the floor, and hides behind the cupboard.

"Who asked you to sniff that!" he says angrily, covering the fish with a sheet of newspaper. "You are a pig to do that, not a cat. . . ."

From the dining-room there is a door leading into the nursery. There, at a table covered with stains and deep scratches, sits Styopa, a high-school boy in the second class, with a peevish expression of face and tear-stained eyes. With his knees raised almost to his chin, and his hands clasped round them, he is swaying to and fro like a Chinese idol and looking crossly at a sum book.

"Are you working?" asks Pavel Vassilitch, sitting down to the table and yawning. "Yes, my boy. . . . We have enjoyed ourselves, slept, and eaten pancakes, and to-morrow comes Lenten fare, repentance, and going to work. Every period of time has its limits. Why are your eyes so red? Are you sick of learning your lessons? To be sure, after pancakes, lessons are nasty to swallow. That's about it."

"What are you laughing at the child for?" Pelageya Ivanovna calls from the next room. "You had better show him instead of laughing at him. He'll get a one again to-morrow, and make me miserable."

"What is it you don't understand?" Pavel Vassilitch asks Styopa.

"Why this . . . division of fractions," the boy answers crossly.

"The division of fractions by fractions. . . ."

"H'm . . . queer boy! What is there in it? There's nothing to understand in it. Learn the rules, and that's all. . . . To divide a fraction by a fraction you must multiply the numerator of the first fraction by the denominator of the second, and that will be the numerator of the quotient. . . . In this case, the numerator of the first fraction. . . ."

"I know that without your telling me," Styopa interrupts him, flicking a walnut shell off the table. "Show me the proof."

"The proof? Very well, give me a pencil. Listen. . . . Suppose we want to divide seven eighths by two fifths. Well, the point of it is, my boy, that it's required to divide these fractions by each other. . . . Have they set the samovar?"

"I don't know."

"It's time for tea. . . . It's past seven. Well, now listen. We will look at it like this. . . . Suppose we want to divide seven eighths not by two fifths but by two, that is, by the numerator only. We divide it, what do we get?

"Seven sixteenths."

"Right. Bravo! Well, the trick of it is, my boy, that if we . . . so if we have divided it by two then. . . . Wait a bit, I am getting muddled. I remember when I was at school, the teacher of arithmetic was called Sigismund Urbanitch, a Pole. He used to get into a muddle over every lesson. He would begin explaining some theory, get in a tangle, and turn crimson all over and race up and down the class-room as though someone were sticking an awl in his back, then he would blow his nose half a dozen times and begin to cry. But you know we were magnanimous to him, we pretended not to see it. 'What is it, Sigismund Urbanitch?' we used to ask him. 'Have you got toothache?' And what a set of young ruffians, regular cut-throats, we were, but yet we were magnanimous, you know! There weren't any boys like you in my day, they were all great hulking fellows, great strapping louts, one taller than another. For instance, in our third class, there was Mamahin. My goodness, he was a solid chap! You know, a regular maypole, seven feet high. When he moved, the floor shook; when he brought his great fist down on your back, he would knock the breath out of your body! Not only we boys, but even the teachers were afraid of him. So this Mamahin used to . . ."

Pelageya Ivanovna's footsteps are heard through the door. Pavel Vassilitch winks towards the door and says:

"There's mother coming. Let's get to work. Well, so you see, my boy," he says, raising his voice. "This fraction has to be multiplied by that one. Well, and to do that you have to take the numerator of the first fraction. . ."

"Come to tea!" cries Pelageya Ivanovna. Pavel Vassilitch and his son abandon arithmetic and go in to tea. Pelageya Ivanovna is already sitting at the table with an aunt who never speaks, another aunt who is deaf and dumb, and Granny Markovna, a midwife who had helped Styopa into the world. The samovar is hissing and puffing out steam which throws flickering shadows on the ceiling. The cats come in from the entry sleepy and melancholy with their tails in the air. . . .

"Have some jam with your tea, Markovna," says Pelageya Ivanovna, addressing the midwife. "To-morrow the great fast begins. Eat well to-day."

Markovna takes a heaped spoonful of jam hesitatingly as though it were a powder, raises it to her lips, and with a sidelong look at Pavel Vassilitch, eats it; at once her face is overspread with a sweet smile, as sweet as the jam itself.

"The jam is particularly good," she says. "Did you make it yourself, Pelageya Ivanovna, ma'am?"

"Yes. Who else is there to do it? I do everything myself. Styopotchka, have I given you your tea too weak? Ah, you have drunk it already. Pass your cup, my angel; let me give you some more."

"So this Mamahin, my boy, could not bear the French master," Pavel Vassilitch goes on, addressing his son. "'I am a nobleman,' he used to shout, 'and I won't allow a Frenchman to lord it over me! We beat the French in 1812!' Well, of course they used to thrash him for it . . . thrash him dre-ead-fully, and sometimes when he saw they were meaning to thrash him, he would jump out of window, and off he would go! Then for five or six days afterwards he would not show himself at the school. His mother would come to the head-master and beg him for God's sake: 'Be so kind, sir, as to find my Mishka, and flog him, the rascal!' And the head-master would say to her: 'Upon my word, madam, our five porters aren't a match for him!'"

"Good heavens, to think of such ruffians being born," whispers Pelageya Ivanovna, looking at her husband in horror. "What a trial for the poor mother!"

A silence follows. Styopa yawns loudly, and scrutinises the Chinaman on the tea-caddy whom he has seen a thousand times already. Markovna and the two aunts sip tea carefully out of their saucers. The air is still and stifling from the stove. . . . Faces and gestures betray the sloth and repletion that comes when the stomach is full, and yet one must go on eating. The samovar, the cups, and the table-cloth are cleared away, but still the family sits on at the table. . . . Pelageya Ivanovna is continually jumping up and, with an expression of alarm on her face, running off into the kitchen, to talk to the cook about the supper. The two aunts go on sitting in the same position immovably, with their arms folded across their bosoms and doze, staring with their pewtery little eyes at the lamp.

Markovna hiccups every minute and asks:

"Why is it I have the hiccups? I don't think I have eaten anything to account for it . . . nor drunk anything either. . . . Hic!"

Pavel Vassilitch and Styopa sit side by side, with their heads touching, and, bending over the table, examine a volume of the "Neva" for 1878.

"'The monument of Leonardo da Vinci, facing the gallery of Victor Emmanuel at Milan.' I say! . . . After the style of a triumphal arch. . . . A cavalier with his lady. . . . And there are little men in the distance. . . ."

"That little man is like a schoolfellow of mine called Niskubin," says Styopa.

"Turn over. . . . 'The proboscis of the common house-fly seen under the microscope.' So that's a proboscis! I say—a fly. Whatever would a bug look like under a microscope, my boy? Wouldn't it be horrid!"

The old-fashioned clock in the drawing-room does not strike, but coughs ten times huskily as though it had a cold. The cook, Anna, comes into the dining-room, and plumps down at the master's feet.

"Forgive me, for Christ's sake, Pavel Vassilitch!" she says, getting up, flushed all over.

"You forgive me, too, for Christ's sake," Pavel Vassilitch responds unconcernedly.

In the same manner, Anna goes up to the other members of the family, plumps down at their feet, and begs forgiveness. She only misses out Markovna to whom, not being one of the gentry, she does not feel it necessary to bow down.

Another half-hour passes in stillness and tranquillity. The "Neva" is by now lying on the sofa, and Pavel Vassilitch, holding up his finger, repeats by heart some Latin verses he has learned in his childhood. Styopa stares at the finger with the wedding ring, listens to the unintelligible words, and dozes; he rubs his eyelids with his fists, and they shut all the tighter.

"I am going to bed . . ." he says, stretching and yawning.

"What, to bed?" says Pelageya Ivanovna. "What about supper before the fast?"

"I don't want any."

"Are you crazy?" says his mother in alarm. "How can you go without your supper before the fast? You'll have nothing but Lenten food all through the fast!"

Pavel Vassilitch is scared too.

"Yes, yes, my boy," he says. "For seven weeks mother will give you nothing but Lenten food. You can't miss the last supper before the fast."

"Oh dear, I am sleepy," says Styopa peevishly.

"Since that is how it is, lay the supper quickly," Pavel Vassilitch cries in a fluster. "Anna, why are you sitting there, silly? Make haste and lay the table."

Pelageya Ivanovna clasps her hands and runs into the kitchen with an expression as though the house were on fire.

"Make haste, make haste," is heard all over the house. "Styopotchka is sleepy. Anna! Oh dear me, what is one to do? Make haste."

Five minutes later the table is laid. Again the cats, arching their spines, and stretching themselves with their tails in the air, come into the dining-room. . . . The family begin supper. . . . No one is hungry, everyone's stomach is overfull, but yet they must eat.

THE OLD HOUSE

(A Story told by a Houseowner)

THE old house had to be pulled down that a new one might be built in its place. I led the architect through the empty rooms, and between our business talk told him various stories. The tattered wallpapers, the dingy windows, the dark stoves, all bore the traces of recent habitation and evoked memories. On that staircase, for instance, drunken men were once carrying down a dead body when they stumbled and flew headlong downstairs together with the coffin; the living were badly bruised, while the dead man looked very serious, as though nothing had happened, and shook his head when they lifted him up from the ground and put him back in the coffin. You see those three doors in a row: in there lived young ladies who were always receiving visitors, and so were better dressed than any other lodgers, and could pay their rent regularly. The door at the end of the corridor leads to the wash-house, where by day they washed clothes and at night made an uproar and drank beer. And in that flat of three rooms everything is saturated with bacteria and bacilli. It's not nice there. Many lodgers have died there, and I can positively assert that that flat was at some time cursed by someone, and that together with its human lodgers there was always another lodger, unseen, living in it. I remember particularly the fate of one family. Picture to yourself an ordinary man, not remarkable in any way, with a wife, a mother, and four children. His name was Putohin; he was a copying clerk at a notary's, and received thirty-five roubles a month. He was a sober, religious, serious man. When he brought me his rent for the flat he always apologised for being badly dressed; apologised for being five days late, and when I gave him a receipt he would smile good-humouredly and say: "Oh yes, there's that too, I don't like those receipts." He lived poorly but decently. In that middle room, the grandmother used to be with the four children; there they used to cook, sleep, receive their visitors, and even dance. This was Putohin's own room; he had a table in it, at which he used to work doing private jobs, copying parts for the theatre, advertisements, and so on. This room on the right was let to his lodger, Yegoritch, a locksmith—a steady fellow, but given to drink; he was always too hot, and so used to go about in his waistcoat and barefoot. Yegoritch used to mend locks, pistols, children's bicycles, would not refuse to mend cheap clocks and make skates for a quarter-rouble, but he despised that work, and looked on himself as a specialist in musical instruments. Amongst the litter of steel and iron on his table there was always to be seen a concertina with a broken key, or a trumpet with its sides bent in. He paid Putohin two and a half roubles for his room; he was always at his work-table, and only came out to thrust some piece of iron into the stove.

On the rare occasions when I went into that flat in the evening, this was always the picture I came upon: Putohin would be sitting at his little table, copying something; his mother and his wife, a thin woman with an exhausted-looking face, were sitting near the lamp, sewing; Yegoritch would be making a rasping sound with his file. And the hot, still smouldering embers in the stove filled the room with heat and fumes; the heavy air smelt of cabbage soup, swaddling-clothes, and Yegoritch. It was poor and stuffy, but the working-class faces, the children's little drawers hung up along by the stove, Yegoritch's bits of iron had yet an air of peace, friendliness, content. . . . In the corridor outside the children raced about with well-combed heads, merry and profoundly convinced that everything was satisfactory in this world, and would be so endlessly, that one had only to say one's prayers every morning and at bedtime.

Now imagine in the midst of that same room, two paces from the stove, the coffin in which Putohin's wife is lying. There is no husband whose wife will live for ever, but there was something special about this death. When, during the requiem service, I glanced at the husband's grave face, at his stern eyes, I thought: "Oho, brother!"

It seemed to me that he himself, his children, the grandmother and Yegoritch, were already marked down by that unseen being which lived with them in that flat. I am a thoroughly superstitious man, perhaps, because I am a houseowner and for forty years have had to do with lodgers. I believe if you don't win at cards from the beginning you will go on losing to the end; when fate wants to wipe you and your family off the face of the earth, it remains inexorable in its persecution, and the first misfortune is commonly only the first of a long series. . . . Misfortunes are like stones. One stone has only to drop from a high cliff for others to be set rolling after it. In short, as I came away from the requiem service at Putohin's, I believed that he and his family were in a bad way.

And, in fact, a week afterwards the notary quite unexpectedly dismissed Putohin, and engaged a young lady in his place. And would you believe it, Putohin was not so much put out at the loss of his job as at being superseded by a young lady and not by a man. Why a young lady? He so resented this that on his return home he thrashed his children, swore at his mother, and got drunk. Yegoritch got drunk, too, to keep him company.

Putohin brought me the rent, but did not apologise this time, though it was eighteen days overdue, and said nothing when he took the receipt from me. The following month the rent was brought by his mother; she only brought me half, and promised to bring the remainder a week later. The third month, I did not get a farthing, and the porter complained to me that the lodgers in No. 23 were "not behaving like gentlemen."

These were ominous symptoms.

Picture this scene. A sombre Petersburg morning looks in at the dingy windows. By the stove, the granny is pouring out the children's tea. Only the eldest, Vassya, drinks out of a glass, for the others the tea is poured out into saucers. Yegoritch is squatting on his heels before the stove, thrusting a bit of iron into the fire. His head is heavy and his eyes are lustreless from yesterday's drinking-bout; he sighs and groans, trembles and coughs.

"He has quite put me off the right way, the devil," he grumbles;

"he drinks himself and leads others into sin."

Putohin sits in his room, on the bedstead from which the bedclothes and the pillows have long ago disappeared, and with his hands straying in his hair looks blankly at the floor at his feet. He is tattered, unkempt, and ill.

"Drink it up, make haste or you will be late for school," the old woman urges on Vassya, "and it's time for me, too, to go and scrub the floors for the Jews. . . ."

The old woman is the only one in the flat who does not lose heart. She thinks of old times, and goes out to hard dirty work. On Fridays she scrubs the floors for the Jews at the crockery shop, on Saturdays she goes out washing for shopkeepers, and on Sundays she is racing about the town from morning to night, trying to find ladies who will help her. Every day she has work of some sort; she washes and scrubs, and is by turns a midwife, a matchmaker, or a beggar. It is true she, too, is not disinclined to drown her sorrows, but even when she has had a drop she does not forget her duties. In Russia there are many such tough old women, and how much of its welfare rests upon them!

When he has finished his tea, Vassya packs up his books in a satchel and goes behind the stove; his greatcoat ought to be hanging there beside his granny's clothes. A minute later he comes out from behind the stove and asks:

"Where is my greatcoat?"

The grandmother and the other children look for the greatcoat together, they waste a long time in looking for it, but the greatcoat has utterly vanished. Where is it? The grandmother and Vassya are pale and frightened. Even Yegoritch is surprised. Putohin is the only one who does not move. Though he is quick to notice anything irregular or disorderly, this time he makes a pretence of hearing and seeing nothing. That is suspicious.

"He's sold it for drink," Yegoritch declares.

Putohin says nothing, so it is the truth. Vassya is overcome with horror. His greatcoat, his splendid greatcoat, made of his dead mother's cloth dress, with a splendid calico lining, gone for drink at the tavern! And with the greatcoat is gone too, of course, the blue pencil that lay in the pocket, and the note-book with "Nota bene" in gold letters on it! There's another pencil with india-rubber stuck into the note-book, and, besides that, there are transfer pictures lying in it.

Vassya would like to cry, but to cry is impossible. If his father, who has a headache, heard crying he would shout, stamp with his feet, and begin fighting, and after drinking he fights horribly. Granny would stand up for Vassya, and his father would strike granny too; it would end in Yegoritch getting mixed up in it too, clutching at his father and falling on the floor with him. The two would roll on the floor, struggling together and gasping with drunken animal fury, and granny would cry, the children would scream, the neighbours would send for the porter. No, better not cry.

Because he mustn't cry, or give vent to his indignation aloud, Vassya moans, wrings his hands and moves his legs convulsively, or biting his sleeve shakes it with his teeth as a dog does a hare. His eyes are frantic, and his face is distorted with despair. Looking at him, his granny all at once takes the shawl off her head, and she too makes queer movements with her arms and legs in silence, with her eyes fixed on a point in the distance. And at that moment I believe there is a definite certainty in the minds of the boy and the old woman that their life is ruined, that there is no hope. . . .

Putohin hears no crying, but he can see it all from his room. When, half an hour later, Vassya sets off to school, wrapped in his grandmother's shawl, he goes out with a face I will not undertake to describe, and walks after him. He longs to call the boy, to comfort him, to beg his forgiveness, to promise him on his word of honour, to call his dead mother to witness, but instead of words, sobs break from him. It is a grey, cold morning. When he reaches the town school Vassya untwists his granny's shawl, and goes into the school with nothing over his jacket for fear the boys should say he looks like a woman. And when he gets home Putohin sobs, mutters some incoherent words, bows down to the ground before his mother and Yegoritch, and the locksmith's table. Then, recovering himself a little, he runs to me and begs me breathlessly, for God's sake, to find him some job. I give him hopes, of course.

"At last I am myself again," he said. "It's high time, indeed, to come to my senses. I've made a beast of myself, and now it's over."

He is delighted and thanks me, while I, who have studied these gentry thoroughly during the years I have owned the house, look at him, and am tempted to say:

"It's too late, dear fellow! You are a dead man already."

From me, Putohin runs to the town school. There he paces up and down, waiting till his boy comes out.

"I say, Vassya," he says joyfully, when the boy at last comes out, "I have just been promised a job. Wait a bit, I will buy you a splendid fur-coat. . . . I'll send you to the high school! Do you understand? To the high school! I'll make a gentleman of you! And I won't drink any more. On my honour I won't."

And he has intense faith in the bright future. But the evening comes on. The old woman, coming back from the Jews with twenty kopecks, exhausted and aching all over, sets to work to wash the children's clothes. Vassya is sitting doing a sum. Yegoritch is not working. Thanks to Putohin he has got into the way of drinking, and is feeling at the moment an overwhelming desire for drink. It's hot and stuffy in the room. Steam rises in clouds from the tub where the old woman is washing.

"Are we going?" Yegoritch asks surlily.

My lodger does not answer. After his excitement he feels insufferably dreary. He struggles with the desire to drink, with acute depression and . . . and, of course, depression gets the best of it. It is a familiar story.

Towards night, Yegoritch and Putohin go out, and in the morning Vassya cannot find granny's shawl.

That is the drama that took place in that flat. After selling the shawl for drink, Putohin did not come home again. Where he disappeared to I don't know. After he disappeared, the old woman first got drunk, then took to her bed. She was taken to the hospital, the younger children were fetched by relations of some sort, and Vassya went into the wash-house here. In the day-time he handed the irons, and at night fetched the beer. When he was turned out of the wash-house he went into the service of one of the young ladies, used to run about at night on errands of some sort, and began to be spoken of as "a dangerous customer."

What has happened to him since I don't know.

And in this room here a street musician lived for ten years. When he died they found twenty thousand roubles in his feather bed.

IN PASSION WEEK

"Go along, they are ringing already; and mind, don't be naughty in church or God will punish you."

My mother thrusts a few copper coins upon me, and, instantly forgetting about me, runs into the kitchen with an iron that needs reheating. I know well that after confession I shall not be allowed to eat or drink, and so, before leaving the house, I force myself to eat a crust of white bread, and to drink two glasses of water. It is quite spring in the street. The roads are all covered with brownish slush, in which future paths are already beginning to show; the roofs and side-walks are dry; the fresh young green is piercing through the rotting grass of last year, under the fences. In the gutters there is the merry gurgling and foaming of dirty water, in which the sunbeams do not disdain to bathe. Chips, straws, the husks of sunflower seeds are carried rapidly along in the water, whirling round and sticking in the dirty foam. Where, where are those chips swimming to? It may well be that from the gutter they may pass into the river, from the river into the sea, and from the sea into the ocean. I try to imagine to myself that long terrible journey, but my fancy stops short before reaching the sea.

A cabman drives by. He clicks to his horse, tugs at the reins, and does not see that two street urchins are hanging on the back of his cab. I should like to join them, but think of confession, and the street urchins begin to seem to me great sinners.

"They will be asked on the day of judgment: 'Why did you play pranks and deceive the poor cabman?'" I think. "They will begin to defend themselves, but evil spirits will seize them, and drag them to fire everlasting. But if they obey their parents, and give the beggars a kopeck each, or a roll, God will have pity on them, and will let them into Paradise."

The church porch is dry and bathed in sunshine. There is not a soul in it. I open the door irresolutely and go into the church. Here, in the twilight which seems to me thick and gloomy as at no other time, I am overcome by the sense of sinfulness and insignificance. What strikes the eye first of all is a huge crucifix, and on one side of it the Mother of God, and on the other, St. John the Divine. The candelabra and the candlestands are draped in black mourning covers, the lamps glimmer dimly and faintly, and the sun seems intentionally to pass by the church windows. The Mother of God and the beloved disciple of Jesus Christ, depicted in profile, gaze in silence at the insufferable agony and do not observe my presence;

I feel that to them I am alien, superfluous, unnoticed, that I can be no help to them by word or deed, that I am a loathsome, dishonest boy, only capable of mischief, rudeness, and tale-bearing. I think of all the people I know, and they all seem to me petty, stupid, and wicked, and incapable of bringing one drop of relief to that intolerable sorrow which I now behold.

The twilight of the church grows darker and more gloomy. And the Mother of God and St. John look lonely and forlorn to me.

Prokofy Ignatitch, a veteran soldier, the church verger's assistant, is standing behind the candle cupboard. Raising his eyebrows and stroking his beard he explains in a half-whisper to an old woman:

"Matins will be in the evening to-day, directly after vespers. And they will ring for the 'hours' to-morrow between seven and eight. Do you understand? Between seven and eight."

Between the two broad columns on the right, where the chapel of Varvara the Martyr begins, those who are going to confess stand beside the screen, awaiting their turn. And Mitka is there too— a ragged boy with his head hideously cropped, with ears that jut out, and little spiteful eyes. He is the son of Nastasya the charwoman, and is a bully and a ruffian who snatches apples from the women's baskets, and has more than once carried off my knuckle-bones. He looks at me angrily, and I fancy takes a spiteful pleasure in the fact that he, not I, will first go behind the screen. I feel boiling over with resentment, I try not to look at him, and, at the bottom of my heart, I am vexed that this wretched boy's sins will soon be forgiven.

In front of him stands a grandly dressed, beautiful lady, wearing a hat with a white feather. She is noticeably agitated, is waiting in strained suspense, and one of her cheeks is flushed red with excitement.

I wait for five minutes, for ten. . . . A well-dressed young man with a long thin neck, and rubber goloshes, comes out from behind the screen. I begin dreaming how, when I am grown up, I will buy goloshes exactly like them. I certainly will! The lady shudders and goes behind the screen. It is her turn.

In the crack, between the two panels of the screen, I can see the lady go up to the lectern and bow down to the ground, then get up, and, without looking at the priest, bow her head in anticipation. The priest stands with his back to the screen, and so I can only see his grey curly head, the chain of the cross on his chest, and his broad back. His face is not visible. Heaving a sigh, and not looking at the lady, he begins speaking rapidly, shaking his head, alternately raising and dropping his whispering voice. The lady listens meekly as though conscious of guilt, answers meekly, and looks at the floor.

"In what way can she be sinful?" I wonder, looking reverently at her gentle, beautiful face. "God forgive her sins, God send her happiness." But now the priest covers her head with the stole. "And I, unworthy priest . . ." I hear his voice, ". . . by His power given unto me, do forgive and absolve thee from all thy sins. . . ."

The lady bows down to the ground, kisses the cross, and comes back. Both her cheeks are flushed now, but her face is calm and serene and cheerful.

"She is happy now," I think to myself, looking first at her and then at the priest who had forgiven her sins. "But how happy the man must be who has the right to forgive sins!"

Now it is Mitka's turn, but a feeling of hatred for that young ruffian suddenly boils up in me. I want to go behind the screen before him, I want to be the first. Noticing my movement he hits me on the head with his candle, I respond by doing the same, and, for half a minute, there is a sound of panting, and, as it were, of someone breaking candles. . . . We are separated. My foe goes timidly up to the lectern, and bows down to the floor without bending his knees, but I do not see what happens after that; the thought that my turn is coming after Mitka's makes everything grow blurred and confused before my eyes; Mitka's protruding ears grow large, and melt into his dark head, the priest sways, the floor seems to be undulating. . . .

The priest's voice is audible: "And I, unworthy priest . . ."

Now I too move behind the screen. I do not feel the ground under my feet, it is as though I were walking on air. . . . I go up to the lectern which is taller than I am. For a minute I have a glimpse of the indifferent, exhausted face of the priest. But after that I see nothing but his sleeve with its blue lining, the cross, and the edge of the lectern. I am conscious of the close proximity of the priest, the smell of his cassock; I hear his stern voice, and my cheek turned towards him begins to burn. . . . I am so troubled that I miss a great deal that he says, but I answer his questions sincerely in an unnatural voice, not my own. I think of the forlorn figures of the Holy Mother and St. John the Divine, the crucifix, my mother, and I want to cry and beg forgiveness.

"What is your name?" the priest asks me, covering my head with the soft stole.

How light-hearted I am now, with joy in my soul!

I have no sins now, I am holy, I have the right to enter Paradise! I fancy that I already smell like the cassock. I go from behind the screen to the deacon to enter my name, and sniff at my sleeves. The dusk of the church no longer seems gloomy, and I look indifferently, without malice, at Mitka.

"What is your name?" the deacon asks.

"Fedya."

"And your name from your father?"

"I don't know."

"What is your papa's name?"

"Ivan Petrovitch."

"And your surname?"

I make no answer.

"How old are you?"

"Nearly nine."

When I get home I go to bed quickly, that I may not see them eating supper; and, shutting my eyes, dream of how fine it would be to endure martyrdom at the hands of some Herod or Dioskorus, to live in the desert, and, like St. Serafim, feed the bears, live in a cell, and eat nothing but holy bread, give my property to the poor, go on a pilgrimage to Kiev. I hear them laying the table in the dining-room—they are going to have supper, they will eat salad, cabbage pies, fried and baked fish. How hungry I am! I would consent to endure any martyrdom, to live in the desert without my mother, to feed bears out of my own hands, if only I might first eat just one cabbage pie!

"Lord, purify me a sinner," I pray, covering my head over. "Guardian angel, save me from the unclean spirit."

The next day, Thursday, I wake up with my heart as pure and clean as a fine spring day. I go gaily and boldly into the church, feeling that I am a communicant, that I have a splendid and expensive shirt on, made out of a silk dress left by my grandmother. In the church everything has an air of joy, happiness, and spring. The faces of the Mother of God and St. John the Divine are not so sorrowful as yesterday. The faces of the communicants are radiant with hope, and it seems as though all the past is forgotten, all is forgiven. Mitka, too, has combed his hair, and is dressed in his best. I look gaily at his protruding ears, and to show that I have nothing against him, I say:

"You look nice to-day, and if your hair did not stand up so, and you weren't so poorly dressed, everybody would think that your mother was not a washerwoman but a lady. Come to me at Easter, we will play knuckle-bones."

Mitka looks at me mistrustfully, and shakes his fist at me on the sly.

And the lady I saw yesterday looks lovely. She is wearing a light blue dress, and a big sparkling brooch in the shape of a horse-shoe. I admire her, and think that, when I am grown-up, I will certainly marry a woman like that, but remembering that getting married is shameful, I leave off thinking about it, and go into the choir where the deacon is already reading the "hours."

WHITEBROW

A HUNGRY she-wolf got up to go hunting. Her cubs, all three of them, were sound asleep, huddled in a heap and keeping each other warm. She licked them and went off.

It was already March, a month of spring, but at night the trees snapped with the cold, as they do in December, and one could hardly put one's tongue out without its being nipped. The wolf-mother was in delicate health and nervous; she started at the slightest sound, and kept hoping that no one would hurt the little ones at home while she was away. The smell of the tracks of men and horses, logs, piles of faggots, and the dark road with horse-dung on it frightened her; it seemed to her that men were standing behind the trees in the darkness, and that dogs were howling somewhere beyond the forest.

She was no longer young and her scent had grown feebler, so that it sometimes happened that she took the track of a fox for that of a dog, and even at times lost her way, a thing that had never been in her youth. Owing to the weakness of her health she no longer hunted calves and big sheep as she had in old days, and kept her distance now from mares with colts; she fed on nothing but carrion; fresh meat she tasted very rarely, only in the spring when she would come upon a hare and take away her young, or make her way into a peasant's stall where there were lambs.

Some three miles from her lair there stood a winter hut on the posting road. There lived the keeper Ignat, an old man of seventy, who was always coughing and talking to himself; at night he was usually asleep, and by day he wandered about the forest with a single-barrelled gun, whistling to the hares. He must have worked among machinery in early days, for before he stood still he always shouted to himself: "Stop the machine!" and before going on: "Full speed!" He had a huge black dog of indeterminate breed, called Arapka. When it ran too far ahead he used to shout to it: "Reverse action!" Sometimes he used to sing, and as he did so staggered violently, and often fell down (the wolf thought the wind blew him over), and shouted: "Run off the rails!"

The wolf remembered that, in the summer and autumn, a ram and two ewes were pasturing near the winter hut, and when she had run by not so long ago she fancied that she had heard bleating in the stall. And now, as she got near the place, she reflected that it was already March, and, by that time, there would certainly be lambs in the stall. She was tormented by hunger, she thought with what greediness she would eat a lamb, and these thoughts made her teeth snap, and her eyes glitter in the darkness like two sparks of light.

Ignat's hut, his barn, cattle-stall, and well were surrounded by high snowdrifts. All was still. Arapka was, most likely, asleep in the barn.

The wolf clambered over a snowdrift on to the stall, and began scratching away the thatched roof with her paws and her nose. The straw was rotten and decaying, so that the wolf almost fell through; all at once a smell of warm steam, of manure, and of sheep's milk floated straight to her nostrils. Down below, a lamb, feeling the cold, bleated softly. Leaping through the hole, the wolf fell with her four paws and chest on something soft and warm, probably a sheep, and at the same moment, something in the stall suddenly began whining, barking, and going off into a shrill little yap; the sheep huddled against the wall, and the wolf, frightened, snatched the first thing her teeth fastened on, and dashed away. . . .

She ran at her utmost speed, while Arapka, who by now had scented the wolf, howled furiously, the frightened hens cackled, and Ignat, coming out into the porch, shouted: "Full speed! Blow the whistle!"

And he whistled like a steam-engine, and then shouted: "Ho-ho-ho-ho!" and all this noise was repeated by the forest echo. When, little by little, it all died away, the wolf somewhat recovered herself, and began to notice that the prey she held in her teeth and dragged along the snow was heavier and, as it were, harder than lambs usually were at that season; and it smelt somehow different, and uttered strange sounds. . . . The wolf stopped and laid her burden on the snow, to rest and begin eating it, then all at once she leapt back in disgust. It was not a lamb, but a black puppy, with a big head and long legs, of a large breed, with a white patch on his brow, like Arapka's. Judging from his manners he was a simple, ignorant, yard-dog. He licked his crushed and wounded back, and, as though nothing was the matter, wagged his tail and barked at the wolf. She growled like a dog, and ran away from him. He ran after her. She looked round and snapped her teeth. He stopped in perplexity, and, probably deciding that she was playing with him, craned his head in the direction he had come from, and went off into a shrill, gleeful bark, as though inviting his mother Arapka to play with him and the wolf.

It was already getting light, and when the wolf reached her home in the thick aspen wood, each aspen tree could be seen distinctly, and the woodcocks were already awake, and the beautiful male birds often flew up, disturbed by the incautious gambols and barking of the puppy.

"Why does he run after me?" thought the wolf with annoyance. "I suppose he wants me to eat him."

She lived with her cubs in a shallow hole; three years before, a tall old pine tree had been torn up by the roots in a violent storm, and the hole had been formed by it. Now there were dead leaves and moss at the bottom, and around it lay bones and bullocks' horns, with which the little ones played. They were by now awake, and all three of them, very much alike, were standing in a row at the edge of their hole, looking at their returning mother, and wagging their tails. Seeing them, the puppy stopped a little way off, and stared at them for a very long time; seeing that they, too, were looking very attentively at him, he began barking angrily, as at strangers.

By now it was daylight and the sun had risen, the snow sparkled all around, but still the puppy stood a little way off and barked. The cubs sucked their mother, pressing her thin belly with their paws, while she gnawed a horse's bone, dry and white; she was tormented by hunger, her head ached from the dog's barking, and she felt inclined to fall on the uninvited guest and tear him to pieces.

At last the puppy was hoarse and exhausted; seeing they were not afraid of him, and not even attending to him, he began somewhat timidly approaching the cubs, alternately squatting down and bounding a few steps forward. Now, by daylight, it was easy to have a good look at him. . . . His white forehead was big, and on it was a hump such as is only seen on very stupid dogs; he had little, blue, dingy-looking eyes, and the expression of his whole face was extremely stupid. When he reached the cubs he stretched out his broad paws, laid his head upon them, and began:

"Mnya, myna . . . nga—nga—nga . . . !"

The cubs did not understand what he meant, but they wagged their tails. Then the puppy gave one of the cubs a smack on its big head with his paw. The cub, too, gave him a smack on the head. The puppy stood sideways to him, and looked at him askance, wagging his tail, then dashed off, and ran round several times on the frozen snow. The cubs ran after him, he fell on his back and kicked up his legs, and all three of them fell upon him, squealing with delight, and began biting him, not to hurt but in play. The crows sat on the high pine tree, and looked down on their struggle, and were much troubled by it. They grew noisy and merry. The sun was hot, as though it were spring; and the woodcocks, continually flitting through the pine tree that had been blown down by the storm, looked as though made of emerald in the brilliant sunshine.

As a rule, wolf-mothers train their children to hunt by giving them prey to play with; and now watching the cubs chasing the puppy over the frozen snow and struggling with him, the mother thought:

"Let them learn."

When they had played long enough, the cubs went into the hole and lay down to sleep. The puppy howled a little from hunger, then he, too, stretched out in the sunshine. And when they woke up they began playing again.

All day long, and in the evening, the wolf-mother was thinking how the lamb had bleated in the cattle-shed the night before, and how it had smelt of sheep's milk, and she kept snapping her teeth from hunger, and never left off greedily gnawing the old bone, pretending to herself that it was the lamb. The cubs sucked their mother, and the puppy, who was hungry, ran round them and sniffed at the snow.

"I'll eat him . . ." the mother-wolf decided.

She went up to him, and he licked her nose and yapped at her, thinking that she wanted to play with him. In the past she had eaten dogs, but the dog smelt very doggy, and in the delicate state of her health she could not endure the smell; she felt disgusted and walked away. . . .

Towards night it grew cold. The puppy felt depressed and went home.

When the wolf-cubs were fast asleep, their mother went out hunting again. As on the previous night she was alarmed at every sound, and she was frightened by the stumps, the logs, the dark juniper bushes, which stood out singly, and in the distance were like human beings. She ran on the ice-covered snow, keeping away from the road. . . . All at once she caught a glimpse of something dark, far away on the road. She strained her eyes and ears: yes, something really was walking on in front, she could even hear the regular thud of footsteps. Surely not a badger? Cautiously holding her breath, and keeping always to one side, she overtook the dark patch, looked round, and recognised it. It was the puppy with the white brow, going with a slow, lingering step homewards.

"If only he doesn't hinder me again," thought the wolf, and ran quickly on ahead.

But the homestead was by now near. Again she clambered on to the cattle-shed by the snowdrift. The gap she had made yesterday had been already mended with straw, and two new rafters stretched across the roof. The wolf began rapidly working with her legs and nose, looking round to see whether the puppy were coming, but the smell of the warm steam and manure had hardly reached her nose before she heard a gleeful burst of barking behind her. It was the puppy. He leapt up to the wolf on the roof, then into the hole, and, feeling himself at home in the warmth, recognising his sheep, he barked louder than ever. . . . Arapka woke up in the barn, and, scenting a wolf, howled, the hens began cackling, and by the time Ignat appeared in the porch with his single-barrelled gun the frightened wolf was already far away.

"Fuite!" whistled Ignat. "Fuite! Full steam ahead!"

He pulled the trigger—the gun missed fire; he pulled the trigger again—again it missed fire; he tried a third time—and a great blaze of flame flew out of the barrel and there was a deafening boom, boom. It kicked him violently on the shoulder, and, taking his gun in one hand and his axe in the other, he went to see what the noise was about.

A little later he went back to the hut.

"What was it?" a pilgrim, who was staying the night at the hut and had been awakened by the noise, asked in a husky voice.

"It's all right," answered Ignat. "Nothing of consequence. Our Whitebrow has taken to sleeping with the sheep in the warm. Only he hasn't the sense to go in at the door, but always tries to wriggle in by the roof. The other night he tore a hole in the roof and went off on the spree, the rascal, and now he has come back and scratched away the roof again."

"Stupid dog."

"Yes, there is a spring snapped in his brain. I do detest fools," sighed Ignat, clambering on to the stove. "Come, man of God, it's early yet to get up. Let us sleep full steam! . . ."

In the morning he called Whitebrow, smacked him hard about the ears, and then showing him a stick, kept repeating to him:

"Go in at the door! Go in at the door! Go in at the door!"

KASHTANKA

(A Story)

I

Misbehaviour

A YOUNG dog, a reddish mongrel, between a dachshund and a "yard-dog," very like a fox in face, was running up and down the pavement looking uneasily from side to side. From time to time she stopped and, whining and lifting first one chilled paw and then another, tried to make up her mind how it could have happened that she was lost.

She remembered very well how she had passed the day, and how, in the end, she had found herself on this unfamiliar pavement.

The day had begun by her master Luka Alexandritch's putting on his hat, taking something wooden under his arm wrapped up in a red handkerchief, and calling: "Kashtanka, come along!"

Hearing her name the mongrel had come out from under the work-table, where she slept on the shavings, stretched herself voluptuously and run after her master. The people Luka Alexandritch worked for lived a very long way off, so that, before he could get to any one of them, the carpenter had several times to step into a tavern to fortify himself. Kashtanka remembered that on the way she had behaved extremely improperly. In her delight that she was being taken for a walk she jumped about, dashed barking after the trains, ran into yards, and chased other dogs. The carpenter was continually losing sight of her, stopping, and angrily shouting at her. Once he had even, with an expression of fury in his face, taken her fox-like ear in his fist, smacked her, and said emphatically: "Pla-a-ague take you, you pest!"

After having left the work where it had been bespoken, Luka Alexandritch went into his sister's and there had something to eat and drink; from his sister's he had gone to see a bookbinder he knew; from the bookbinder's to a tavern, from the tavern to another crony's, and so on. In short, by the time Kashtanka found herself on the unfamiliar pavement, it was getting dusk, and the carpenter was as drunk as a cobbler. He was waving his arms and, breathing heavily, muttered:

"In sin my mother bore me! Ah, sins, sins! Here now we are walking along the street and looking at the street lamps, but when we die, we shall burn in a fiery Gehenna. . ."

Or he fell into a good-natured tone, called Kashtanka to him, and said to her: "You, Kashtanka, are an insect of a creature, and nothing else. Beside a man, you are much the same as a joiner beside a cabinet-maker. . . ."

While he talked to her in that way, there was suddenly a burst of music. Kashtanka looked round and saw that a regiment of soldiers was coming straight towards her. Unable to endure the music, which unhinged her nerves, she turned round and round and wailed. To her great surprise, the carpenter, instead of being frightened, whining and barking, gave a broad grin, drew himself up to attention, and saluted with all his five fingers. Seeing that her master did not protest, Kashtanka whined louder than ever, and dashed across the road to the opposite pavement.

When she recovered herself, the band was not playing and the regiment was no longer there. She ran across the road to the spot where she had left her master, but alas, the carpenter was no longer there. She dashed forward, then back again and ran across the road once more, but the carpenter seemed to have vanished into the earth. Kashtanka began sniffing the pavement, hoping to find her master by the scent of his tracks, but some wretch had been that way just before in new rubber goloshes, and now all delicate scents were mixed with an acute stench of india-rubber, so that it was impossible to make out anything.

Kashtanka ran up and down and did not find her master, and meanwhile it had got dark. The street lamps were lighted on both sides of the road, and lights appeared in the windows. Big, fluffy snowflakes were falling and painting white the pavement, the horses' backs and the cabmen's caps, and the darker the evening grew the whiter were all these objects. Unknown customers kept walking incessantly to and fro, obstructing her field of vision and shoving against her with their feet. (All mankind Kashtanka divided into two uneven parts: masters and customers; between them there was an essential difference: the first had the right to beat her, and the second she had the right to nip by the calves of their legs.) These customers were hurrying off somewhere and paid no attention to her.

When it got quite dark, Kashtanka was overcome by despair and horror. She huddled up in an entrance and began whining piteously. The long day's journeying with Luka Alexandritch had exhausted her, her ears and her paws were freezing, and, what was more, she was terribly hungry. Only twice in the whole day had she tasted a morsel: she had eaten a little paste at the bookbinder's, and in one of the taverns she had found a sausage skin on the floor, near the counter that was all. If she had been a human being she would have certainly thought: "No, it is impossible to live like this! I must shoot myself!"

II

A Mysterious Stranger

But she thought of nothing, she simply whined. When her head and back were entirely plastered over with the soft feathery snow, and she had sunk into a painful doze of exhaustion, all at once the door of the entrance clicked, creaked, and struck her on the side. She jumped up. A man belonging to the class of customers came out. As Kashtanka whined and got under his feet, he could not help noticing her. He bent down to her and asked:

"Doggy, where do you come from? Have I hurt you? O, poor thing, poor thing. . . . Come, don't be cross, don't be cross. . . . I am sorry."

Kashtanka looked at the stranger through the snow-flakes that hung on her eyelashes, and saw before her a short, fat little man, with a plump, shaven face wearing a top hat and a fur coat that swung open.

"What are you whining for?" he went on, knocking the snow off her back with his fingers. "Where is your master? I suppose you are lost? Ah, poor doggy! What are we going to do now?"

Catching in the stranger's voice a warm, cordial note, Kashtanka licked his hand, and whined still more pitifully.

"Oh, you nice funny thing!" said the stranger. "A regular fox! Well, there's nothing for it, you must come along with me! Perhaps you will be of use for something. . . . Well!"

He clicked with his lips, and made a sign to Kashtanka with his hand, which could only mean one thing: "Come along!" Kashtanka went.

Not more than half an hour later she was sitting on the floor in a big, light room, and, leaning her head against her side, was looking with tenderness and curiosity at the stranger who was sitting at the table, dining. He ate and threw pieces to her. . . . At first he gave her bread and the green rind of cheese, then a piece of meat, half a pie and chicken bones, while through hunger she ate so quickly that she had not time to distinguish the taste, and the more she ate the more acute was the feeling of hunger.

"Your masters don't feed you properly," said the stranger, seeing with what ferocious greediness she swallowed the morsels without munching them. "And how thin you are! Nothing but skin and bones. . . ."

Kashtanka ate a great deal and yet did not satisfy her hunger, but was simply stupefied with eating. After dinner she lay down in the middle of the room, stretched her legs and, conscious of an agreeable weariness all over her body, wagged her tail. While her new master, lounging in an easy-chair, smoked a cigar, she wagged her tail and considered the question, whether it was better at the stranger's or at the carpenter's. The stranger's surroundings were poor and ugly; besides the easy-chairs, the sofa, the lamps and the rugs, there was nothing, and the room seemed empty. At the carpenter's the whole place was stuffed full of things: he had a table, a bench, a heap of shavings, planes, chisels, saws, a cage with a goldfinch, a basin. . . . The stranger's room smelt of nothing, while there was always a thick fog in the carpenter's room, and a glorious smell of glue, varnish, and shavings. On the other hand, the stranger had one great superiority—he gave her a great deal to eat and, to do him full justice, when Kashtanka sat facing the table and looking wistfully at him, he did not once hit or kick her, and did not once shout: "Go away, damned brute!"

When he had finished his cigar her new master went out, and a minute later came back holding a little mattress in his hands.

"Hey, you dog, come here!" he said, laying the mattress in the corner near the dog. "Lie down here, go to sleep!"

Then he put out the lamp and went away. Kashtanka lay down on the mattress and shut her eyes; the sound of a bark rose from the street, and she would have liked to answer it, but all at once she was overcome with unexpected melancholy. She thought of Luka Alexandritch, of his son Fedyushka, and her snug little place under the bench. . . . She remembered on the long winter evenings, when the carpenter was planing or reading the paper aloud, Fedyushka usually played with her. . . . He used to pull her from under the bench by her hind legs, and play such tricks with her, that she saw green before her eyes, and ached in every joint. He would make her walk on her hind legs, use her as a bell, that is, shake her violently by the tail so that she squealed and barked, and give her tobacco to sniff . . . . The following trick was particularly agonising: Fedyushka would tie a piece of meat to a thread and give it to Kashtanka, and then, when she had swallowed it he would, with a loud laugh, pull it back again from her stomach, and the more lurid were her memories the more loudly and miserably Kashtanka whined.

But soon exhaustion and warmth prevailed over melancholy. She began to fall asleep. Dogs ran by in her imagination: among them a shaggy old poodle, whom she had seen that day in the street with a white patch on his eye and tufts of wool by his nose. Fedyushka ran after the poodle with a chisel in his hand, then all at once he too was covered with shaggy wool, and began merrily barking beside Kashtanka. Kashtanka and he goodnaturedly sniffed each other's noses and merrily ran down the street. . . .

III

New and Very Agreeable Acquaintances

When Kashtanka woke up it was already light, and a sound rose from the street, such as only comes in the day-time. There was not a soul in the room. Kashtanka stretched, yawned and, cross and ill-humoured, walked about the room. She sniffed the corners and the furniture, looked into the passage and found nothing of interest there. Besides the door that led into the passage there was another door. After thinking a little Kashtanka scratched on it with both paws, opened it, and went into the adjoining room. Here on the bed, covered with a rug, a customer, in whom she recognised the stranger of yesterday, lay asleep.

"Rrrrr . . ." she growled, but recollecting yesterday's dinner, wagged her tail, and began sniffing.

She sniffed the stranger's clothes and boots and thought they smelt of horses. In the bedroom was another door, also closed. Kashtanka scratched at the door, leaned her chest against it, opened it, and was instantly aware of a strange and very suspicious smell. Foreseeing an unpleasant encounter, growling and looking about her, Kashtanka walked into a little room with a dirty wall-paper and drew back in alarm. She saw something surprising and terrible. A grey gander came straight towards her, hissing, with its neck bowed down to the floor and its wings outspread. Not far from him, on a little mattress, lay a white tom-cat; seeing Kashtanka, he jumped up, arched his back, wagged his tail with his hair standing on end and he, too, hissed at her. The dog was frightened in earnest, but not caring to betray her alarm, began barking loudly and dashed at the cat . . . . The cat arched his back more than ever, mewed and gave Kashtanka a smack on the head with his paw. Kashtanka jumped back, squatted on all four paws, and craning her nose towards the cat, went off into loud, shrill barks; meanwhile the gander came up behind and gave her a painful peck in the back. Kashtanka leapt up and dashed at the gander.

"What's this?" They heard a loud angry voice, and the stranger came into the room in his dressing-gown, with a cigar between his teeth. "What's the meaning of this? To your places!"

He went up to the cat, flicked him on his arched back, and said:

"Fyodor Timofeyitch, what's the meaning of this? Have you got up a fight? Ah, you old rascal! Lie down!"

And turning to the gander he shouted: "Ivan Ivanitch, go home!"

The cat obediently lay down on his mattress and closed his eyes. Judging from the expression of his face and whiskers, he was displeased with himself for having lost his temper and got into a fight.

Kashtanka began whining resentfully, while the gander craned his neck and began saying something rapidly, excitedly, distinctly, but quite unintelligibly.

"All right, all right," said his master, yawning. "You must live in peace and friendship." He stroked Kashtanka and went on: "And you, redhair, don't be frightened. . . . They are capital company, they won't annoy you. Stay, what are we to call you? You can't go on without a name, my dear."

The stranger thought a moment and said: "I tell you what . . . you shall be Auntie. . . . Do you understand? Auntie!"

And repeating the word "Auntie" several times he went out. Kashtanka sat down and began watching. The cat sat motionless on his little mattress, and pretended to be asleep. The gander, craning his neck and stamping, went on talking rapidly and excitedly about something. Apparently it was a very clever gander; after every long tirade, he always stepped back with an air of wonder and made a show of being highly delighted with his own speech. . . . Listening to him and answering "R-r-r-r," Kashtanka fell to sniffing the corners. In one of the corners she found a little trough in which she saw some soaked peas and a sop of rye crusts. She tried the peas; they were not nice; she tried the sopped bread and began eating it. The gander was not at all offended that the strange dog was eating his food, but, on the contrary, talked even more excitedly, and to show his confidence went to the trough and ate a few peas himself.

IV

Marvels on a Hurdle

A little while afterwards the stranger came in again, and brought a strange thing with him like a hurdle, or like the figure II. On the crosspiece on the top of this roughly made wooden frame hung a bell, and a pistol was also tied to it; there were strings from the tongue of the bell, and the trigger of the pistol. The stranger put the frame in the middle of the room, spent a long time tying and untying something, then looked at the gander and said: "Ivan Ivanitch, if you please!"

The gander went up to him and stood in an expectant attitude.

"Now then," said the stranger, "let us begin at the very beginning.

First of all, bow and make a curtsey! Look sharp!"

Ivan Ivanitch craned his neck, nodded in all directions, and scraped with his foot.

"Right. Bravo. . . . Now die!"

The gander lay on his back and stuck his legs in the air. After performing a few more similar, unimportant tricks, the stranger suddenly clutched at his head, and assuming an expression of horror, shouted: "Help! Fire! We are burning!"

Ivan Ivanitch ran to the frame, took the string in his beak, and set the bell ringing.

The stranger was very much pleased. He stroked the gander's neck and said:

"Bravo, Ivan Ivanitch! Now pretend that you are a jeweller selling gold and diamonds. Imagine now that you go to your shop and find thieves there. What would you do in that case?"

The gander took the other string in his beak and pulled it, and at once a deafening report was heard. Kashtanka was highly delighted with the bell ringing, and the shot threw her into so much ecstasy that she ran round the frame barking.

"Auntie, lie down!" cried the stranger; "be quiet!"

Ivan Ivanitch's task was not ended with the shooting. For a whole hour afterwards the stranger drove the gander round him on a cord, cracking a whip, and the gander had to jump over barriers and through hoops; he had to rear, that is, sit on his tail and wave his legs in the air. Kashtanka could not take her eyes off Ivan Ivanitch, wriggled with delight, and several times fell to running after him with shrill barks. After exhausting the gander and himself, the stranger wiped the sweat from his brow and cried:

"Marya, fetch Havronya Ivanovna here!"

A minute later there was the sound of grunting. Kashtanka growled, assumed a very valiant air, and to be on the safe side, went nearer to the stranger. The door opened, an old woman looked in, and, saying something, led in a black and very ugly sow. Paying no attention to Kashtanka's growls, the sow lifted up her little hoof and grunted good-humouredly. Apparently it was very agreeable to her to see her master, the cat, and Ivan Ivanitch. When she went up to the cat and gave him a light tap on the stomach with her hoof, and then made some remark to the gander, a great deal of good-nature was expressed in her movements, and the quivering of her tail. Kashtanka realised at once that to growl and bark at such a character was useless.

The master took away the frame and cried. "Fyodor Timofeyitch, if you please!"

The cat stretched lazily, and reluctantly, as though performing a duty, went up to the sow.

"Come, let us begin with the Egyptian pyramid," began the master.

He spent a long time explaining something, then gave the word of command, "One . . . two . . . three!" At the word "three" Ivan Ivanitch flapped his wings and jumped on to the sow's back. . . . When, balancing himself with his wings and his neck, he got a firm foothold on the bristly back, Fyodor Timofeyitch listlessly and lazily, with manifest disdain, and with an air of scorning his art and not caring a pin for it, climbed on to the sow's back, then reluctantly mounted on to the gander, and stood on his hind legs. The result was what the stranger called the Egyptian pyramid. Kashtanka yapped with delight, but at that moment the old cat yawned and, losing his balance, rolled off the gander. Ivan Ivanitch lurched and fell off too. The stranger shouted, waved his hands, and began explaining something again. After spending an hour over the pyramid their indefatigable master proceeded to teach Ivan Ivanitch to ride on the cat, then began to teach the cat to smoke, and so on.

The lesson ended in the stranger's wiping the sweat off his brow and going away. Fyodor Timofeyitch gave a disdainful sniff, lay down on his mattress, and closed his eyes; Ivan Ivanitch went to the trough, and the pig was taken away by the old woman. Thanks to the number of her new impressions, Kashranka hardly noticed how the day passed, and in the evening she was installed with her mattress in the room with the dirty wall-paper, and spent the night in the society of Fyodor Timofeyitch and the gander.

V

Talent! Talent!

A month passed.

Kashtanka had grown used to having a nice dinner every evening, and being called Auntie. She had grown used to the stranger too, and to her new companions. Life was comfortable and easy.

Every day began in the same way. As a rule, Ivan Ivanitch was the first to wake up, and at once went up to Auntie or to the cat, twisting his neck, and beginning to talk excitedly and persuasively, but, as before, unintelligibly. Sometimes he would crane up his head in the air and utter a long monologue. At first Kashtanka thought he talked so much because he was very clever, but after a little time had passed, she lost all her respect for him; when he went up to her with his long speeches she no longer wagged her tail, but treated him as a tiresome chatterbox, who would not let anyone sleep and, without the slightest ceremony, answered him with "R-r-r-r!"

Fyodor Timofeyitch was a gentleman of a very different sort. When he woke he did not utter a sound, did not stir, and did not even open his eyes. He would have been glad not to wake, for, as was evident, he was not greatly in love with life. Nothing interested him, he showed an apathetic and nonchalant attitude to everything, he disdained everything and, even while eating his delicious dinner, sniffed contemptuously.

When she woke Kashtanka began walking about the room and sniffing the corners. She and the cat were the only ones allowed to go all over the flat; the gander had not the right to cross the threshold of the room with the dirty wall-paper, and Hayronya Ivanovna lived somewhere in a little outhouse in the yard and made her appearance only during the lessons. Their master got up late, and immediately after drinking his tea began teaching them their tricks. Every day the frame, the whip, and the hoop were brought in, and every day almost the same performance took place. The lesson lasted three or four hours, so that sometimes Fyodor Timofeyitch was so tired that he staggered about like a drunken man, and Ivan Ivanitch opened his beak and breathed heavily, while their master became red in the face and could not mop the sweat from his brow fast enough.

The lesson and the dinner made the day very interesting, but the evenings were tedious. As a rule, their master went off somewhere in the evening and took the cat and the gander with him. Left alone, Auntie lay down on her little mattress and began to feel sad.

Melancholy crept on her imperceptibly and took possession of her by degrees, as darkness does of a room. It began with the dog's losing every inclination to bark, to eat, to run about the rooms, and even to look at things; then vague figures, half dogs, half human beings, with countenances attractive, pleasant, but incomprehensible, would appear in her imagination; when they came Auntie wagged her tail, and it seemed to her that she had somewhere, at some time, seen them and loved them. And as she dropped asleep, she always felt that those figures smelt of glue, shavings, and varnish.

When she had grown quite used to her new life, and from a thin, long mongrel, had changed into a sleek, well-groomed dog, her master looked at her one day before the lesson and said:

"It's high time, Auntie, to get to business. You have kicked up your heels in idleness long enough. I want to make an artiste of you. . . . Do you want to be an artiste?"

And he began teaching her various accomplishments. At the first lesson he taught her to stand and walk on her hind legs, which she liked extremely. At the second lesson she had to jump on her hind legs and catch some sugar, which her teacher held high above her head. After that, in the following lessons she danced, ran tied to a cord, howled to music, rang the bell, and fired the pistol, and in a month could successfully replace Fyodor Timofeyitch in the "Egyptian Pyramid." She learned very eagerly and was pleased with her own success; running with her tongue out on the cord, leaping through the hoop, and riding on old Fyodor Timofeyitch, gave her the greatest enjoyment. She accompanied every successful trick with a shrill, delighted bark, while her teacher wondered, was also delighted, and rubbed his hands.

"It's talent! It's talent!" he said. "Unquestionable talent! You will certainly be successful!"

And Auntie grew so used to the word talent, that every time her master pronounced it, she jumped up as if it had been her name.

VI

An Uneasy Night

Auntie had a doggy dream that a porter ran after her with a broom, and she woke up in a fright.

It was quite dark and very stuffy in the room. The fleas were biting. Auntie had never been afraid of darkness before, but now, for some reason, she felt frightened and inclined to bark.

Her master heaved a loud sigh in the next room, then soon afterwards the sow grunted in her sty, and then all was still again. When one thinks about eating one's heart grows lighter, and Auntie began thinking how that day she had stolen the leg of a chicken from Fyodor Timofeyitch, and had hidden it in the drawing-room, between the cupboard and the wall, where there were a great many spiders' webs and a great deal of dust. Would it not be as well to go now and look whether the chicken leg were still there or not? It was very possible that her master had found it and eaten it. But she must not go out of the room before morning, that was the rule. Auntie shut her eyes to go to sleep as quickly as possible, for she knew by experience that the sooner you go to sleep the sooner the morning comes. But all at once there was a strange scream not far from her which made her start and jump up on all four legs. It was Ivan Ivanitch, and his cry was not babbling and persuasive as usual, but a wild, shrill, unnatural scream like the squeak of a door opening. Unable to distinguish anything in the darkness, and not understanding what was wrong, Auntie felt still more frightened and growled: "R-r-r-r. . . ."

Some time passed, as long as it takes to eat a good bone; the scream was not repeated. Little by little Auntie's uneasiness passed off and she began to doze. She dreamed of two big black dogs with tufts of last year's coat left on their haunches and sides; they were eating out of a big basin some swill, from which there came a white steam and a most appetising smell; from time to time they looked round at Auntie, showed their teeth and growled: "We are not going to give you any!" But a peasant in a fur-coat ran out of the house and drove them away with a whip; then Auntie went up to the basin and began eating, but as soon as the peasant went out of the gate, the two black dogs rushed at her growling, and all at once there was again a shrill scream.

"K-gee! K-gee-gee!" cried Ivan Ivanitch.

Auntie woke, jumped up and, without leaving her mattress, went off into a yelping bark. It seemed to her that it was not Ivan Ivanitch that was screaming but someone else, and for some reason the sow again grunted in her sty.

Then there was the sound of shuffling slippers, and the master came into the room in his dressing-gown with a candle in his hand. The flickering light danced over the dirty wall-paper and the ceiling, and chased away the darkness. Auntie saw that there was no stranger in the room. Ivan Ivanitch was sitting on the floor and was not asleep. His wings were spread out and his beak was open, and altogether he looked as though he were very tired and thirsty. Old Fyodor Timofeyitch was not asleep either. He, too, must have been awakened by the scream.

"Ivan Ivanitch, what's the matter with you?" the master asked the gander. "Why are you screaming? Are you ill?"

The gander did not answer. The master touched him on the neck, stroked his back, and said: "You are a queer chap. You don't sleep yourself, and you don't let other people. . . ."

When the master went out, carrying the candle with him, there was darkness again. Auntie felt frightened. The gander did not scream, but again she fancied that there was some stranger in the room. What was most dreadful was that this stranger could not be bitten, as he was unseen and had no shape. And for some reason she thought that something very bad would certainly happen that night. Fyodor Timofeyitch was uneasy too.

Auntie could hear him shifting on his mattress, yawning and shaking his head.

Somewhere in the street there was a knocking at a gate and the sow grunted in her sty. Auntie began to whine, stretched out her front-paws and laid her head down upon them. She fancied that in the knocking at the gate, in the grunting of the sow, who was for some reason awake, in the darkness and the stillness, there was something as miserable and dreadful as in Ivan Ivanitch's scream. Everything was in agitation and anxiety, but why? Who was the stranger who could not be seen? Then two dim flashes of green gleamed for a minute near Auntie. It was Fyodor Timofeyitch, for the first time of their whole acquaintance coming up to her. What did he want? Auntie licked his paw, and not asking why he had come, howled softly and on various notes.

"K-gee!" cried Ivan Ivanitch, "K-g-ee!"

The door opened again and the master came in with a candle.

The gander was sitting in the same attitude as before, with his beak open, and his wings spread out, his eyes were closed.

"Ivan Ivanitch!" his master called him.

The gander did not stir. His master sat down before him on the floor, looked at him in silence for a minute, and said:

"Ivan Ivanitch, what is it? Are you dying? Oh, I remember now, I remember!" he cried out, and clutched at his head. "I know why it is! It's because the horse stepped on you to-day! My God! My God!"

Auntie did not understand what her master was saying, but she saw from his face that he, too, was expecting something dreadful. She stretched out her head towards the dark window, where it seemed to her some stranger was looking in, and howled.

"He is dying, Auntie!" said her master, and wrung his hands. "Yes, yes, he is dying! Death has come into your room. What are we to do?"

Pale and agitated, the master went back into his room, sighing and shaking his head. Auntie was afraid to remain in the darkness, and followed her master into his bedroom. He sat down on the bed and repeated several times: "My God, what's to be done?"

Auntie walked about round his feet, and not understanding why she was wretched and why they were all so uneasy, and trying to understand, watched every movement he made. Fyodor Timofeyitch, who rarely left his little mattress, came into the master's bedroom too, and began rubbing himself against his feet. He shook his head as though he wanted to shake painful thoughts out of it, and kept peeping suspiciously under the bed.

The master took a saucer, poured some water from his wash-stand into it, and went to the gander again.

"Drink, Ivan Ivanitch!" he said tenderly, setting the saucer before him; "drink, darling."

But Ivan Ivanitch did not stir and did not open his eyes. His master bent his head down to the saucer and dipped his beak into the water, but the gander did not drink, he spread his wings wider than ever, and his head remained lying in the saucer.

"No, there's nothing to be done now," sighed his master. "It's all over. Ivan Ivanitch is gone!"

And shining drops, such as one sees on the window-pane when it rains, trickled down his cheeks. Not understanding what was the matter, Auntie and Fyodor Timofeyitch snuggled up to him and looked with horror at the gander.

"Poor Ivan Ivanitch!" said the master, sighing mournfully. "And I was dreaming I would take you in the spring into the country, and would walk with you on the green grass. Dear creature, my good comrade, you are no more! How shall I do without you now?"

It seemed to Auntie that the same thing would happen to her, that is, that she too, there was no knowing why, would close her eyes, stretch out her paws, open her mouth, and everyone would look at her with horror. Apparently the same reflections were passing through the brain of Fyodor Timofeyitch. Never before had the old cat been so morose and gloomy.

It began to get light, and the unseen stranger who had so frightened Auntie was no longer in the room. When it was quite daylight, the porter came in, took the gander, and carried him away. And soon afterwards the old woman came in and took away the trough.

Auntie went into the drawing-room and looked behind the cupboard:

her master had not eaten the chicken bone, it was lying in its place among the dust and spiders' webs. But Auntie felt sad and dreary and wanted to cry. She did not even sniff at the bone, but went under the sofa, sat down there, and began softly whining in a thin voice.

VII

An Unsuccessful Debut

One fine evening the master came into the room with the dirty wall-paper, and, rubbing his hands, said:

"Well. . . ."

He meant to say something more, but went away without saying it. Auntie, who during her lessons had thoroughly studied his face and intonations, divined that he was agitated, anxious and, she fancied, angry. Soon afterwards he came back and said:

"To-day I shall take with me Auntie and F'yodor Timofeyitch. To-day, Auntie, you will take the place of poor Ivan Ivanitch in the 'Egyptian Pyramid.' Goodness knows how it will be! Nothing is ready, nothing has been thoroughly studied, there have been few rehearsals! We shall be disgraced, we shall come to grief!"

Then he went out again, and a minute later, came back in his fur-coat and top hat. Going up to the cat he took him by the fore-paws and put him inside the front of his coat, while Fyodor Timofeyitch appeared completely unconcerned, and did not even trouble to open his eyes. To him it was apparently a matter of absolute indifference whether he remained lying down, or were lifted up by his paws, whether he rested on his mattress or under his master's fur-coat.

"Come along, Auntie," said her master.

Wagging her tail, and understanding nothing, Auntie followed him. A minute later she was sitting in a sledge by her master's feet and heard him, shrinking with cold and anxiety, mutter to himself:

"We shall be disgraced! We shall come to grief!"

The sledge stopped at a big strange-looking house, like a soup-ladle turned upside down. The long entrance to this house, with its three glass doors, was lighted up with a dozen brilliant lamps. The doors opened with a resounding noise and, like jaws, swallowed up the people who were moving to and fro at the entrance. There were a great many people, horses, too, often ran up to the entrance, but no dogs were to be seen.

The master took Auntie in his arms and thrust her in his coat, where Fyodor Timofeyirch already was. It was dark and stuffy there, but warm. For an instant two green sparks flashed at her; it was the cat, who opened his eyes on being disturbed by his neighbour's cold rough paws. Auntie licked his ear, and, trying to settle herself as comfortably as possible, moved uneasily, crushed him under her cold paws, and casually poked her head out from under the coat, but at once growled angrily, and tucked it in again. It seemed to her that she had seen a huge, badly lighted room, full of monsters; from behind screens and gratings, which stretched on both sides of the room, horrible faces looked out: faces of horses with horns, with long ears, and one fat, huge countenance with a tail instead of a nose, and two long gnawed bones sticking out of his mouth.

The cat mewed huskily under Auntie's paws, but at that moment the coat was flung open, the master said, "Hop!" and Fyodor Timofeyitch and Auntie jumped to the floor. They were now in a little room with grey plank walls; there was no other furniture in it but a little table with a looking-glass on it, a stool, and some rags hung about the corners, and instead of a lamp or candles, there was a bright fan-shaped light attached to a little pipe fixed in the wall. Fyodor Timofeyitch licked his coat which had been ruffled by Auntie, went under the stool, and lay down. Their master, still agitated and rubbing his hands, began undressing. . . . He undressed as he usually did at home when he was preparing to get under the rug, that is, took off everything but his underlinen, then he sat down on the stool, and, looking in the looking-glass, began playing the most surprising tricks with himself. . . . First of all he put on his head a wig, with a parting and with two tufts of hair standing up like horns, then he smeared his face thickly with something white, and over the white colour painted his eyebrows, his moustaches, and red on his cheeks. His antics did not end with that. After smearing his face and neck, he began putting himself into an extraordinary and incongruous costume, such as Auntie had never seen before, either in houses or in the street. Imagine very full trousers, made of chintz covered with big flowers, such as is used in working-class houses for curtains and covering furniture, trousers which buttoned up just under his armpits. One trouser leg was made of brown chintz, the other of bright yellow. Almost lost in these, he then put on a short chintz jacket, with a big scalloped collar, and a gold star on the back, stockings of different colours, and green slippers.

Everything seemed going round before Auntie's eyes and in her soul. The white-faced, sack-like figure smelt like her master, its voice, too, was the familiar master's voice, but there were moments when Auntie was tortured by doubts, and then she was ready to run away from the parti-coloured figure and to bark. The new place, the fan-shaped light, the smell, the transformation that had taken place in her master—all this aroused in her a vague dread and a foreboding that she would certainly meet with some horror such as the big face with the tail instead of a nose. And then, somewhere through the wall, some hateful band was playing, and from time to time she heard an incomprehensible roar. Only one thing reassured her—that was the imperturbability of Fyodor Timofeyitch. He dozed with the utmost tranquillity under the stool, and did not open his eyes even when it was moved.

A man in a dress coat and a white waistcoat peeped into the little room and said:

"Miss Arabella has just gone on. After her—you."

Their master made no answer. He drew a small box from under the table, sat down, and waited. From his lips and his hands it could be seen that he was agitated, and Auntie could hear how his breathing came in gasps.

"Monsieur George, come on!" someone shouted behind the door. Their master got up and crossed himself three times, then took the cat from under the stool and put him in the box.

"Come, Auntie," he said softly.

Auntie, who could make nothing out of it, went up to his hands, he kissed her on the head, and put her beside Fyodor Timofeyitch. Then followed darkness. . . . Auntie trampled on the cat, scratched at the walls of the box, and was so frightened that she could not utter a sound, while the box swayed and quivered, as though it were on the waves. . . .

"Here we are again!" her master shouted aloud: "here we are again!"

Auntie felt that after that shout the box struck against something hard and left off swaying. There was a loud deep roar, someone was being slapped, and that someone, probably the monster with the tail instead of a nose, roared and laughed so loud that the locks of the box trembled. In response to the roar, there came a shrill, squeaky laugh from her master, such as he never laughed at home.

"Ha!" he shouted, trying to shout above the roar. "Honoured friends! I have only just come from the station! My granny's kicked the bucket and left me a fortune! There is something very heavy in the box, it must be gold, ha! ha! I bet there's a million here! We'll open it and look. . . ."

The lock of the box clicked. The bright light dazzled Auntie's eyes, she jumped out of the box, and, deafened by the roar, ran quickly round her master, and broke into a shrill bark.

"Ha!" exclaimed her master. "Uncle Fyodor Timofeyitch! Beloved Aunt, dear relations! The devil take you!"

He fell on his stomach on the sand, seized the cat and Auntie, and fell to embracing them. While he held Auntie tight in his arms, she glanced round into the world into which fate had brought her and, impressed by its immensity, was for a minute dumbfounded with amazement and delight, then jumped out of her master's arms, and to express the intensity of her emotions, whirled round and round on one spot like a top. This new world was big and full of bright light; wherever she looked, on all sides, from floor to ceiling there were faces, faces, faces, and nothing else.

"Auntie, I beg you to sit down!" shouted her master. Remembering what that meant, Auntie jumped on to a chair, and sat down. She looked at her master. His eyes looked at her gravely and kindly as always, but his face, especially his mouth and teeth, were made grotesque by a broad immovable grin. He laughed, skipped about, twitched his shoulders, and made a show of being very merry in the presence of the thousands of faces. Auntie believed in his merriment, all at once felt all over her that those thousands of faces were looking at her, lifted up her fox-like head, and howled joyously.

"You sit there, Auntie," her master said to her, "while Uncle and I will dance the Kamarinsky."

Fyodor Timofeyitch stood looking about him indifferently, waiting to be made to do something silly. He danced listlessly, carelessly, sullenly, and one could see from his movements, his tail and his ears, that he had a profound contempt for the crowd, the bright light, his master and himself. When he had performed his allotted task, he gave a yawn and sat down.

"Now, Auntie!" said her master, "we'll have first a song, and then a dance, shall we?"

He took a pipe out of his pocket, and began playing. Auntie, who could not endure music, began moving uneasily in her chair and howled. A roar of applause rose from all sides. Her master bowed, and when all was still again, went on playing. . . . Just as he took one very high note, someone high up among the audience uttered a loud exclamation:

"Auntie!" cried a child's voice, "why it's Kashtanka!"

"Kashtanka it is!" declared a cracked drunken tenor. "Kashtanka!

Strike me dead, Fedyushka, it is Kashtanka. Kashtanka! here!"

Someone in the gallery gave a whistle, and two voices, one a boy's and one a man's, called loudly: "Kashtanka! Kashtanka!"

Auntie started, and looked where the shouting came from. Two faces, one hairy, drunken and grinning, the other chubby, rosy-cheeked and frightened-looking, dazed her eyes as the bright light had dazed them before. . . . She remembered, fell off the chair, struggled on the sand, then jumped up, and with a delighted yap dashed towards those faces. There was a deafening roar, interspersed with whistles and a shrill childish shout: "Kashtanka! Kashtanka!"

Auntie leaped over the barrier, then across someone's shoulders. She found herself in a box: to get into the next tier she had to leap over a high wall. Auntie jumped, but did not jump high enough, and slipped back down the wall. Then she was passed from hand to hand, licked hands and faces, kept mounting higher and higher, and at last got into the gallery. . . .

Half an hour afterwards, Kashtanka was in the street, following the people who smelt of glue and varnish. Luka Alexandritch staggered and instinctively, taught by experience, tried to keep as far from the gutter as possible.

"In sin my mother bore me," he muttered. "And you, Kashtanka, are a thing of little understanding. Beside a man, you are like a joiner beside a cabinetmaker."

Fedyushka walked beside him, wearing his father's cap. Kashtanka looked at their backs, and it seemed to her that she had been following them for ages, and was glad that there had not been a break for a minute in her life.

She remembered the little room with dirty wall-paper, the gander, Fyodor Timofeyitch, the delicious dinners, the lessons, the circus, but all that seemed to her now like a long, tangled, oppressive dream.

A CHAMELEON

THE police superintendent Otchumyelov is walking across the market square wearing a new overcoat and carrying a parcel under his arm. A red-haired policeman strides after him with a sieve full of confiscated gooseberries in his hands. There is silence all around. Not a soul in the square. . . . The open doors of the shops and taverns look out upon God's world disconsolately, like hungry mouths; there is not even a beggar near them.

"So you bite, you damned brute?" Otchumyelov hears suddenly. "Lads, don't let him go! Biting is prohibited nowadays! Hold him! ah . . . ah!"

There is the sound of a dog yelping. Otchumyelov looks in the direction of the sound and sees a dog, hopping on three legs and looking about her, run out of Pitchugin's timber-yard. A man in a starched cotton shirt, with his waistcoat unbuttoned, is chasing her. He runs after her, and throwing his body forward falls down and seizes the dog by her hind legs. Once more there is a yelping and a shout of "Don't let go!" Sleepy countenances are protruded from the shops, and soon a crowd, which seems to have sprung out of the earth, is gathered round the timber-yard.

"It looks like a row, your honour . . ." says the policeman.

Otchumyelov makes a half turn to the left and strides towards the crowd.

He sees the aforementioned man in the unbuttoned waistcoat standing close by the gate of the timber-yard, holding his right hand in the air and displaying a bleeding finger to the crowd. On his half-drunken face there is plainly written: "I'll pay you out, you rogue!" and indeed the very finger has the look of a flag of victory. In this man Otchumyelov recognises Hryukin, the goldsmith. The culprit who has caused the sensation, a white borzoy puppy with a sharp muzzle and a yellow patch on her back, is sitting on the ground with her fore-paws outstretched in the middle of the crowd, trembling all over. There is an expression of misery and terror in her tearful eyes.

"What's it all about?" Otchumyelov inquires, pushing his way through the crowd. "What are you here for? Why are you waving your finger . . . ? Who was it shouted?"

"I was walking along here, not interfering with anyone, your honour," Hryukin begins, coughing into his fist. "I was talking about firewood to Mitry Mitritch, when this low brute for no rhyme or reason bit my finger. . . . You must excuse me, I am a working man. . . . Mine is fine work. I must have damages, for I shan't be able to use this finger for a week, may be. . . . It's not even the law, your honour, that one should put up with it from a beast. . . . If everyone is going to be bitten, life won't be worth living. . . ."

"H'm. Very good," says Otchumyelov sternly, coughing and raising his eyebrows. "Very good. Whose dog is it? I won't let this pass! I'll teach them to let their dogs run all over the place! It's time these gentry were looked after, if they won't obey the regulations! When he's fined, the blackguard, I'll teach him what it means to keep dogs and such stray cattle! I'll give him a lesson! . . . Yeldyrin," cries the superintendent, addressing the policeman, "find out whose dog this is and draw up a report! And the dog must be strangled. Without delay! It's sure to be mad. . . . Whose dog is it, I ask?"

"I fancy it's General Zhigalov's," says someone in the crowd.

"General Zhigalov's, h'm. . . . Help me off with my coat, Yeldyrin . . . it's frightfully hot! It must be a sign of rain. . . . There's one thing I can't make out, how it came to bite you?" Otchumyelov turns to Hryukin. "Surely it couldn't reach your finger. It's a little dog, and you are a great hulking fellow! You must have scratched your finger with a nail, and then the idea struck you to get damages for it. We all know . . . your sort! I know you devils!"

"He put a cigarette in her face, your honour, for a joke, and she had the sense to snap at him. . . . He is a nonsensical fellow, your honour!"

"That's a lie, Squinteye! You didn't see, so why tell lies about it? His honour is a wise gentleman, and will see who is telling lies and who is telling the truth, as in God's sight. . . . And if I am lying let the court decide. It's written in the law. . . . We are all equal nowadays. My own brother is in the gendarmes . . . let me tell you. . . ."

"Don't argue!"

"No, that's not the General's dog," says the policeman, with profound conviction, "the General hasn't got one like that. His are mostly setters."

"Do you know that for a fact?"

"Yes, your honour."

"I know it, too. The General has valuable dogs, thoroughbred, and this is goodness knows what! No coat, no shape. . . . A low creature. And to keep a dog like that! . . . where's the sense of it. If a dog like that were to turn up in Petersburg or Moscow, do you know what would happen? They would not worry about the law, they would strangle it in a twinkling! You've been injured, Hryukin, and we can't let the matter drop. . . . We must give them a lesson! It is high time . . . . !"

"Yet maybe it is the General's," says the policeman, thinking aloud. "It's not written on its face. . . . I saw one like it the other day in his yard."

"It is the General's, that's certain!" says a voice in the crowd.

"H'm, help me on with my overcoat, Yeldyrin, my lad . . . the wind's getting up. . . . I am cold. . . . You take it to the General's, and inquire there. Say I found it and sent it. And tell them not to let it out into the street. . . . It may be a valuable dog, and if every swine goes sticking a cigar in its mouth, it will soon be ruined. A dog is a delicate animal. . . . And you put your hand down, you blockhead. It's no use your displaying your fool of a finger. It's your own fault. . . ."

"Here comes the General's cook, ask him. . . Hi, Prohor! Come here, my dear man! Look at this dog. . . . Is it one of yours?"

"What an idea! We have never had one like that!"

"There's no need to waste time asking," says Otchumyelov. "It's a stray dog! There's no need to waste time talking about it. . . . Since he says it's a stray dog, a stray dog it is. . . . It must be destroyed, that's all about it."

"It is not our dog," Prohor goes on. "It belongs to the General's brother, who arrived the other day. Our master does not care for hounds. But his honour is fond of them. . . ."

"You don't say his Excellency's brother is here? Vladimir Ivanitch?" inquires Otchumyelov, and his whole face beams with an ecstatic smile. "'Well, I never! And I didn't know! Has he come on a visit?

"Yes."

"Well, I never. . . . He couldn't stay away from his brother. . . . And there I didn't know! So this is his honour's dog? Delighted to hear it. . . . Take it. It's not a bad pup. . . . A lively creature. . . . Snapped at this fellow's finger! Ha-ha-ha. . . . Come, why are you shivering? Rrr . . . Rrrr. . . . The rogue's angry . . . a nice little pup."

Prohor calls the dog, and walks away from the timber-yard with her.

The crowd laughs at Hryukin.

"I'll make you smart yet!" Otchumyelov threatens him, and wrapping himself in his greatcoat, goes on his way across the square.

THE DEPENDENTS

MIHAIL PETROVITCH ZOTOV, a decrepit and solitary old man of seventy, belonging to the artisan class, was awakened by the cold and the aching in his old limbs. It was dark in his room, but the little lamp before the ikon was no longer burning. Zotov raised the curtain and looked out of the window. The clouds that shrouded the sky were beginning to show white here and there, and the air was becoming transparent, so it must have been nearly five, not more.

Zotov cleared his throat, coughed, and shrinking from the cold, got out of bed. In accordance with years of habit, he stood for a long time before the ikon, saying his prayers. He repeated "Our Father," "Hail Mary," the Creed, and mentioned a long string of names. To whom those names belonged he had forgotten years ago, and he only repeated them from habit. From habit, too, he swept his room and entry, and set his fat little four-legged copper samovar. If Zotov had not had these habits he would not have known how to occupy his old age.

The little samovar slowly began to get hot, and all at once, unexpectedly, broke into a tremulous bass hum.

"Oh, you've started humming!" grumbled Zotov. "Hum away then, and bad luck to you!"

At that point the old man appropriately recalled that, in the preceding night, he had dreamed of a stove, and to dream of a stove is a sign of sorrow.

Dreams and omens were the only things left that could rouse him to reflection; and on this occasion he plunged with a special zest into the considerations of the questions: What the samovar was humming for? and what sorrow was foretold by the stove? The dream seemed to come true from the first. Zotov rinsed out his teapot and was about to make his tea, when he found there was not one teaspoonful left in the box.

"What an existence!" he grumbled, rolling crumbs of black bread round in his mouth. "It's a dog's life. No tea! And it isn't as though I were a simple peasant: I'm an artisan and a house-owner. The disgrace!"

Grumbling and talking to himself, Zotov put on his overcoat, which was like a crinoline, and, thrusting his feet into huge clumsy golosh-boots (made in the year 1867 by a bootmaker called Prohoritch), went out into the yard. The air was grey, cold, and sullenly still. The big yard, full of tufts of burdock and strewn with yellow leaves, was faintly silvered with autumn frost. Not a breath of wind nor a sound. The old man sat down on the steps of his slanting porch, and at once there happened what happened regularly every morning: his dog Lyska, a big, mangy, decrepit-looking, white yard-dog, with black patches, came up to him with its right eye shut. Lyska came up timidly, wriggling in a frightened way, as though her paws were not touching the earth but a hot stove, and the whole of her wretched figure was expressive of abjectness. Zotov pretended not to notice her, but when she faintly wagged her tail, and, wriggling as before, licked his golosh, he stamped his foot angrily.

"Be off! The plague take you!" he cried. "Con-found-ed bea-east!"

Lyska moved aside, sat down, and fixed her solitary eye upon her master.

"You devils!" he went on. "You are the last straw on my back, you Herods."

And he looked with hatred at his shed with its crooked, overgrown roof; there from the door of the shed a big horse's head was looking out at him. Probably flattered by its master's attention, the head moved, pushed forward, and there emerged from the shed the whole horse, as decrepit as Lyska, as timid and as crushed, with spindly legs, grey hair, a pinched stomach, and a bony spine. He came out of the shed and stood still, hesitating as though overcome with embarrassment.

"Plague take you," Zotov went on. "Shall I ever see the last of you, you jail-bird Pharaohs! . . . I wager you want your breakfast!" he jeered, twisting his angry face into a contemptuous smile. "By all means, this minute! A priceless steed like you must have your fill of the best oats! Pray begin! This minute! And I have something to give to the magnificent, valuable dog! If a precious dog like you does not care for bread, you can have meat."

Zotov grumbled for half an hour, growing more and more irritated. In the end, unable to control the anger that boiled up in him, he jumped up, stamped with his goloshes, and growled out to be heard all over the yard:

"I am not obliged to feed you, you loafers! I am not some millionaire for you to eat me out of house and home! I have nothing to eat myself, you cursed carcases, the cholera take you! I get no pleasure or profit out of you; nothing but trouble and ruin, Why don't you give up the ghost? Are you such personages that even death won't take you? You can live, damn you! but I don't want to feed you! I have had enough of you! I don't want to!"

Zotov grew wrathful and indignant, and the horse and the dog listened. Whether these two dependents understood that they were being reproached for living at his expense, I don't know, but their stomachs looked more pinched than ever, and their whole figures shrivelled up, grew gloomier and more abject than before. . . . Their submissive air exasperated Zotov more than ever.

"Get away!" he shouted, overcome by a sort of inspiration. "Out of my house! Don't let me set eyes on you again! I am not obliged to keep all sorts of rubbish in my yard! Get away!"

The old man moved with little hurried steps to the gate, opened it, and picking up a stick from the ground, began driving out his dependents. The horse shook its head, moved its shoulder-blades, and limped to the gate; the dog followed him. Both of them went out into the street, and, after walking some twenty paces, stopped at the fence.

"I'll give it you!" Zotov threatened them.

When he had driven out his dependents he felt calmer, and began sweeping the yard. From time to time he peeped out into the street: the horse and the dog were standing like posts by the fence, looking dejectedly towards the gate.

"Try how you can do without me," muttered the old man, feeling as though a weight of anger were being lifted from his heart. "Let somebody else look after you now! I am stingy and ill-tempered. . . . It's nasty living with me, so you try living with other people . . . . Yes. . . ."

After enjoying the crushed expression of his dependents, and grumbling to his heart's content, Zotov went out of the yard, and, assuming a ferocious air, shouted:

"Well, why are you standing there? Whom are you waiting for? Standing right across the middle of the road and preventing the public from passing! Go into the yard!"

The horse and the dog with drooping heads and a guilty air turned towards the gate. Lyska, probably feeling she did not deserve forgiveness, whined piteously.

"Stay you can, but as for food, you'll get nothing from me! You may die, for all I care!"

Meanwhile the sun began to break through the morning mist; its slanting rays gilded over the autumn frost. There was a sound of steps and voices. Zotov put back the broom in its place, and went out of the yard to see his crony and neighbour, Mark Ivanitch, who kept a little general shop. On reaching his friend's shop, he sat down on a folding-stool, sighed sedately, stroked his beard, and began about the weather. From the weather the friends passed to the new deacon, from the deacon to the choristers; and the conversation lengthened out. They did not notice as they talked how time was passing, and when the shop-boy brought in a big teapot of boiling water, and the friends proceeded to drink tea, the time flew as quickly as a bird. Zotov got warm and felt more cheerful.

"I have a favour to ask of you, Mark Ivanitch," he began, after the sixth glass, drumming on the counter with his fingers. "If you would just be so kind as to give me a gallon of oats again to-day. . . ."

From behind the big tea-chest behind which Mark Ivanitch was sitting came the sound of a deep sigh.

"Do be so good," Zotov went on; "never mind tea—don't give it me to-day, but let me have some oats. . . . I am ashamed to ask you, I have wearied you with my poverty, but the horse is hungry."

"I can give it you," sighed the friend—"why not? But why the devil do you keep those carcases?--tfoo!--Tell me that, please. It would be all right if it were a useful horse, but—tfoo!-- one is ashamed to look at it. . . . And the dog's nothing but a skeleton! Why the devil do you keep them?"

"What am I to do with them?"

"You know. Take them to Ignat the slaughterer—that is all there is to do. They ought to have been there long ago. It's the proper place for them."

"To be sure, that is so! . . . I dare say! . . ."

"You live like a beggar and keep animals," the friend went on. "I don't grudge the oats. . . . God bless you. But as to the future, brother . . . I can't afford to give regularly every day! There is no end to your poverty! One gives and gives, and one doesn't know when there will be an end to it all."

The friend sighed and stroked his red face.

"If you were dead that would settle it," he said. "You go on living, and you don't know what for. . . . Yes, indeed! But if it is not the Lord's will for you to die, you had better go somewhere into an almshouse or a refuge."

"What for? I have relations. I have a great-niece. . . ."

And Zotov began telling at great length of his great-niece Glasha, daughter of his niece Katerina, who lived somewhere on a farm.

"She is bound to keep me!" he said. "My house will be left to her, so let her keep me; I'll go to her. It's Glasha, you know . . . Katya's daughter; and Katya, you know, was my brother Panteley's stepdaughter. . . . You understand? The house will come to her . . . . Let her keep me!"

"To be sure; rather than live, as you do, a beggar, I should have gone to her long ago."

"I will go! As God's above, I will go. It's her duty."

When an hour later the old friends were drinking a glass of vodka, Zotov stood in the middle of the shop and said with enthusiasm:

"I have been meaning to go to her for a long time; I will go this very day."

"To be sure; rather than hanging about and dying of hunger, you ought to have gone to the farm long ago."

"I'll go at once! When I get there, I shall say: Take my house, but keep me and treat me with respect. It's your duty! If you don't care to, then there is neither my house, nor my blessing for you! Good-bye, Ivanitch!"

Zotov drank another glass, and, inspired by the new idea, hurried home. The vodka had upset him and his head was reeling, but instead of lying down, he put all his clothes together in a bundle, said a prayer, took his stick, and went out. Muttering and tapping on the stones with his stick, he walked the whole length of the street without looking back, and found himself in the open country. It was eight or nine miles to the farm. He walked along the dry road, looked at the town herd lazily munching the yellow grass, and pondered on the abrupt change in his life which he had only just brought about so resolutely. He thought, too, about his dependents. When he went out of the house, he had not locked the gate, and so had left them free to go whither they would.

He had not gone a mile into the country when he heard steps behind him. He looked round and angrily clasped his hands. The horse and Lyska, with their heads drooping and their tails between their legs, were quietly walking after him.

"Go back!" he waved to them.

They stopped, looked at one another, looked at him. He went on, they followed him. Then he stopped and began ruminating. It was impossible to go to his great-niece Glasha, whom he hardly knew, with these creatures; he did not want to go back and shut them up, and, indeed, he could not shut them up, because the gate was no use.

"To die of hunger in the shed," thought Zotov. "Hadn't I really better take them to Ignat?"

Ignat's hut stood on the town pasture-ground, a hundred paces from the flagstaff. Though he had not quite made up his mind, and did not know what to do, he turned towards it. His head was giddy and there was a darkness before his eyes. . . .

He remembers little of what happened in the slaughterer's yard. He has a memory of a sickening, heavy smell of hides and the savoury steam of the cabbage-soup Ignat was sipping when he went in to him. As in a dream he saw Ignat, who made him wait two hours, slowly preparing something, changing his clothes, talking to some women about corrosive sublimate; he remembered the horse was put into a stand, after which there was the sound of two dull thuds, one of a blow on the skull, the other of the fall of a heavy body. When Lyska, seeing the death of her friend, flew at Ignat, barking shrilly, there was the sound of a third blow that cut short the bark abruptly. Further,

Zotov remembers that in his drunken foolishness, seeing the two corpses, he went up to the stand, and put his own forehead ready for a blow.

And all that day his eyes were dimmed by a haze, and he could not even see his own fingers.

WHO WAS TO BLAME?

As my uncle Pyotr Demyanitch, a lean, bilious collegiate councillor, exceedingly like a stale smoked fish with a stick through it, was getting ready to go to the high school, where he taught Latin, he noticed that the corner of his grammar was nibbled by mice.

"I say, Praskovya," he said, going into the kitchen and addressing the cook, "how is it we have got mice here? Upon my word! yesterday my top hat was nibbled, to-day they have disfigured my Latin grammar . . . . At this rate they will soon begin eating my clothes!"

"What can I do? I did not bring them in!" answered Praskovya.

"We must do something! You had better get a cat, hadn't you?"

"I've got a cat, but what good is it?"

And Praskovya pointed to the corner where a white kitten, thin as a match, lay curled up asleep beside a broom.

"Why is it no good?" asked Pyotr Demyanitch.

"It's young yet, and foolish. It's not two months old yet."

"H'm. . . . Then it must be trained. It had much better be learning instead of lying there."

Saying this, Pyotr Demyanitch sighed with a careworn air and went out of the kitchen. The kitten raised his head, looked lazily after him, and shut his eyes again.

The kitten lay awake thinking. Of what? Unacquainted with real life, having no store of accumulated impressions, his mental processes could only be instinctive, and he could but picture life in accordance with the conceptions that he had inherited, together with his flesh and blood, from his ancestors, the tigers (vide Darwin). His thoughts were of the nature of day-dreams. His feline imagination pictured something like the Arabian desert, over which flitted shadows closely resembling Praskovya, the stove, the broom. In the midst of the shadows there suddenly appeared a saucer of milk; the saucer began to grow paws, it began moving and displayed a tendency to run; the kitten made a bound, and with a thrill of blood-thirsty sensuality thrust his claws into it.

When the saucer had vanished into obscurity a piece of meat appeared, dropped by Praskovya; the meat ran away with a cowardly squeak, but the kitten made a bound and got his claws into it. . . . Everything that rose before the imagination of the young dreamer had for its starting-point leaps, claws, and teeth. . . The soul of another is darkness, and a cat's soul more than most, but how near the visions just described are to the truth may be seen from the following fact: under the influence of his day-dreams the kitten suddenly leaped up, looked with flashing eyes at Praskovya, ruffled up his coat, and making one bound, thrust his claws into the cook's skirt. Obviously he was born a mouse catcher, a worthy son of his bloodthirsty ancestors. Fate had destined him to be the terror of cellars, store-rooms and cornbins, and had it not been for education . . . we will not anticipate, however.

On his way home from the high school, Pyotr Demyanitch went into a general shop and bought a mouse-trap for fifteen kopecks. At dinner he fixed a little bit of his rissole on the hook, and set the trap under the sofa, where there were heaps of the pupils' old exercise-books, which Praskovya used for various domestic purposes. At six o'clock in the evening, when the worthy Latin master was sitting at the table correcting his pupils' exercises, there was a sudden "klop!" so loud that my uncle started and dropped his pen. He went at once to the sofa and took out the trap. A neat little mouse, the size of a thimble, was sniffing the wires and trembling with fear.

"Aha," muttered Pyotr Demyanitch, and he looked at the mouse malignantly, as though he were about to give him a bad mark. "You are cau—aught, wretch! Wait a bit! I'll teach you to eat my grammar!"

Having gloated over his victim, Poytr Demyanitch put the mouse-trap on the floor and called:

"Praskovya, there's a mouse caught! Bring the kitten here!"

"I'm coming," responded Praskovya, and a minute later she came in with the descendant of tigers in her arms.

"Capital!" said Pyotr Demyanitch, rubbing his hands. "We will give him a lesson. . . . Put him down opposite the mouse-trap . . . that's it. . . . Let him sniff it and look at it. . . . That's it. . . ."

The kitten looked wonderingly at my uncle, at his arm-chair, sniffed the mouse-trap in bewilderment, then, frightened probably by the glaring lamplight and the attention directed to him, made a dash and ran in terror to the door.

"Stop!" shouted my uncle, seizing him by the tail, "stop, you rascal!
He's afraid of a mouse, the idiot! Look! It's a mouse! Look! Well?
Look, I tell you!"
Pyotr Demyanitch took the kitten by the scruff of the neck and pushed him with his nose against the mouse-trap.

"Look, you carrion! Take him and hold him, Praskovya. . . . Hold him opposite the door of the trap. . . . When I let the mouse out, you let him go instantly. . . . Do you hear? . . . Instantly let go! Now!"

My uncle assumed a mysterious expression and lifted the door of the trap. . . . The mouse came out irresolutely, sniffed the air, and flew like an arrow under the sofa. . . . The kitten on being released darted under the table with his tail in the air.

"It has got away! got away!" cried Pyotr Demyanitch, looking ferocious. "Where is he, the scoundrel? Under the table? You wait. . ."

My uncle dragged the kitten from under the table and shook him in the air.

"Wretched little beast," he muttered, smacking him on the ear. "Take that, take that! Will you shirk it next time? Wr-r-r-etch. . . ."

Next day Praskovya heard again the summons.

"Praskovya, there is a mouse caught! Bring the kitten here!"

After the outrage of the previous day the kitten had taken refuge under the stove and had not come out all night. When Praskovya pulled him out and, carrying him by the scruff of the neck into the study, set him down before the mouse-trap, he trembled all over and mewed piteously.

"Come, let him feel at home first," Pyotr Demyanitch commanded. "Let him look and sniff. Look and learn! Stop, plague take you!" he shouted, noticing that the kitten was backing away from the mouse-trap. "I'll thrash you! Hold him by the ear! That's it. . . . Well now, set him down before the trap. . . ."

My uncle slowly lifted the door of the trap . . . the mouse whisked under the very nose of the kitten, flung itself against Praskovya's hand and fled under the cupboard; the kitten, feeling himself free, took a desperate bound and retreated under the sofa.

"He's let another mouse go!" bawled Pyotr Demyanitch. "Do you call that a cat? Nasty little beast! Thrash him! thrash him by the mousetrap!"

When the third mouse had been caught, the kitten shivered all over at the sight of the mousetrap and its inmate, and scratched Praskovya's hand. . . . After the fourth mouse my uncle flew into a rage, kicked the kitten, and said:

"Take the nasty thing away! Get rid of it! Chuck it away! It's no earthly use!"

A year passed, the thin, frail kitten had turned into a solid and sagacious tom-cat. One day he was on his way by the back yards to an amatory interview. He had just reached his destination when he suddenly heard a rustle, and thereupon caught sight of a mouse which ran from a water-trough towards a stable; my hero's hair stood on end, he arched his back, hissed, and trembling all over, took to ignominious flight.

Alas! sometimes I feel myself in the ludicrous position of the flying cat. Like the kitten, I had in my day the honour of being taught Latin by my uncle. Now, whenever I chance to see some work of classical antiquity, instead of being moved to eager enthusiasm, I begin recalling, *ut consecutivum*, the irregular verbs, the sallow grey face of my uncle, the ablative absolute. . . . I turn pale, my hair stands up on my head, and, like the cat, I take to ignominious flight.

THE BIRD MARKET

THERE is a small square near the monastery of the Holy Birth which is called Trubnoy, or simply Truboy; there is a market there on Sundays. Hundreds of sheepskins, wadded coats, fur caps, and chimneypot hats swarm there, like crabs in a sieve. There is the sound of the twitter of birds in all sorts of keys, recalling the spring. If the sun is shining, and there are no clouds in the sky, the singing of the birds and the smell of hay make a more vivid impression, and this reminder of spring sets one thinking and carries one's fancy far, far away. Along one side of the square there stands a string of waggons. The waggons are loaded, not with hay, not with cabbages, nor with beans, but with goldfinches, siskins, larks, blackbirds and thrushes, bluetits, bullfinches. All of them are hopping about in rough, home-made cages, twittering and looking with envy at the free sparrows. The goldfinches cost five kopecks, the siskins are rather more expensive, while the value of the other birds is quite indeterminate.

"How much is a lark?"

The seller himself does not know the value of a lark. He scratches his head and asks whatever comes into it, a rouble, or three kopecks, according to the purchaser. There are expensive birds too. A faded old blackbird, with most of its feathers plucked out of its tail, sits on a dirty perch. He is dignified, grave, and motionless as a retired general. He has waved his claw in resignation to his captivity long ago, and looks at the blue sky with indifference. Probably, owing to this indifference, he is considered a sagacious bird. He is not to be bought for less than forty kopecks. Schoolboys, workmen, young men in stylish greatcoats, and bird-fanciers in incredibly shabby caps, in ragged trousers that are turned up at the ankles, and look as though they had been gnawed by mice, crowd round the birds, splashing through the mud. The young people and the workmen are sold hens for cocks, young birds for old ones. . . . They know very little about birds. But there is no deceiving the bird-fancier. He sees and understands his bird from a distance.

"There is no relying on that bird," a fancier will say, looking into a siskin's beak, and counting the feathers on its tail. "He sings now, it's true, but what of that? I sing in company too. No, my boy, shout, sing to me without company; sing in solitude, if you can. . . . You give me that one yonder that sits and holds its tongue! Give me the quiet one! That one says nothing, so he thinks the more. . . ."

Among the waggons of birds there are some full of other live creatures. Here you see hares, rabbits, hedgehogs, guinea-pigs, polecats. A hare sits sorrowfully nibbling the straw. The guinea-pigs shiver with cold, while the hedgehogs look out with curiosity from under their prickles at the public.

"I have read somewhere," says a post-office official in a faded overcoat, looking lovingly at the hare, and addressing no one in particular, "I have read that some learned man had a cat and a mouse and a falcon and a sparrow, who all ate out of one bowl."

"That's very possible, sir. The cat must have been beaten, and the falcon, I dare say, had all its tail pulled out. There's no great cleverness in that, sir. A friend of mine had a cat who, saving your presence, used to eat his cucumbers. He thrashed her with a big whip for a fortnight, till he taught her not to. A hare can learn to light matches if you beat it. Does that surprise you? It's very simple! It takes the match in its mouth and strikes it. An animal is like a man. A man's made wiser by beating, and it's the same with a beast."

Men in long, full-skirted coats move backwards and forwards in the crowd with cocks and ducks under their arms. The fowls are all lean and hungry. Chickens poke their ugly, mangy-looking heads out of their cages and peck at something in the mud. Boys with pigeons stare into your face and try to detect in you a pigeon-fancier.

"Yes, indeed! It's no use talking to you," someone shouts angrily. "You should look before you speak! Do you call this a pigeon? It is an eagle, not a pigeon!"

A tall thin man, with a shaven upper lip and side whiskers, who looks like a sick and drunken footman, is selling a snow-white lap-dog. The old lap-dog whines.

"She told me to sell the nasty thing," says the footman, with a contemptuous snigger. "She is bankrupt in her old age, has nothing to eat, and here now is selling her dogs and cats. She cries, and kisses them on their filthy snouts. And then she is so hard up that she sells them. 'Pon my soul, it is a fact! Buy it, gentlemen! The money is wanted for coffee."

But no one laughs. A boy who is standing by screws up one eye and looks at him gravely with compassion.

The most interesting of all is the fish section. Some dozen peasants are sitting in a row. Before each of them is a pail, and in each pail there is a veritable little hell. There, in the thick, greenish water are swarms of little carp, eels, small fry, water-snails, frogs, and newts. Big water-beetles with broken legs scurry over the small surface, clambering on the carp, and jumping over the frogs. The creatures have a strong hold on life. The frogs climb on the beetles, the newts on the frogs. The dark green tench, as more expensive fish, enjoy an exceptional position; they are kept in a special jar where they can't swim, but still they are not so cramped. . . .

"The carp is a grand fish! The carp's the fish to keep, your honour, plague take him! You can keep him for a year in a pail and he'll live! It's a week since I caught these very fish. I caught them, sir, in Pererva, and have come from there on foot. The carp are two kopecks each, the eels are three, and the minnows are ten kopecks the dozen, plague take them! Five kopecks' worth of minnows, sir? Won't you take some worms?"

The seller thrusts his coarse rough fingers into the pail and pulls out of it a soft minnow, or a little carp, the size of a nail. Fishing lines, hooks, and tackle are laid out near the pails, and pond-worms glow with a crimson light in the sun.

An old fancier in a fur cap, iron-rimmed spectacles, and goloshes that look like two dread-noughts, walks about by the waggons of birds and pails of fish. He is, as they call him here, "a type." He hasn't a farthing to bless himself with, but in spite of that he haggles, gets excited, and pesters purchasers with advice. He has thoroughly examined all the hares, pigeons, and fish; examined them in every detail, fixed the kind, the age, and the price of each one of them a good hour ago. He is as interested as a child in the goldfinches, the carp, and the minnows. Talk to him, for instance, about thrushes, and the queer old fellow will tell you things you could not find in any book. He will tell you them with enthusiasm, with passion, and will scold you too for your ignorance. Of goldfinches and bullfinches he is ready to talk endlessly, opening his eyes wide and gesticulating violently with his hands. He is only to be met here at the market in the cold weather; in the summer he is somewhere in the country, catching quails with a bird-call and angling for fish.

And here is another "type," a very tall, very thin, close-shaven gentleman in dark spectacles, wearing a cap with a cockade, and looking like a scrivener of by-gone days. He is a fancier; he is a man of decent position, a teacher in a high school, and that is well known to the *habitues* of the market, and they treat him with respect, greet him with bows, and have even invented for him a special title: "Your Scholarship." At Suharev market he rummages among the books, and at Trubnoy looks out for good pigeons.

"Please, sir!" the pigeon-sellers shout to him, "Mr. Schoolmaster, your Scholarship, take notice of my tumblers! your Scholarship!"

"Your Scholarship!" is shouted at him from every side.

"Your Scholarship!" an urchin repeats somewhere on the boulevard.

And his "Scholarship," apparently quite accustomed to his title, grave and severe, takes a pigeon in both hands, and lifting it above his head, begins examining it, and as he does so frowns and looks graver than ever, like a conspirator.

And Trubnoy Square, that little bit of Moscow where animals are so tenderly loved, and where they are so tortured, lives its little life, grows noisy and excited, and the business-like or pious people who pass by along the boulevard cannot make out what has brought this crowd of people, this medley of caps, fur hats, and chimneypots together; what they are talking about there, what they are buying and selling.

AN ADVENTURE

(A Driver's Story)

IT was in that wood yonder, behind the creek, that it happened, sir. My father, the kingdom of Heaven be his, was taking five hundred roubles to the master; in those days our fellows and the Shepelevsky peasants used to rent land from the master, so father was taking money for the half-year. He was a God-fearing man, he used to read the scriptures, and as for cheating or wronging anyone, or defrauding --God forbid, and the peasants honoured him greatly, and when someone had to be sent to the town about taxes or such-like, or with money, they used to send him. He was a man above the ordinary, but, not that I'd speak ill of him, he had a weakness. He was fond of a drop. There was no getting him past a tavern: he would go in, drink a glass, and be completely done for! He was aware of this weakness in himself, and when he was carrying public money, that he might not fall asleep or lose it by some chance, he always took me or my sister Anyutka with him.

To tell the truth, all our family have a great taste for vodka. I can read and write, I served for six years at a tobacconist's in the town, and I can talk to any educated gentleman, and can use very fine language, but, it is perfectly true, sir, as I read in a book, that vodka is the blood of Satan. Through vodka my face has darkened. And there is nothing seemly about me, and here, as you may see, sir, I am a cab-driver like an ignorant, uneducated peasant.

And so, as I was telling you, father was taking the money to the master, Anyutka was going with him, and at that time Anyutka was seven or maybe eight—a silly chit, not that high. He got as far as Kalantchiko successfully, he was sober, but when he reached Kalantchiko and went into Moiseika's tavern, this same weakness of his came upon him. He drank three glasses and set to bragging before people:

"I am a plain humble man," he says, "but I have five hundred roubles in my pocket; if I like," says he, "I could buy up the tavern and all the crockery and Moiseika and his Jewess and his little Jews. I can buy it all out and out," he said. That was his way of joking, to be sure, but then he began complaining: "It's a worry, good Christian people," said he, "to be a rich man, a merchant, or anything of that kind. If you have no money you have no care, if you have money you must watch over your pocket the whole time that wicked men may not rob you. It's a terror to live in the world for a man who has a lot of money."

The drunken people listened of course, took it in, and made a note of it. And in those days they were making a railway line at Kalantchiko, and there were swarms and swarms of tramps and vagabonds of all sorts like locusts. Father pulled himself up afterwards, but it was too late. A word is not a sparrow, if it flies out you can't catch it. They drove, sir, by the wood, and all at once there was someone galloping on horseback behind them. Father was not of the chicken-hearted brigade—that I couldn't say—but he felt uneasy; there was no regular road through the wood, nothing went that way but hay and timber, and there was no cause for anyone to be galloping there, particularly in working hours. One wouldn't be galloping after any good.

"It seems as though they are after someone," said father to Anyutka, "they are galloping so furiously. I ought to have kept quiet in the tavern, a plague on my tongue. Oy, little daughter, my heart misgives me, there is something wrong!"

He did not spend long in hesitation about his dangerous position, and he said to my sister Anyutka:

"Things don't look very bright, they really are in pursuit. Anyway, Anyutka dear, you take the money, put it away in your skirts, and go and hide behind a bush. If by ill-luck they attack me, you run back to mother, and give her the money. Let her take it to the village elder. Only mind you don't let anyone see you; keep to the wood and by the creek, that no one may see you. Run your best and call on the merciful God. Christ be with you!"

Father thrust the parcel of notes on Anyutka, and she looked out the thickest of the bushes and hid herself. Soon after, three men on horseback galloped up to father. One a stalwart, big-jawed fellow, in a crimson shirt and high boots, and the other two, ragged, shabby fellows, navvies from the line. As my father feared, so it really turned out, sir. The one in the crimson shirt, the sturdy, strong fellow, a man above the ordinary, left his horse, and all three made for my father.

"Halt you, so-and-so! Where's the money!"

"What money? Go to the devil!"

"Oh, the money you are taking the master for the rent. Hand it over, you bald devil, or we will throttle you, and you'll die in your sins."

And they began to practise their villainy on father, and, instead of beseeching them, weeping, or anything of the sort, father got angry and began to reprove them with the greatest severity.

"What are you pestering me for?" said he. "You are a dirty lot. There is no fear of God in you, plague take you! It's not money you want, but a beating, to make your backs smart for three years after. Be off, blockheads, or I shall defend myself. I have a revolver that takes six bullets, it's in my bosom!"

But his words did not deter the robbers, and they began beating him with anything they could lay their hands on.

They looked through everything in the cart, searched my father thoroughly, even taking off his boots; when they found that beating father only made him swear at them the more, they began torturing him in all sorts of ways. All the time Anyutka was sitting behind the bush, and she saw it all, poor dear. When she saw father lying on the ground and gasping, she started off and ran her hardest through the thicket and the creek towards home. She was only a little girl, with no understanding; she did not know the way, just ran on not knowing where she was going. It was some six miles to our home. Anyone else might have run there in an hour, but a little child, as we all know, takes two steps back for one forwards, and indeed it is not everyone who can run barefoot through the prickly bushes; you want to be used to it, too, and our girls used always to be crowding together on the stove or in the yard, and were afraid to run in the forest.

Towards evening Anyutka somehow reached a habitation, she looked, it was a hut. It was the forester's hut, in the Crown forest; some merchants were renting it at the time and burning charcoal. She knocked. A woman, the forester's wife, came out to her. Anyutka, first of all, burst out crying, and told her everything just as it was, and even told her about the money. The forester's wife was full of pity for her.

"My poor little dear! Poor mite, God has preserved you, poor little one! My precious! Come into the hut, and I will give you something to eat."

She began to make up to Anyutka, gave her food and drink, and even wept with her, and was so attentive to her that the girl, only think, gave her the parcel of notes.

"I will put it away, darling, and to-morrow morning I will give it you back and take you home, dearie."

The woman took the money, and put Anyutka to sleep on the stove where at the time the brooms were drying. And on the same stove, on the brooms, the forester's daughter, a girl as small as our Anyutka, was asleep. And Anyutka used to tell us afterwards that there was such a scent from the brooms, they smelt of honey! Anyutka lay down, but she could not get to sleep, she kept crying quietly; she was sorry for father, and terrified. But, sir, an hour or two passed, and she saw those very three robbers who had tortured father walk into the hut; and the one in the crimson shirt, with big jaws, their leader, went up to the woman and said:

"Well, wife, we have simply murdered a man for nothing. To-day we killed a man at dinner-time, we killed him all right, but not a farthing did we find."

So this fellow in the crimson shirt turned out to be the forester, the woman's husband.

"The man's dead for nothing," said his ragged companions. "In vain we have taken a sin on our souls."

The forester's wife looked at all three and laughed.

"What are you laughing at, silly?"

"I am laughing because I haven't murdered anyone, and I have not taken any sin on my soul, but I have found the money."

"What money? What nonsense are you talking!"

"Here, look whether I am talking nonsense."

The forester's wife untied the parcel and, wicked woman, showed them the money. Then she described how Anyutka had come, what she had said, and so on. The murderers were delighted and began to divide the money between them, they almost quarrelled, then they sat down to the table, you know, to drink. And Anyutka lay there, poor child, hearing every word and shaking like a Jew in a frying-pan. What was she to do? And from their words she learned that father was dead and lying across the road, and she fancied, in her foolishness, that the wolves and the dogs would eat father, and that our horse had gone far away into the forest, and would be eaten by wolves too, and that she, Anyutka herself, would be put in prison and beaten, because she had not taken care of the money. The robbers got drunk and sent the woman for vodka. They gave her five roubles for vodka and sweet wine. They set to singing and drinking on other people's money. They drank and drank, the dogs, and sent the woman off again that they might drink beyond all bounds.

"We will keep it up till morning," they cried. "We have plenty of money now, there is no need to spare! Drink, and don't drink away your wits."

And so at midnight, when they were all fairly fuddled, the woman ran off for vodka the third time, and the forester strode twice up and down the cottage, and he was staggering.

"Look here, lads," he said, "we must make away with the girl, too!

If we leave her, she will be the first to bear witness against us."

They talked it over and discussed it, and decided that Anyutka must not be left alive, that she must be killed. Of course, to murder an innocent child's a fearful thing, even a man drunken or crazy would not take such a job on himself. They were quarrelling for maybe an hour which was to kill her, one tried to put it on the other, they almost fought again, and no one would agree to do it; then they cast lots. It fell to the forester. He drank another full glass, cleared his throat, and went to the outer room for an axe.

But Anyutka was a sharp wench. For all she was so simple, she thought of something that, I must say, not many an educated man would have thought of. Maybe the Lord had compassion on her, and gave her sense for the moment, or perhaps it was the fright sharpened her wits, anyway when it came to the test it turned out that she was cleverer than anyone. She got up stealthily, prayed to God, took the little sheepskin, the one the forester's wife had put over her, and, you understand, the forester's little daughter, a girl of the same age as herself, was lying on the stove beside her. She covered this girl with the sheepskin, and took the woman's jacket off her and threw it over herself. Disguised herself, in fact. She put it over her head, and so walked across the hut by the drunken men, and they thought it was the forester's daughter, and did not even look at her. Luckily for her the woman was not in the hut, she had gone for vodka, or maybe she would not have escaped the axe, for a woman's eyes are as far-seeing as a buzzard's. A woman's eyes are sharp.

Anyutka came out of the hut, and ran as fast as her legs could carry her. All night she was lost in the forest, but towards morning she came out to the edge and ran along the road. By the mercy of God she met the clerk Yegor Danilitch, the kingdom of Heaven be his. He was going along with his hooks to catch fish. Anyutka told him all about it. He went back quicker than he came—thought no more of the fish—gathered the peasants together in the village, and off they went to the forester's.

They got there, and all the murderers were lying side by side, dead drunk, each where he had fallen; the woman, too, was drunk. First thing they searched them; they took the money and then looked on the stove—the Holy Cross be with us! The forester's child was lying on the brooms, under the sheepskin, and her head was in a pool of blood, chopped off by the axe. They roused the peasants and the woman, tied their hands behind them, and took them to the district court; the woman howled, but the forester only shook his head and asked:

"You might give me a drop, lads! My head aches!"

Afterwards they were tried in the town in due course, and punished with the utmost rigour of the law.

So that's what happened, sir, beyond the forest there, that lies behind the creek. Now you can scarcely see it, the sun is setting red behind it. I have been talking to you, and the horses have stopped, as though they were listening too. Hey there, my beauties! Move more briskly, the good gentleman will give us something extra.

Hey, you darlings!

THE FISH

A SUMMER morning. The air is still; there is no sound but the churring of a grasshopper on the river bank, and somewhere the timid cooing of a turtle-dove. Feathery clouds stand motionless in the sky, looking like snow scattered about. . . . Gerassim, the carpenter, a tall gaunt peasant, with a curly red head and a face overgrown with hair, is floundering about in the water under the green willow branches near an unfinished bathing shed. . . . He puffs and pants and, blinking furiously, is trying to get hold of something under the roots of the willows. His face is covered with perspiration. A couple of yards from him, Lubim, the carpenter, a young hunchback with a triangular face and narrow Chinese-looking eyes, is standing up to his neck in water. Both Gerassim and Lubim are in shirts and linen breeches. Both are blue with cold, for they have been more than an hour already in the water.

"But why do you keep poking with your hand?" cries the hunchback Lubim, shivering as though in a fever. "You blockhead! Hold him, hold him, or else he'll get away, the anathema! Hold him, I tell you!"

"He won't get away. . . . Where can he get to? He's under a root," says Gerassim in a hoarse, hollow bass, which seems to come not from his throat, but from the depths of his stomach. "He's slippery, the beggar, and there's nothing to catch hold of."

"Get him by the gills, by the gills!"

"There's no seeing his gills. . . . Stay, I've got hold of something . . . . I've got him by the lip. . . He's biting, the brute!"

"Don't pull him out by the lip, don't—or you'll let him go! Take him by the gills, take him by the gills. . . . You've begun poking with your hand again! You are a senseless man, the Queen of Heaven forgive me! Catch hold!"

"Catch hold!" Gerassim mimics him. "You're a fine one to give orders . . . . You'd better come and catch hold of him yourself, you hunchback devil. . . . What are you standing there for?"

"I would catch hold of him if it were possible. But can I stand by the bank, and me as short as I am? It's deep there."

"It doesn't matter if it is deep. . . . You must swim."

The hunchback waves his arms, swims up to Gerassim, and catches hold of the twigs. At the first attempt to stand up, he goes into the water over his head and begins blowing up bubbles.

"I told you it was deep," he says, rolling his eyes angrily. "Am I to sit on your neck or what?"

"Stand on a root . . . there are a lot of roots like a ladder." The hunchback gropes for a root with his heel, and tightly gripping several twigs, stands on it. . . . Having got his balance, and established himself in his new position, he bends down, and trying not to get the water into his mouth, begins fumbling with his right hand among the roots.

Getting entangled among the weeds and slipping on the mossy roots he finds his hand in contact with the sharp pincers of a crayfish.

"As though we wanted to see you, you demon!" says Lubim, and he angrily flings the crayfish on the bank.

At last his hand feels Gerassim' s arm, and groping its way along it comes to something cold and slimy.

"Here he is!" says Lubim with a grin. "A fine fellow! Move your fingers, I'll get him directly . . . by the gills. Stop, don't prod me with your elbow. . . . I'll have him in a minute, in a minute, only let me get hold of him. . . . The beggar has got a long way under the roots, there is nothing to get hold of. . . . One can't get to the head . . . one can only feel its belly . . . . kill that gnat on my neck—it's stinging! I'll get him by the gills, directly . . . . Come to one side and give him a push! Poke him with your finger!"

The hunchback puffs out his cheeks, holds his breath, opens his eyes wide, and apparently has already got his fingers in the gills, but at that moment the twigs to which he is holding on with his left hand break, and losing his balance he plops into the water! Eddies race away from the bank as though frightened, and little bubbles come up from the spot where he has fallen in. The hunchback swims out and, snorting, clutches at the twigs.

"You'll be drowned next, you stupid, and I shall have to answer for you," wheezes Gerassim. "Clamber out, the devil take you! I'll get him out myself."

High words follow. . . . The sun is baking hot. The shadows begin to grow shorter and to draw in on themselves, like the horns of a snail. . . . The high grass warmed by the sun begins to give out a strong, heavy smell of honey. It will soon be midday, and Gerassim and Lubim are still floundering under the willow tree. The husky bass and the shrill, frozen tenor persistently disturb the stillness of the summer day.

"Pull him out by the gills, pull him out! Stay, I'll push him out! Where are you shoving your great ugly fist? Poke him with your finger—you pig's face! Get round by the side! get to the left, to the left, there's a big hole on the right! You'll be a supper for the water-devil! Pull it by the lip!"

There is the sound of the flick of a whip. . . . A herd of cattle, driven by Yefim, the shepherd, saunter lazily down the sloping bank to drink. The shepherd, a decrepit old man, with one eye and a crooked mouth, walks with his head bowed, looking at his feet. The first to reach the water are the sheep, then come the horses, and last of all the cows.

"Push him from below!" he hears Lubim's voice. "Stick your finger in! Are you deaf, fellow, or what? Tfoo!"

"What are you after, lads?" shouts Yefim.

"An eel-pout! We can't get him out! He's hidden under the roots.

Get round to the side! To the side!"

For a minute Yefim screws up his eye at the fishermen, then he takes off his bark shoes, throws his sack off his shoulders, and takes off his shirt. He has not the patience to take off his breeches, but, making the sign of the cross, he steps into the water, holding out his thin dark arms to balance himself. . . . For fifty paces he walks along the slimy bottom, then he takes to swimming.

"Wait a minute, lads!" he shouts. "Wait! Don't be in a hurry to pull him out, you'll lose him. You must do it properly!"

Yefim joins the carpenters and all three, shoving each other with their knees and their elbows, puffing and swearing at one another, bustle about the same spot. Lubim, the hunchback, gets a mouthful of water, and the air rings with his hard spasmodic coughing.

"Where's the shepherd?" comes a shout from the bank. "Yefim! Shepherd! Where are you? The cattle are in the garden! Drive them out, drive them out of the garden! Where is he, the old brigand?"

First men's voices are heard, then a woman's. The master himself, Andrey Andreitch, wearing a dressing-gown made of a Persian shawl and carrying a newspaper in his hand, appears from behind the garden fence. He looks inquiringly towards the shouts which come from the river, and then trips rapidly towards the bathing shed.

"What's this? Who's shouting?" he asks sternly, seeing through the branches of the willow the three wet heads of the fishermen. "What are you so busy about there?"

"Catching a fish," mutters Yefim, without raising his head.

"I'll give it to you! The beasts are in the garden and he is fishing! . . . When will that bathing shed be done, you devils? You've been at work two days, and what is there to show for it?"

"It . . . will soon be done," grunts Gerassim; summer is long, you'll have plenty of time to wash, your honour. . . . Pfrrr! . . . We can't manage this eel-pout here anyhow. . . . He's got under a root and sits there as if he were in a hole and won't budge one way or another . . . ."

"An eel-pout?" says the master, and his eyes begin to glisten. "Get him out quickly then."

"You'll give us half a rouble for it presently if we oblige you . . . . A huge eel-pout, as fat as a merchant's wife. . . . It's worth half a rouble, your honour, for the trouble. . . . Don't squeeze him, Lubim, don't squeeze him, you'll spoil him! Push him up from below! Pull the root upwards, my good man . . . what's your name? Upwards, not downwards, you brute! Don't swing your legs!"

Five minutes pass, ten. . . . The master loses all patience.

"Vassily!" he shouts, turning towards the garden. "Vaska! Call Vassily to me!"

The coachman Vassily runs up. He is chewing something and breathing hard.

"Go into the water," the master orders him. "Help them to pull out that eel-pout. They can't get him out."

Vassily rapidly undresses and gets into the water.

"In a minute. . . . I'll get him in a minute," he mutters. "Where's the eel-pout? We'll have him out in a trice! You'd better go, Yefim. An old man like you ought to be minding his own business instead of being here. Where's that eel-pout? I'll have him in a minute . . . . Here he is! Let go."

"What's the good of saying that? We know all about that! You get it out!"

But there is no getting it out like this! One must get hold of it by the head."

"And the head is under the root! We know that, you fool!"
"Now then, don't talk or you'll catch it! You dirty cur!"
"Before the master to use such language," mutters Yefim. "You won't get him out, lads! He's fixed himself much too cleverly!"
"Wait a minute, I'll come directly," says the master, and he begins hurriedly undressing. "Four fools, and can't get an eel-pout!"

When he is undressed, Andrey Andreitch gives himself time to cool and gets into the water. But even his interference leads to nothing.

"We must chop the root off," Lubim decides at last. "Gerasim, go and get an axe! Give me an axe!"

"Don't chop your fingers off," says the master, when the blows of the axe on the root under water are heard. "Yefim, get out of this! Stay, I'll get the eel-pout. . . . You'll never do it."

The root is hacked a little. They partly break it off, and Andrey Andreitch, to his immense satisfaction, feels his fingers under the gills of the fish.

"I'm pulling him out, lads! Don't crowd round . . . stand still . . . . I am pulling him out!"

The head of a big eel-pout, and behind it its long black body, nearly a yard long, appears on the surface of the water. The fish flaps its tail heavily and tries to tear itself away.

"None of your nonsense, my boy! Fiddlesticks! I've got you! Aha!"

A honied smile overspreads all the faces. A minute passes in silent contemplation.

"A famous eel-pout," mutters Yefim, scratching under his shoulder-blades.

"I'll be bound it weighs ten pounds."

"Mm! . . . Yes," the master assents. "The liver is fairly swollen!

It seems to stand out! A-ach!"

The fish makes a sudden, unexpected upward movement with its tail and the fishermen hear a loud splash . . . they all put out their hands, but it is too late; they have seen the last of the eel-pout.

ART

A GLOOMY winter morning.

On the smooth and glittering surface of the river Bystryanka, sprinkled here and there with snow, stand two peasants, scrubby little Seryozhka and the church beadle, Matvey. Seryozhka, a short-legged, ragged, mangy-looking fellow of thirty, stares angrily at the ice. Tufts of wool hang from his shaggy sheepskin like a mangy dog. In his hands he holds a compass made of two pointed sticks. Matvey, a fine-looking old man in a new sheepskin and high felt boots, looks with mild blue eyes upwards where on the high sloping bank a village nestles picturesquely. In his hands there is a heavy crowbar.

"Well, are we going to stand like this till evening with our arms folded?" says Seryozhka, breaking the silence and turning his angry eyes on Matvey. "Have you come here to stand about, old fool, or to work?"

"Well, you . . . er . . . show me . . ." Matvey mutters, blinking mildly.

"Show you. . . . It's always me: me to show you, and me to do it. They have no sense of their own! Mark it out with the compasses, that's what's wanted! You can't break the ice without marking it out. Mark it! Take the compass."

Matvey takes the compasses from Seryozhka's hands, and, shuffling heavily on the same spot and jerking with his elbows in all directions, he begins awkwardly trying to describe a circle on the ice. Seryozhka screws up his eyes contemptuously and obviously enjoys his awkwardness and incompetence.

"Eh-eh-eh!" he mutters angrily. "Even that you can't do! The fact is you are a stupid peasant, a wooden-head! You ought to be grazing geese and not making a Jordan! Give the compasses here! Give them here, I say!"

Seryozhka snatches the compasses out of the hands of the perspiring Matvey, and in an instant, jauntily twirling round on one heel, he describes a circle on the ice. The outline of the new Jordan is ready now, all that is left to do is to break the ice. . .

But before proceeding to the work Seryozhka spends a long time in airs and graces, whims and reproaches. . .

"I am not obliged to work for you! You are employed in the church, you do it!"

He obviously enjoys the peculiar position in which he has been placed by the fate that has bestowed on him the rare talent of surprising the whole parish once a year by his art. Poor mild Matvey has to listen to many venomous and contemptuous words from him. Seryozhka sets to work with vexation, with anger. He is lazy. He has hardly described the circle when he is already itching to go up to the village to drink tea, lounge about, and babble. . .

"I'll be back directly," he says, lighting his cigarette, "and meanwhile you had better bring something to sit on and sweep up, instead of standing there counting the crows."

Matvey is left alone. The air is grey and harsh but still. The white church peeps out genially from behind the huts scattered on the river bank. Jackdaws are incessantly circling round its golden crosses. On one side of the village where the river bank breaks off and is steep a hobbled horse is standing at the very edge, motionless as a stone, probably asleep or deep in thought.

Matvey, too, stands motionless as a statue, waiting patiently. The dreamily brooding look of the river, the circling of the jackdaws, and the sight of the horse make him drowsy. One hour passes, a second, and still Seryozhka does not come. The river has long been swept and a box brought to sit on, but the drunken fellow does not appear. Matvey waits and merely yawns. The feeling of boredom is one of which he knows nothing. If he were told to stand on the river for a day, a month, or a year he would stand there.

At last Seryozhka comes into sight from behind the huts. He walks with a lurching gait, scarcely moving. He is too lazy to go the long way round, and he comes not by the road, but prefers a short cut in a straight line down the bank, and sticks in the snow, hangs on to the bushes, slides on his back as he comes—and all this slowly, with pauses.

"What are you about?" he cries, falling on Matvey at once. "Why are you standing there doing nothing! When are you going to break the ice?"

Matvey crosses himself, takes the crowbar in both hands, and begins breaking the ice, carefully keeping to the circle that has been drawn. Seryozhka sits down on the box and watches the heavy clumsy movements of his assistant.

"Easy at the edges! Easy there!" he commands. "If you can't do it properly, you shouldn't undertake it, once you have undertaken it you should do it. You!"

A crowd collects on the top of the bank. At the sight of the spectators Seryozhka becomes even more excited.

"I declare I am not going to do it . . ." he says, lighting a stinking cigarette and spitting on the ground. "I should like to see how you get on without me. Last year at Kostyukovo, Styopka Gulkov undertook to make a Jordan as I do. And what did it amount to—it was a laughing-stock. The Kostyukovo folks came to ours crowds and crowds of them! The people flocked from all the villages."

"Because except for ours there is nowhere a proper Jordan . . ."

"Work, there is no time for talking. . . . Yes, old man . . . you won't find another Jordan like it in the whole province. The soldiers say you would look in vain, they are not so good even in the towns. Easy, easy!"

Matvey puffs and groans. The work is not easy. The ice is firm and thick; and he has to break it and at once take the pieces away that the open space may not be blocked up.

But, hard as the work is and senseless as Seryozhka's commands are, by three o'clock there is a large circle of dark water in the Bystryanka.

"It was better last year," says Seryozhka angrily. "You can't do even that! Ah, dummy! To keep such fools in the temple of God! Go and bring a board to make the pegs! Bring the ring, you crow! And er . . . get some bread somewhere . . . and some cucumbers, or something."

Matvey goes off and soon afterwards comes back, carrying on his shoulders an immense wooden ring which had been painted in previous years in patterns of various colours. In the centre of the ring is a red cross, at the circumference holes for the pegs. Seryozhka takes the ring and covers the hole in the ice with it.

"Just right . . . it fits. . . . We have only to renew the paint and it will be first-rate. . . . Come, why are you standing still? Make the lectern. Or—er—go and get logs to make the cross . . ."

Matvey, who has not tasted food or drink all day, trudges up the hill again. Lazy as Seryozhka is, he makes the pegs with his own hands. He knows that those pegs have a miraculous power: whoever gets hold of a peg after the blessing of the water will be lucky for the whole year. Such work is really worth doing.

But the real work begins the following day. Then Seryozhka displays himself before the ignorant Matvey in all the greatness of his talent. There is no end to his babble, his fault-finding, his whims and fancies. If Matvey nails two big pieces of wood to make a cross, he is dissatisfied and tells him to do it again. If Matvey stands still, Seryozhka asks him angrily why he does not go; if he moves, Seryozhka shouts to him not to go away but to do his work. He is not satisfied with his tools, with the weather, or with his own talent; nothing pleases him.

Matvey saws out a great piece of ice for a lectern.

"Why have you broken off the corner?" cries Seryozhka, and glares at him furiously. "Why have you broken off the corner? I ask you."

"Forgive me, for Christ's sake."

"Do it over again!"

Matvey saws again . . . and there is no end to his sufferings. A lectern is to stand by the hole in the ice that is covered by the painted ring; on the lectern is to be carved the cross and the open gospel. But that is not all. Behind the lectern there is to be a high cross to be seen by all the crowd and to glitter in the sun as though sprinkled with diamonds and rubies. On the cross is to be a dove carved out of ice. The path from the church to the Jordan is to be strewn with branches of fir and juniper. All this is their task.

First of all Seryozhka sets to work on the lectern. He works with a file, a chisel, and an awl. He is perfectly successful in the cross on the lectern, the gospel, and the drapery that hangs down from the lectern. Then he begins on the dove. While he is trying to carve an expression of meekness and humility on the face of the dove, Matvey, lumbering about like a bear, is coating with ice the cross he has made of wood. He takes the cross and dips it in the hole. Waiting till the water has frozen on the cross he dips it in a second time, and so on till the cross is covered with a thick layer of ice. It is a difficult job, calling for a great deal of strength and patience.

But now the delicate work is finished. Seryozhka races about the village like one possessed. He swears and vows he will go at once to the river and smash all his work. He is looking for suitable paints.

His pockets are full of ochre, dark blue, red lead, and verdigris; without paying a farthing he rushes headlong from one shop to another. The shop is next door to the tavern. Here he has a drink; with a wave of his hand he darts off without paying. At one hut he gets beetroot leaves, at another an onion skin, out of which he makes a yellow colour. He swears, shoves, threatens, and not a soul murmurs! They all smile at him, they sympathise with him, call him Sergey Nikititch; they all feel that his art is not his personal affair but something that concerns them all, the whole people. One creates, the others help him. Seryozhka in himself is a nonentity, a sluggard, a drunkard, and a wastrel, but when he has his red lead or compasses in his hand he is at once something higher, a servant of God.

Epiphany morning comes. The precincts of the church and both banks of the river for a long distance are swarming with people. Everything that makes up the Jordan is scrupulously concealed under new mats. Seryozhka is meekly moving about near the mats, trying to control his emotion. He sees thousands of people. There are many here from other parishes; these people have come many a mile on foot through the frost and the snow merely to see his celebrated Jordan. Matvey, who had finished his coarse, rough work, is by now back in the church, there is no sight, no sound of him; he is already forgotten . . . . The weather is lovely. . . . There is not a cloud in the sky. The sunshine is dazzling.

The church bells ring out on the hill . . . Thousands of heads are bared, thousands of hands are moving, there are thousands of signs of the cross!

And Seryozhka does not know what to do with himself for impatience. But now they are ringing the bells for the Sacrament; then half an hour later a certain agitation is perceptible in the belfry and among the people. Banners are borne out of the church one after the other, while the bells peal in joyous haste. Seryozhka, trembling, pulls away the mat . . . and the people behold something extraordinary. The lectern, the wooden ring, the pegs, and the cross in the ice are iridescent with thousands of colors. The cross and the dove glitter so dazzlingly that it hurts the eyes to look at them. Merciful God, how fine it is! A murmur of wonder and delight runs through the crowd; the bells peal more loudly still, the day grows brighter; the banners oscillate and move over the crowd as over the waves. The procession, glittering with the settings of the ikons and the vestments of the clergy, comes slowly down the road and turns towards the Jordan. Hands are waved to the belfry for the ringing to cease, and the blessing of the water begins. The priests conduct the service slowly, deliberately, evidently trying to prolong the ceremony and the joy of praying all gathered together. There is perfect stillness.

But now they plunge the cross in, and the air echoes with an extraordinary din. Guns are fired, the bells peal furiously, loud exclamations of delight, shouts, and a rush to get the pegs. Seryozhka listens to this uproar, sees thousands of eyes fixed upon him, and the lazy fellow's soul is filled with a sense of glory and triumph.

THE SWEDISH MATCH

(The Story of a Crime)

I

ON the morning of October 6, 1885, a well-dressed young man presented himself at the office of the police superintendent of the 2nd division of the S. district, and announced that his employer, a retired cornet of the guards, called Mark Ivanovitch Klyauzov, had been murdered. The young man was pale and extremely agitated as he made this announcement. His hands trembled and there was a look of horror in his eyes.

"To whom have I the honour of speaking?" the superintendent asked him.

"Psyekov, Klyauzov's steward. Agricultural and engineering expert."

The police superintendent, on reaching the spot with Psyekov and the necessary witnesses, found the position as follows.

Masses of people were crowding about the lodge in which Klyauzov lived. The news of the event had flown round the neighbourhood with the rapidity of lightning, and, thanks to its being a holiday, the people were flocking to the lodge from all the neighbouring villages. There was a regular hubbub of talk. Pale and tearful faces were to be seen here and there. The door into Klyauzov's bedroom was found to be locked. The key was in the lock on the inside.

"Evidently the criminals made their way in by the window" Psyekov observed, as they examined the door.

They went into the garden into which the bedroom window looked. The window had a gloomy, ominous air. It was covered by a faded green curtain. One corner of the curtain was slightly turned back, which made it possible to peep into the bedroom.

"Has anyone of you looked in at the window?" inquired the superintendent.

"No, your honour," said Yefrem, the gardener, a little, grey-haired old man with the face of a veteran non-commissioned officer. "No one feels like looking when they are shaking in every limb!"

"Ech, Mark Ivanitch! Mark Ivanitch!" sighed the superintendent, as he looked at the window. "I told you that you would come to a bad end! I told you, poor dear—you wouldn't listen! Dissipation leads to no good!"

"It's thanks to Yefrem," said Psyekov. "We should never have guessed it but for him. It was he who first thought that something was wrong. He came to me this morning and said: 'Why is it our master hasn't waked up for so long? He hasn't been out of his bedroom for a whole week! When he said that to me I was struck all of a heap . . . . The thought flashed through my mind at once. He hasn't made an appearance since Saturday of last week, and to-day's Sunday. Seven days is no joke!"

"Yes, poor man," the superintendent sighed again. "A clever fellow, well-educated, and so good-hearted. There was no one like him, one may say, in company. But a rake; the kingdom of heaven be his! I'm not surprised at anything with him! Stepan," he said, addressing one of the witnesses, "ride off this minute to my house and send Andryushka to the police captain's, let him report to him. Say Mark Ivanitch has been murdered! Yes, and run to the inspector—why should he sit in comfort doing nothing? Let him come here. And you go yourself as fast as you can to the examining magistrate, Nikolay Yermolaitch, and tell him to come here. Wait a bit, I will write him a note."

The police superintendent stationed watchmen round the lodge, and went off to the steward's to have tea. Ten minutes later he was sitting on a stool, carefully nibbling lumps of sugar, and sipping tea as hot as a red-hot coal.

"There it is! . . ." he said to Psyekov, "there it is! . . . a gentleman, and a well-to-do one, too . . . a favourite of the gods, one may say, to use Pushkin's expression, and what has he made of it? Nothing! He gave himself up to drinking and debauchery, and . . . here now . . . he has been murdered!"

Two hours later the examining magistrate drove up. Nikolay Yermolaitch Tchubikov (that was the magistrate's name), a tall, thick-set old man of sixty, had been hard at work for a quarter of a century. He was known to the whole district as an honest, intelligent, energetic man, devoted to his work. His invariable companion, assistant, and secretary, a tall young man of six and twenty, called Dyukovsky, arrived on the scene of action with him.

"Is it possible, gentlemen?" Tchubikov began, going into Psyekov's room and rapidly shaking hands with everyone. "Is it possible? Mark Ivanitch? Murdered? No, it's impossible! Imposs-i-ble!"

"There it is," sighed the superintendent

"Merciful heavens! Why I saw him only last Friday. At the fair at Tarabankovo! Saving your presence, I drank a glass of vodka with him!"

"There it is," the superintendent sighed once more.

They heaved sighs, expressed their horror, drank a glass of tea each, and went to the lodge.

"Make way!" the police inspector shouted to the crowd.

On going into the lodge the examining magistrate first of all set to work to inspect the door into the bedroom. The door turned out to be made of deal, painted yellow, and not to have been tampered with. No special traces that might have served as evidence could be found. They proceeded to break open the door.

"I beg you, gentlemen, who are not concerned, to retire," said the examining magistrate, when, after long banging and cracking, the door yielded to the axe and the chisel. "I ask this in the interests of the investigation. . . . Inspector, admit no one!"

Tchubikov, his assistant, and the police superintendent opened the door and hesitatingly, one after the other, walked into the room. The following spectacle met their eyes. In the solitary window stood a big wooden bedstead with an immense feather bed on it. On the rumpled feather bed lay a creased and crumpled quilt. A pillow, in a cotton pillow case—also much creased, was on the floor. On a little table beside the bed lay a silver watch, and silver coins to the value of twenty kopecks. Some sulphur matches lay there too. Except the bed, the table, and a solitary chair, there was no furniture in the room. Looking under the bed, the superintendent saw two dozen empty bottles, an old straw hat, and a jar of vodka. Under the table lay one boot, covered with dust. Taking a look round the room, Tchubikov frowned and flushed crimson.

"The blackguards!" he muttered, clenching his fists.

"And where is Mark Ivanitch?" Dyukovsky asked quietly.

"I beg you not to put your spoke in," Tchubikov answered roughly. "Kindly examine the floor. This is the second case in my experience, Yevgraf Kuzmitch," he added to the police superintendent, dropping his voice. "In 1870 I had a similar case. But no doubt you remember it. . . . The murder of the merchant Portretov. It was just the same. The blackguards murdered him, and dragged the dead body out of the window."

Tchubikov went to the window, drew the curtain aside, and cautiously pushed the window. The window opened.

"It opens, so it was not fastened. . . . H'm there are traces on the window-sill. Do you see? Here is the trace of a knee. . . . Some one climbed out. . . . We shall have to inspect the window thoroughly."

"There is nothing special to be observed on the floor," said Dyukovsky. "No stains, nor scratches. The only thing I have found is a used Swedish match. Here it is. As far as I remember, Mark Ivanitch didn't smoke; in a general way he used sulphur ones, never Swedish matches. This match may serve as a clue. . . ."

"Oh, hold your tongue, please!" cried Tchubikov, with a wave of his hand. "He keeps on about his match! I can't stand these excitable people! Instead of looking for matches, you had better examine the bed!"

On inspecting the bed, Dyukovsky reported:

"There are no stains of blood or of anything else. . . . Nor are there any fresh rents. On the pillow there are traces of teeth. A liquid, having the smell of beer and also the taste of it, has been spilt on the quilt. . . . The general appearance of the bed gives grounds for supposing there has been a struggle."

"I know there was a struggle without your telling me! No one asked you whether there was a struggle. Instead of looking out for a struggle you had better be . . ."

"One boot is here, the other one is not on the scene."

"Well, what of that?"

"Why, they must have strangled him while he was taking off his boots. He hadn't time to take the second boot off when . . . ."

"He's off again! . . . And how do you know that he was strangled?"

"There are marks of teeth on the pillow. The pillow itself is very much crumpled, and has been flung to a distance of six feet from the bed."

"He argues, the chatterbox! We had better go into the garden. You had better look in the garden instead of rummaging about here. . . . I can do that without your help."

When they went out into the garden their first task was the inspection of the grass. The grass had been trampled down under the windows. The clump of burdock against the wall under the window turned out to have been trodden on too. Dyukovsky succeeded in finding on it some broken shoots, and a little bit of wadding. On the topmost burrs, some fine threads of dark blue wool were found.

"What was the colour of his last suit? Dyukovsky asked Psyekov.

"It was yellow, made of canvas."

"Capital! Then it was they who were in dark blue. . . ."

Some of the burrs were cut off and carefully wrapped up in paper. At that moment Artsybashev-Svistakovsky, the police captain, and Tyutyuev, the doctor, arrived. The police captain greeted the others, and at once proceeded to satisfy his curiosity; the doctor, a tall and extremely lean man with sunken eyes, a long nose, and a sharp chin, greeting no one and asking no questions, sat down on a stump, heaved a sigh and said:

"The Serbians are in a turmoil again! I can't make out what they want! Ah, Austria, Austria! It's your doing!"

The inspection of the window from outside yielded absolutely no result; the inspection of the grass and surrounding bushes furnished many valuable clues. Dyukovsky succeeded, for instance, in detecting a long, dark streak in the grass, consisting of stains, and stretching from the window for a good many yards into the garden. The streak ended under one of the lilac bushes in a big, brownish stain. Under the same bush was found a boot, which turned out to be the fellow to the one found in the bedroom.

"This is an old stain of blood," said Dyukovsky, examining the stain.

At the word "blood," the doctor got up and lazily took a cursory glance at the stain.

"Yes, it's blood," he muttered.

"Then he wasn't strangled since there's blood," said Tchubikov, looking malignantly at Dyukovsky.

"He was strangled in the bedroom, and here, afraid he would come to, they stabbed him with something sharp. The stain under the bush shows that he lay there for a comparatively long time, while they were trying to find some way of carrying him, or something to carry him on out of the garden."

"Well, and the boot?"

"That boot bears out my contention that he was murdered while he was taking off his boots before going to bed. He had taken off one boot, the other, that is, this boot he had only managed to get half off. While he was being dragged and shaken the boot that was only half on came off of itself. . . ."

"What powers of deduction! Just look at him!" Tchubikov jeered. "He brings it all out so pat! And when will you learn not to put your theories forward? You had better take a little of the grass for analysis instead of arguing!"

After making the inspection and taking a plan of the locality they went off to the steward's to write a report and have lunch. At lunch they talked.

"Watch, money, and everything else . . . are untouched," Tchubikov began the conversation. "It is as clear as twice two makes four that the murder was committed not for mercenary motives."

"It was committed by a man of the educated class," Dyukovsky put in.

"From what do you draw that conclusion?"

"I base it on the Swedish match which the peasants about here have not learned to use yet. Such matches are only used by landowners and not by all of them. He was murdered, by the way, not by one but by three, at least: two held him while the third strangled him. Klyauzov was strong and the murderers must have known that."

"What use would his strength be to him, supposing he were asleep?"

"The murderers came upon him as he was taking off his boots. He was taking off his boots, so he was not asleep."

"It's no good making things up! You had better eat your lunch!"

"To my thinking, your honour," said Yefrem, the gardener, as he set the samovar on the table, "this vile deed was the work of no other than Nikolashka."

"Quite possible," said Psyekov.

"Who's this Nikolashka?"

"The master's valet, your honour," answered Yefrem. "Who else should it be if not he? He's a ruffian, your honour! A drunkard, and such a dissipated fellow! May the Queen of Heaven never bring the like again! He always used to fetch vodka for the master, he always used to put the master to bed. . . . Who should it be if not he? And what's more, I venture to bring to your notice, your honour, he boasted once in a tavern, the rascal, that he would murder his master. It's all on account of Akulka, on account of a woman. . . . He had a soldier's wife. . . . The master took a fancy to her and got intimate with her, and he . . . was angered by it, to be sure. He's lolling about in the kitchen now, drunk. He's crying . . . making out he is grieving over the master .
. . ."

"And anyone might be angry over Akulka, certainly," said Psyekov. "She is a soldier's wife, a peasant woman, but . . . Mark Ivanitch might well call her Nana. There is something in her that does suggest Nana . . . fascinating . . . ."

"I have seen her . . . I know . . ." said the examining magistrate, blowing his nose in a red handkerchief.

Dyukovsky blushed and dropped his eyes. The police superintendent drummed on his saucer with his fingers. The police captain coughed and rummaged in his portfolio for something. On the doctor alone the mention of Akulka and Nana appeared to produce no impression. Tchubikov ordered Nikolashka to be fetched. Nikolashka, a lanky young man with a long pock-marked nose and a hollow chest, wearing a reefer jacket that had been his master's, came into Psyekov's room and bowed down to the ground before Tchubikov. His face looked sleepy and showed traces of tears. He was drunk and could hardly stand up.

"Where is your master?" Tchubikov asked him.

"He's murdered, your honour."

As he said this Nikolashka blinked and began to cry.

"We know that he is murdered. But where is he now? Where is his body?"

"They say it was dragged out of window and buried in the garden."

"H'm . . . the results of the investigation are already known in the kitchen then. . . . That's bad. My good fellow, where were you on the night when your master was killed? On Saturday, that is?"

Nikolashka raised his head, craned his neck, and pondered.

"I can't say, your honour," he said. "I was drunk and I don't remember."

"An alibi!" whispered Dyukovsky, grinning and rubbing his hands.

"Ah! And why is it there's blood under your master's window!"

Nikolashka flung up his head and pondered.

"Think a little quicker," said the police captain.

"In a minute. That blood's from a trifling matter, your honour. I killed a hen; I cut her throat very simply in the usual way, and she fluttered out of my hands and took and ran off. . . .That's what the blood's from."

Yefrem testified that Nikolashka really did kill a hen every evening and killed it in all sorts of places, and no one had seen the half-killed hen running about the garden, though of course it could not be positively denied that it had done so.

"An alibi," laughed Dyukovsky, "and what an idiotic alibi."

"Have you had relations with Akulka?"

"Yes, I have sinned."

"And your master carried her off from you?"

"No, not at all. It was this gentleman here, Mr. Psyekov, Ivan Mihalitch, who enticed her from me, and the master took her from Ivan Mihalitch. That's how it was."

Psyekov looked confused and began rubbing his left eye. Dyukovsky fastened his eyes upon him, detected his confusion, and started. He saw on the steward's legs dark blue trousers which he had not previously noticed. The trousers reminded him of the blue threads found on the burdock. Tchubikov in his turn glanced suspiciously at Psyekov.

"You can go!" he said to Nikolashka. "And now allow me to put one question to you, Mr. Psyekov. You were here, of course, on the Saturday of last week?

"Yes, at ten o'clock I had supper with Mark Ivanitch."

"And afterwards?"

Psyekov was confused, and got up from the table.

"Afterwards . . . afterwards . . . I really don't remember," he muttered. "I had drunk a good deal on that occasion. . . . I can't remember where and when I went to bed. . . . Why do you all look at me like that? As though I had murdered him!"

"Where did you wake up?"

"I woke up in the servants' kitchen on the stove . . . . They can all confirm that. How I got on to the stove I can't say. . . ."

"Don't disturb yourself . . . Do you know Akulina?"

"Oh well, not particularly."

"Did she leave you for Klyauzov?"

"Yes. . . . Yefrem, bring some more mushrooms! Will you have some tea, Yevgraf Kuzmitch?"

There followed an oppressive, painful silence that lasted for some five minutes. Dyukovsky held his tongue, and kept his piercing eyes on Psyekov's face, which gradually turned pale. The silence was broken by Tchubikov.

"We must go to the big house," he said, "and speak to the deceased's sister, Marya Ivanovna. She may give us some evidence."

Tchubikov and his assistant thanked Psyekov for the lunch, then went off to the big house. They found Klyauzov's sister, a maiden lady of five and forty, on her knees before a high family shrine of ikons. When she saw portfolios and caps adorned with cockades in her visitors' hands, she turned pale.

"First of all, I must offer an apology for disturbing your devotions, so to say," the gallant Tchubikov began with a scrape. "We have come to you with a request. You have heard, of course, already. . . . There is a suspicion that your brother has somehow been murdered. God's will, you know. . . . Death no one can escape, neither Tsar nor ploughman. Can you not assist us with some fact, something that will throw light?"

"Oh, do not ask me!" said Marya Ivanovna, turning whiter still, and hiding her face in her hands. "I can tell you nothing! Nothing! I implore you! I can say nothing . . . What can I do? Oh, no, no . . . not a word . . . of my brother! I would rather die than speak!"

Marya Ivanovna burst into tears and went away into another room. The officials looked at each other, shrugged their shoulders, and beat a retreat.

"A devil of a woman!" said Dyukovsky, swearing as they went out of the big house. "Apparently she knows something and is concealing it. And there is something peculiar in the maid-servant's expression too. . . . You wait a bit, you devils! We will get to the bottom of it all!"

In the evening, Tchubikov and his assistant were driving home by the light of a pale-faced moon; they sat in their waggonette, summing up in their minds the incidents of the day. Both were exhausted and sat silent. Tchubikov never liked talking on the road. In spite of his talkativeness, Dyukovsky held his tongue in deference to the old man. Towards the end of the journey, however, the young man could endure the silence no longer, and began:

"That Nikolashka has had a hand in the business," he said, "non dubitandum est. One can see from his mug too what sort of a chap he is. . . . His alibi gives him away hand and foot. There is no doubt either that he was not the instigator of the crime. He was only the stupid hired tool. Do you agree? The discreet Psyekov plays a not unimportant part in the affair too. His blue trousers, his embarrassment, his lying on the stove from fright after the murder, his alibi, and Akulka."

"Keep it up, you're in your glory! According to you, if a man knows Akulka he is the murderer. Ah, you hot-head! You ought to be sucking your bottle instead of investigating cases! You used to be running after Akulka too, does that mean that you had a hand in this business?"

"Akulka was a cook in your house for a month, too, but . . . I don't say anything. On that Saturday night I was playing cards with you, I saw you, or I should be after you too. The woman is not the point, my good sir. The point is the nasty, disgusting, mean feeling. . . . The discreet young man did not like to be cut out, do you see. Vanity, do you see. . . . He longed to be revenged. Then . . . His thick lips are a strong indication of sensuality. Do you remember how he smacked his lips when he compared Akulka to Nana? That he is burning with passion, the scoundrel, is beyond doubt! And so you have wounded vanity and unsatisfied passion. That's enough to lead to murder. Two of them are in our hands, but who is the third? Nikolashka and Psyekov held him. Who was it smothered him? Psyekov is timid, easily embarrassed, altogether a coward. People like Nikolashka are not equal to smothering with a pillow, they set to work with an axe or a mallet. . . . Some third person must have smothered him, but who?"

Dyukovsky pulled his cap over his eyes, and pondered. He was silent till the waggonette had driven up to the examining magistrate's house.

"Eureka!" he said, as he went into the house, and took off his overcoat. "Eureka, Nikolay Yermolaitch! I can't understand how it is it didn't occur to me before. Do you know who the third is?"

"Do leave off, please! There's supper ready. Sit down to supper!"

Tchubikov and Dyukovsky sat down to supper. Dyukovsky poured himself out a wine-glassful of vodka, got up, stretched, and with sparkling eyes, said:

"Let me tell you then that the third person who collaborated with the scoundrel Psyekov and smothered him was a woman! Yes! I am speaking of the murdered man's sister, Marya Ivanovna!"

Tchubikov coughed over his vodka and fastened his eyes on Dyukovsky.

"Are you . . . not quite right? Is your head . . . not quite right?

Does it ache?"

"I am quite well. Very good, suppose I have gone out of my mind, but how do you explain her confusion on our arrival? How do you explain her refusal to give information? Admitting that that is trivial—very good! All right!--but think of the terms they were on! She detested her brother! She is an Old Believer, he was a profligate, a godless fellow . . . that is what has bred hatred between them! They say he succeeded in persuading her that he was an angel of Satan! He used to practise spiritualism in her presence!"

"Well, what then?"

"Don't you understand? She's an Old Believer, she murdered him through fanaticism! She has not merely slain a wicked man, a profligate, she has freed the world from Antichrist—and that she fancies is her merit, her religious achievement! Ah, you don't know these old maids, these Old Believers! You should read Dostoevsky! And what does Lyeskov say . . . and Petchersky! It's she, it's she, I'll stake my life on it. She smothered him! Oh, the fiendish woman! Wasn't she, perhaps, standing before the ikons when we went in to put us off the scent? 'I'll stand up and say my prayers,' she said to herself, 'they will think I am calm and don't expect them.' That's the method of all novices in crime. Dear Nikolay Yermolaitch! My dear man! Do hand this case over to me! Let me go through with it to the end! My dear fellow! I have begun it, and I will carry it through to the end."

Tchubikov shook his head and frowned.

"I am equal to sifting difficult cases myself," he said. "And it's your place not to put yourself forward. Write what is dictated to you, that is your business!"

Dyukovsky flushed crimson, walked out, and slammed the door.

"A clever fellow, the rogue," Tchubikov muttered, looking after him. "Ve-ery clever! Only inappropriately hasty. I shall have to buy him a cigar-case at the fair for a present."

Next morning a lad with a big head and a hare lip came from Klyauzovka. He gave his name as the shepherd Danilko, and furnished a very interesting piece of information.

"I had had a drop," said he. "I stayed on till midnight at my crony's. As I was going home, being drunk, I got into the river for a bathe. I was bathing and what do I see! Two men coming along the dam carrying something black. 'Tyoo!' I shouted at them. They were scared, and cut along as fast as they could go into the Makarev kitchen-gardens. Strike me dead, if it wasn't the master they were carrying!"

Towards evening of the same day Psyekov and Nikolashka were arrested and taken under guard to the district town. In the town they were put in the prison tower.

II

Twelve days passed.

It was morning. The examining magistrate, Nikolay Yermolaitch, was sitting at a green table at home, looking through the papers, relating to the "Klyauzov case"; Dyukovsky was pacing up and down the room restlessly, like a wolf in a cage.

"You are convinced of the guilt of Nikolashka and Psyekov," he said, nervously pulling at his youthful beard. "Why is it you refuse to be convinced of the guilt of Marya Ivanovna? Haven't you evidence enough?"

"I don't say that I don't believe in it. I am convinced of it, but somehow I can't believe it. . . . There is no real evidence. It's all theoretical, as it were. . . . Fanaticism and one thing and another. . . ."

"And you must have an axe and bloodstained sheets! . . . You lawyers! Well, I will prove it to you then! Do give up your slip-shod attitude to the psychological aspect of the case. Your Marya Ivanovna ought to be in Siberia! I'll prove it. If theoretical proof is not enough for you, I have something material. . . . It will show you how right my theory is! Only let me go about a little!"

"What are you talking about?"

"The Swedish match! Have you forgotten? I haven't forgotten it! I'll find out who struck it in the murdered man's room! It was not struck by Nikolashka, nor by Psyekov, neither of whom turned out to have matches when searched, but a third person, that is Marya Ivanovna. And I will prove it! . . . Only let me drive about the district, make some inquiries. . . ."

"Oh, very well, sit down. . . . Let us proceed to the examination."

Dyukovsky sat down to the table, and thrust his long nose into the papers.

"Bring in Nikolay Tetchov!" cried the examining magistrate.

Nikolashka was brought in. He was pale and thin as a chip. He was trembling.

"Tetchov!" began Tchubikov. "In 1879 you were convicted of theft and condemned to a term of imprisonment. In 1882 you were condemned for theft a second time, and a second time sent to prison . . . We know all about it. . . ."

A look of surprise came up into Nikolashka's face. The examining magistrate's omniscience amazed him, but soon wonder was replaced by an expression of extreme distress. He broke into sobs, and asked leave to go to wash, and calm himself. He was led out.

"Bring in Psyekov!" said the examining magistrate.

Psyekov was led in. The young man's face had greatly changed during those twelve days. He was thin, pale, and wasted. There was a look of apathy in his eyes.

"Sit down, Psyekov," said Tchubikov. "I hope that to-day you will be sensible and not persist in lying as on other occasions. All this time you have denied your participation in the murder of Klyauzov, in spite of the mass of evidence against you. It is senseless. Confession is some mitigation of guilt. To-day I am talking to you for the last time. If you don't confess to-day, to-morrow it will be too late. Come, tell us. . . ."

"I know nothing, and I don't know your evidence," whispered Psyekov.

"That's useless! Well then, allow me to tell you how it happened. On Saturday evening, you were sitting in Klyauzov's bedroom drinking vodka and beer with him." (Dyukovsky riveted his eyes on Psyekov's face, and did not remove them during the whole monologue.) "Nikolay was waiting upon you. Between twelve and one Mark Ivanitch told you he wanted to go to bed. He always did go to bed at that time. While he was taking off his boots and giving you some instructions regarding the estate, Nikolay and you at a given signal seized your intoxicated master and flung him back upon the bed. One of you sat on his feet, the other on his head. At that moment the lady, you know who, in a black dress, who had arranged with you beforehand the part she would take in the crime, came in from the passage. She picked up the pillow, and proceeded to smother him with it. During the struggle, the light went out. The woman took a box of Swedish matches out of her pocket and lighted the candle. Isn't that right? I see from your face that what I say is true. Well, to proceed. . . . Having smothered him, and being convinced that he had ceased to breathe, Nikolay and you dragged him out of window and put him down near the burdocks. Afraid that he might regain consciousness, you struck him with something sharp. Then you carried him, and laid him for some time under a lilac bush. After resting and considering a little, you carried him . . . lifted him over the hurdle. . . . Then went along the road. . . Then comes the dam; near the dam you were frightened by a peasant. But what is the matter with you?"

Psyekov, white as a sheet, got up, staggering.

"I am suffocating!" he said. "Very well. . . . So be it. . . . Only I must go. . . . Please."

Psyekov was led out.

"At last he has admitted it!" said Tchubikov, stretching at his ease. "He has given himself away! How neatly I caught him there."

"And he didn't deny the woman in black!" said Dyukovsky, laughing. "I am awfully worried over that Swedish match, though! I can't endure it any longer. Good-bye! I am going!"

Dyukovsky put on his cap and went off. Tchubikov began interrogating Akulka.

Akulka declared that she knew nothing about it. . . .

"I have lived with you and with nobody else!" she said.

At six o'clock in the evening Dyukovsky returned. He was more excited than ever. His hands trembled so much that he could not unbutton his overcoat. His cheeks were burning. It was evident that he had not come back without news.

"Veni, vidi, vici!" he cried, dashing into Tchubikov's room and sinking into an armchair. "I vow on my honour, I begin to believe in my own genius. Listen, damnation take us! Listen and wonder, old friend! It's comic and it's sad. You have three in your grasp already . . . haven't you? I have found a fourth murderer, or rather murderess, for it is a woman! And what a woman! I would have given ten years of my life merely to touch her shoulders. But . . . listen. I drove to Klyauzovka and proceeded to describe a spiral round it. On the way I visited all the shopkeepers and innkeepers, asking for Swedish matches. Everywhere I was told 'No.' I have been on my round up to now. Twenty times I lost hope, and as many times regained it. I have been on the go all day long, and only an hour ago came upon what I was looking for. A couple of miles from here they gave me a packet of a dozen boxes of matches. One box was missing . . . I asked at once: 'Who bought that box?' 'So-and-so. She took a fancy to them. . . They crackle.' My dear fellow! Nikolay Yermolaitch! What can sometimes be done by a man who has been expelled from a seminary and studied Gaboriau is beyond all conception! From to-day I shall began to respect myself! . . . Ough. . . . Well, let us go!"

"Go where?"

"To her, to the fourth. . . . We must make haste, or . . . I shall explode with impatience! Do you know who she is? You will never guess. The young wife of our old police superintendent, Yevgraf Kuzmitch, Olga Petrovna; that's who it is! She bought that box of matches!"

"You . . . you. . . . Are you out of your mind?"

"It's very natural! In the first place she smokes, and in the second she was head over ears in love with Klyauzov. He rejected her love for the sake of an Akulka. Revenge. I remember now, I once came upon them behind the screen in the kitchen. She was cursing him, while he was smoking her cigarette and puffing the smoke into her face. But do come along; make haste, for it is getting dark already . . . . Let us go!"

"I have not gone so completely crazy yet as to disturb a respectable, honourable woman at night for the sake of a wretched boy!"

"Honourable, respectable. . . . You are a rag then, not an examining magistrate! I have never ventured to abuse you, but now you force me to it! You rag! you old fogey! Come, dear Nikolay Yermolaitch, I entreat you!"

The examining magistrate waved his hand in refusal and spat in disgust.

"I beg you! I beg you, not for my own sake, but in the interests of justice! I beseech you, indeed! Do me a favour, if only for once in your life!"

Dyukovsky fell on his knees.

"Nikolay Yermolaitch, do be so good! Call me a scoundrel, a worthless wretch if I am in error about that woman! It is such a case, you know! It is a case! More like a novel than a case. The fame of it will be all over Russia. They will make you examining magistrate for particularly important cases! Do understand, you unreasonable old man!"

The examining magistrate frowned and irresolutely put out his hand towards his hat.

"Well, the devil take you!" he said, "let us go."

It was already dark when the examining magistrate's waggonette rolled up to the police superintendent's door.

"What brutes we are!" said Tchubikov, as he reached for the bell.

"We are disturbing people."

"Never mind, never mind, don't be frightened. We will say that one of the springs has broken."

Tchubikov and Dyukovsky were met in the doorway by a tall, plump woman of three and twenty, with eyebrows as black as pitch and full red lips. It was Olga Petrovna herself.

"Ah, how very nice," she said, smiling all over her face. "You are just in time for supper. My Yevgraf Kuzmitch is not at home. . . . He is staying at the priest's. But we can get on without him. Sit down. Have you come from an inquiry?"

"Yes. . . . We have broken one of our springs, you know," began Tchubikov, going into the drawing-room and sitting down in an easy-chair.

"Take her by surprise at once and overwhelm her," Dyukovsky whispered to him.

"A spring .. . er . . . yes. . . . We just drove up. . . ."

"Overwhelm her, I tell you! She will guess if you go drawing it out."

"Oh, do as you like, but spare me," muttered Tchubikov, getting up and walking to the window. "I can't! You cooked the mess, you eat it!"

"Yes, the spring," Dyukovsky began, going up to the superintendent's wife and wrinkling his long nose. "We have not come in to . . . er-er-er . . . supper, nor to see Yevgraf Kuzmitch. We have come to ask you, madam, where is Mark Ivanovitch whom you have murdered?"

"What? What Mark Ivanovitch?" faltered the superintendent's wife, and her full face was suddenly in one instant suffused with crimson. "I . . . don't understand."

"I ask you in the name of the law! Where is Klyauzov? We know all about it!"

"Through whom?" the superintendent's wife asked slowly, unable to face Dyukovsky's eyes.

"Kindly inform us where he is!"

"But how did you find out? Who told you?"

"We know all about it. I insist in the name of the law."

The examining magistrate, encouraged by the lady's confusion, went up to her.

"Tell us and we will go away. Otherwise we . . ."

"What do you want with him?"

"What is the object of such questions, madam? We ask you for information. You are trembling, confused. . . . Yes, he has been murdered, and if you will have it, murdered by you! Your accomplices have betrayed you!"

The police superintendent's wife turned pale.

"Come along," she said quietly, wringing her hands. "He is hidden in the bath-house. Only for God's sake, don't tell my husband! I implore you! It would be too much for him."

The superintendent's wife took a big key from the wall, and led her visitors through the kitchen and the passage into the yard. It was dark in the yard. There was a drizzle of fine rain. The superintendent's wife went on ahead. Tchubikov and Dyukovsky strode after her through the long grass, breathing in the smell of wild hemp and slops, which made a squelching sound under their feet. It was a big yard. Soon there were no more pools of slops, and their feet felt ploughed land. In the darkness they saw the silhouette of trees, and among the trees a little house with a crooked chimney.

"This is the bath-house," said the superintendent's wife, "but, I implore you, do not tell anyone."

Going up to the bath-house, Tchubikov and Dyukovsky saw a large padlock on the door.

"Get ready your candle-end and matches," Tchubikov whispered to his assistant.

The superintendent's wife unlocked the padlock and let the visitors into the bath-house. Dyukovsky struck a match and lighted up the entry. In the middle of it stood a table. On the table, beside a podgy little samovar, was a soup tureen with some cold cabbage-soup in it, and a dish with traces of some sauce on it.

"Go on!"

They went into the next room, the bath-room. There, too, was a table. On the table there stood a big dish of ham, a bottle of vodka, plates, knives and forks.

"But where is he . . . where's the murdered man?"

"He is on the top shelf," whispered the superintendent's wife, turning paler than ever and trembling.

Dyukovsky took the candle-end in his hand and climbed up to the upper shelf. There he saw a long, human body, lying motionless on a big feather bed. The body emitted a faint snore. . . .

"They have made fools of us, damn it all!" Dyukovsky cried. "This is not he! It is some living blockhead lying here. Hi! who are you, damnation take you!"

The body drew in its breath with a whistling sound and moved. Dyukovsky prodded it with his elbow. It lifted up its arms, stretched, and raised its head.

"Who is that poking?" a hoarse, ponderous bass voice inquired. "What do you want?"

Dyukovsky held the candle-end to the face of the unknown and uttered a shriek. In the crimson nose, in the ruffled, uncombed hair, in the pitch-black moustaches of which one was jauntily twisted and pointed insolently towards the ceiling, he recognised Cornet Klyauzov.

"You. . . . Mark . . . Ivanitch! Impossible!"

The examining magistrate looked up and was dumbfoundered.

"It is I, yes. . . . And it's you, Dyukovsky! What the devil do you want here? And whose ugly mug is that down there? Holy Saints, it's the examining magistrate! How in the world did you come here?"

Klyauzov hurriedly got down and embraced Tchubikov. Olga Petrovna whisked out of the door.

"However did you come? Let's have a drink!--dash it all! Tra-ta-ti-to-tom . . . . Let's have a drink! Who brought you here, though? How did you get to know I was here? It doesn't matter, though! Have a drink!"

Klyauzov lighted the lamp and poured out three glasses of vodka.

"The fact is, I don't understand you," said the examining magistrate, throwing out his hands. "Is it you, or not you?"

"Stop that. . . . Do you want to give me a sermon? Don't trouble yourself! Dyukovsky boy, drink up your vodka! Friends, let us pass the . . . What are you staring at . . . ? Drink!"

"All the same, I can't understand," said the examining magistrate, mechanically drinking his vodka. "Why are you here?"

"Why shouldn't I be here, if I am comfortable here?"

Klyauzov sipped his vodka and ate some ham.

"I am staying with the superintendent's wife, as you see. In the wilds among the ruins, like some house goblin. Drink! I felt sorry for her, you know, old man! I took pity on her, and, well, I am living here in the deserted bath-house, like a hermit. . . . I am well fed. Next week I am thinking of moving on. . . . I've had enough of it. . . ."

"Inconceivable!" said Dyukovsky.

"What is there inconceivable in it?"

"Inconceivable! For God's sake, how did your boot get into the garden?"

"What boot?"

"We found one of your boots in the bedroom and the other in the garden."

"And what do you want to know that for? It is not your business. But do drink, dash it all. Since you have waked me up, you may as well drink! There's an interesting tale about that boot, my boy. I didn't want to come to Olga's. I didn't feel inclined, you know, I'd had a drop too much. . . . She came under the window and began scolding me. . . . You know how women . . . as a rule. Being drunk, I up and flung my boot at her. Ha-ha! . . . 'Don't scold,' I said. She clambered in at the window, lighted the lamp, and gave me a good drubbing, as I was drunk. I have plenty to eat here. . . . Love, vodka, and good things! But where are you off to? Tchubikov, where are you off to?"

The examining magistrate spat on the floor and walked out of the bath-house. Dyukovsky followed him with his head hanging. Both got into the waggonette in silence and drove off. Never had the road seemed so long and dreary. Both were silent. Tchubikov was shaking with anger all the way. Dyukovsky hid his face in his collar as though he were afraid the darkness and the drizzling rain might read his shame on his face.

On getting home the examining magistrate found the doctor, Tyutyuev, there. The doctor was sitting at the table and heaving deep sighs as he turned over the pages of the *Neva*.

"The things that are going on in the world," he said, greeting the examining magistrate with a melancholy smile. "Austria is at it again . . . and Gladstone, too, in a way. . . ."

Tchubikov flung his hat under the table and began to tremble.

"You devil of a skeleton! Don't bother me! I've told you a thousand times over, don't bother me with your politics! It's not the time for politics! And as for you," he turned upon Dyukovsky and shook his fist at him, "as for you. . . . I'll never forget it, as long as I live!"

"But the Swedish match, you know! How could I tell. . . ."

"Choke yourself with your match! Go away and don't irritate me, or goodness knows what I shall do to you. Don't let me set eyes on you."

Dyukovsky heaved a sigh, took his hat, and went out.

"I'll go and get drunk!" he decided, as he went out of the gate, and he sauntered dejectedly towards the tavern.

When the superintendent's wife got home from the bath-house she found her husband in the drawing-room.

"What did the examining magistrate come about?" asked her husband.

"He came to say that they had found Klyauzov. Only fancy, they found him staying with another man's wife."

"Ah, Mark Ivanitch, Mark Ivanitch!" sighed the police superintendent, turning up his eyes. "I told you that dissipation would lead to no good! I told you so—you wouldn't heed me!"

Anton Chekhov - A Biography

Anton Pavlovich Chekhov was born the third of six surviving children on 29th January 1860 in Taganrog, a port town on the Sea of Azov on the south coast of Russia. During his intense career he would make a name for himself as a playwright and author, though the whole time he practised as a physician. Indeed, he once wrote "medicine is my lawful wife, and literature is my mistress". This affair was an extended and colourful one, begun as a means of bolstering his income but developed as a form of artistic expression, through which he would make several key formal innovations which prevail in the writing of various authors who succeed him such as the method of stream-of-consciousness writing, heavily employed by the Irish novelist and poet James Joyce.

Chekhov's father Pavel Yegorovich, from whose Christian name Chekhov received his patronymic middle name, was the son of a former serf and ran a grocery store in Taganrog. As a devout orthodox Christian and director of the parish church choir in which Chekhov and his brothers sang, the stark contrast between this and his physically abusive attitude at home served as an example for many of Chekhov's portraits of hypocrisy, while also providing Chekhov with a model of how not to conduct himself in public and in private. This proved a valuable life lesson for him, for at every juncture Chekhov would treat those around him with dignity and respect. His mother, Yevgeniya, was a talented and passionate story-teller, and entertained the children with extensive stories about her travels across the entirety of Russia with her cloth merchant father. As his father provided character inspiration, his mother instilled in him a love of stories and a skill for telling them. He would later affirm that "our talents we got from our father, but our soul from our mother". The extent of the influence that this childhood had on him can be seen in his later chastisement of his elder brother Alexander, whose tyrannical treatment of his own wife and children reminded Chekhov all too painfully of their own fraught upbringing; he wrote, tentatively,

> Let me ask you to recall that it was despotism and lying that ruined your mother's youth. Despotism and lying so mutilated our childhood that it's sickening and frightening to think about it. Remember the horror and disgust we felt in those times when Father threw a tantrum at dinner over too much salt in the soup and called Mother a fool.

Between the ages of six and eight, he attended a Greek school in Taganrog, run by the Greek Church of Taganrog and funded by wealthy Greek merchants. Among the subjects taught were Greek language, God's law, mathematics, history, calligraphy and singing. Then, from 1868 he attended Taganrog gymnasium, the local grammar school, where he proved a distinctly average pupil. Despite being academically reserved and largely undemonstrative he nonetheless forged himself a reputation as a prankster, for making up humourous nicknames for his teachers and for being a reliable source of witty, satirical remarks. It soon became apparent that his interests lay away from academia for he became involved in amateur dramatics, frequently attending performances at the Taganrog Theatre. The first of these performances was

Offenbach's operetta *Elena the Beautiful* which he saw when he was thirteen, and from then on he became an avid theatre attendee and spent much of his savings on visits, despite the theatre being out of bounds for Gymnasium students without special dispensation to visit; permission was rarely given, and mostly on weekends. So regular was he that he had a favourite seat, whose most attractive characteristic was its location; situated in the back gallery it was cheap, and being so far out of sight it proved an effective place to hide from the Gymnasium staff who would routinely check for unauthorised students. To further conceal themselves from these spot-checks, Anton and his schoolmates would disguise themselves with make-up, wigs and props such as spectacles and fake beards. Much of the savings which he spent at the theatre came from the annual 300 ruble grant he received from the Taganrog City Council after a failed assassination attempt on the then Tsar, Alexander II of Russia. Inspired by the drama he witnessed at the theatre, he tried his hand at writing short, amusing 'anecdotes' and stories. Alongside this he is known to have written a long, tragicomic play, entitled *Fatherless*, though he later destroyed it and no manuscript remains, and which his brother Alexander denounced as "an inexcusable though innocent fabrication".

His preoccupation with the theatre had a marked result on his school career, and the greatest blow came when he was fifteen and kept down a year for failing a Greek examination. During this time he sang under his Father's direction in the Greek orthodox ministry choir, a time which he would later recall as one of "suffering". A letter written in 1892 describes how "when my brothers and I used to stand in the middle of the church and sing the trio 'May my prayer be exalted', or 'The Archangel's Voice', everyone looked at us with emotion and envied our parents, but we at that moment felt like little convicts". The family gave an appearance of idyllic happiness and talent, though this contrast between this outward façade and the tyranny and despotism they experienced at home under Pavel's strict rule serves as another example of exactly the source of the picture of hypocrisy Chekhov paints in his work. When Chekhov was sixteen, Pavel mismanaged his own finances quite spectacularly during the process of building a new house which resulted in a declaration of bankruptcy and a subsequent fleeing to Moscow to avoid debtor's prison.

By now Chekhov's elder brothers Alexander and Nikolay were already studying at Moscow University so the majority of the family reunited there, living in poverty, a change of circumstance which left Yevgeniya in a state of emotional and physical infirmity. Chekhov, however, remained in Taganrog living with a man called Selivanov who, like Lopakhin in *The Cherry Orchard*, had bailed out the family for the price of their house, to complete his education. Although his board was free with Selivanov, he was left to pay for his schooling, covering the costs and surviving on a disparate income cobbled together from the selling off of family possessions and bolstered by private tutoring, catching and selling goldfinches, and by writing and selling short sketches to the newspapers. Every ruble he could spare from his education and his now less frequent theatre visits he sent to his family in Moscow, enclosed with humourous letters designed to cheer them up in their poverty and misery. He now began to take a more earnest interest in his education, reading extensively and analytically, including the works of Cervantes, Turgenev, Goncharov and Schopenhauer. Meanwhile he enjoyed a series of closeted love affairs, including one with the wife of one of his teachers. His schooling completed and a scholarship to Moscow University obtained, he moved there in 1879 and rejoined his family.

He now assumed responsibility for the family, supporting them by writing regular satirical sketches and vignettes of contemporary Russian lifestyle under pseudonyms such as 'Antosha Chekhonte' and 'Man Without a Spleen', and his prodigious output earned him first a reputation as a reputable chronicler and then, in 1882, a regular position writing for Oskolki, a journal owned by Nicolai Leykin, the most successful Russian publisher at the time. Although the wit and brevity of his work here prevails through much of his later writing, it was considerably harsher in tone, perhaps a reflection of the stressful position of poverty, study and patriarch in which he found himself. In 1884, he qualified as a physician and, although he earned little from the profession and often treated the poor free of charge, he considered this his principle profession. At this time and for the next two years he would regularly cough up blood, a symptom of tuberculosis with which he was all too familiar as a physician. However, not wishing to "submit himself to be sounded by his colleagues", he kept the condition to himself. The continued success of his periodical writing enabled him to move the family into progressively more comfortable accommodation, and then in 1886 he received an invitation to write for *Novoye Vremya* (*New Times*), owned and edited by the millionaire media magnate Alexey Suvorin. Paying double per line what Anton received from Leykin and being given three times the column inches he took the offer immediately and became close friends with Suvorin, a friendship which would last his lifetime.

His work at these periodicals was not the sole extent of his literary output, for in 1885 he published a short story, *The Huntsman*, which quickly attracted scholarly attention and recognition. The sixty-four year old celebrated writer Grigorovich wrote to him shortly after it first appeared on the shelves, saying "you have *real* talent—a talent which places you in the front rank among writers in the new generation." The letter continues in this effusive manner before resolving to offer Chekhov the practical advice to slow down, write less, and concentrate on literary quality. In reply, Chekhov admitted that he had been struck "like a thunderbolt" on reading the letter, confessing to hitherto writing his stories "the way reporters write up their notes about fires - mechanically, half-consciously, caring nothing about either the reader or myself." In making such an honest admission, Chekhov arguably undersold himself as a serious author, for despite the appearance of a nonchalant and casual approach, later analysis and comparison of early manuscripts reveals a huge extent of careful revision indicating a far more involved, authorial approach than he allows himself in correspondence with Grigorovich. Nonetheless, receiving such warm congratulation and encouragement along with such earnest advice from so respected an author caused Chekhov to sit up straight and approach his writing with far more serious, artistic ambition. Now twenty-six, and with the patronage of such a revered and loved author, his collection of short stories entitled *V Sumerkakh* (*At Dusk*) won him the much coveted Pushkin Prize, awarded "for the best literary production distinguished by high artistic worth".

Following this act of formal recognition and somewhat burnt out by the years of continued literary output his enduring success afforded him the time and the money to take a sabbatical, so he engaged in a journey to the Ukraine in 1887 whereupon he was reminded of the beauty of the Steppe. This excursion inspired the novella *The*

Steppe which he started on his return, and which he described in a letter to Grigorovich as "something rather odd and much too original", and which was eventually published in *Severny Vestnik* (*The Northern Herald*). Later that year he was commissioned by a theatre manager to write a play, and a fortnight later Chekhov produced *Ivanov* which, though he considered the process "sickening" and described in a letter to his brother Alexander in the manner of a comic portrait, it was a huge success and was widely regarded as a work of excellent and noteworthy originality. Furthermore this period is considered the source of a literary device noted by Ilia Gurliand, who overheard it in conversation, as Chekhov's Gun; "if in act 1 you have a pistol hanging on the wall, then it must fire in the last act". Then, in 1889, his brother Nikolay died as a result of tuberculosis. Their brother Mikhail, who recorded Anton's depression during the period of mourning after the death, had been researching prisons as part of his studies in law, and Anton too became interested and eventually somewhat obsessed with the idea of prison reform.

This newfound interest in the humanitarian questions surrounding the prison system, combined with a conceivable yet subconscious desire to escape the close environment of mourning surrounding his brother's death, led Chekhov to journey to the penal colony Sakhalin, an island off the far East coast of Russia, where he spent three months interviewing convicts and settlers with the aim of compiling a census of the island. He made several now notorious remarks to his sister about what he witnessed (among others, a relatively lighthearted and blunt description of Tomsk, "a very dull town. To judge from the drunkards whose acquaintance I have made, and from the intellectual people who have come to the hotel to pay their respects to me, the inhabitants are very dull, too." [-the inhabitants of Tomsk later retaliated by erecting a mocking statue of Chekhov]). More seriously, though, many of the things he saw during this trip horrified him, writing that "there were times I felt that I saw before me the extreme limits of man's degradation." Among these was the plight of the children of the island, describing one such incident in his journals:

> On the Amur steamer going to Sakhalin, there was a convict who
> had murdered his wife and wore fetters on his legs. His daughter, a
> little girl of six, was with him. I noticed wherever the convict moved
> the little girl scrambled after him, holding on to his fetters. At night
> the child slept with the convicts and soldiers all in a heap together.

Concluding that the solution to this inhumanity lay not with charity and philanthropy, but with Government intervention and reform, he wrote *Ostrov Sakhalin* (*The Island of Sakhalin*), a work of social science which was praised, not for its literary brilliance, but for its steady and worthy informativeness, which was serialised and published in 1893-4. Though this initial work which stemmed from the trip was not literary in nature, the extended contact and expansive experience he received found itself expressed in *The Murder*, a story which, though longer than his others, is still considered short in nature.

In 1892 Chekhov had bought Melikhovo, a small country estate forty miles north of Moscow, which was his and his family's home until 1899. He joked about his residence there, quipping to his friend Ivan Leontyev that "it's nice to be a Lord" though this lighthearted remark belies the seriousness with which he undertook his responsibilities as a landlord. Within a few years of his taking residence there he had established his usefulness and sense of duty to the peasants, affording them relief from the 1892 outbreaks of cholera and bouts of famine, and building three schools, a fire station and a clinic, and offering his services as a physician to the peasantry of the surrounding countryside. Often he would find queues of patients lining up outside his door in the morning who had travelled by foot or by cart to receive treatment, and frequently he was called out to visit those too sick to travel. His brother Mikhail who resided with the family at Melikhovo recorded this honourable commitment to his role as estate physician, writing

> from the first day that Chekhov moved to Melikhovo, the sick began flocking to him from twenty miles around. They came on foot or were brought in carts, and often he was fetched to patients at a distance. Sometimes from early in the morning peasant women and children were standing before his door waiting.

Though these demanding hours left him with significantly less time for writing, they enriched his literary output for he was able to write informatively and genuinely about the peasantry and their living conditions, most notably in his short story *Peasants*. He did, however, visit those belonging to the upper-classes as well, though he was not enamoured by them, writing in his journal "Aristocrats? The same ugly bodies and physical uncleanliness, the same toothless old age and disgusting death, as with market-women".

He began to write arguably his most famous work, *The Seagull*, in 1894, in a lodge he had built himself in the orchard on the estate. Its first night on 17th October 1896 at the Alexandrinsky Theatre in Petersburg was something of a fiasco; it was booed by the audience, many of whom left, and this poor reception saw Chekhov fall out of love with the theatre. However, despite its poor reception by the play-going audience, it impressed the theatre director Vladimir Nemirovich-Danchenko so much that he proceeded to convince his colleague Constantin Stanislavski to take the play on and direct it in the innovative, progressive Moscow Art Theatre. This revival, in 1898, for the less-closeted Moscow audience was enormously well-received. Whereas the Petersburg performance had rendered the play literally and played down its more psychoanalytical aspects, Stanislavski payed far closer attention to the play's psychological realism and brought the deeply buried subtleties, lost on the Petersburg boards and on the audience's narrow-mindedness, to the surface. The play was such a success here that the Art Theatre commissioned further work from Chekhov, staging *Uncle Vanya* which he had completed in 1896. Furthermore, the positive critical reception had a restorative effect on Chekhov's interest in stage writing.

However, by now Chekhov's health condition was worsening, having suffered a major haemorrhage of the lungs in 1897 while visiting Moscow. His early reluctance to be seen by doctors prevailed and he protested to the notion of entering a clinic, though he eventually assented whereupon a formal diagnosis of the tuberculosis on the upper part of his lungs was reached, and the doctors ordered various changes in his lifestyle. His father then died in 1898, after which Chekhov bought a plot of land on the outskirts of Yalta and proceeded to build a villa, moving his mother and sister in with him the following year. Even though he pursued the enjoyment of gardening he had developed while at Melikhovo by planting trees and flowers, he kept dogs and tame cranes and regularly received highly regarded company such as Leo Tolstoy and

Maxim Gorky, he spoke of a sense of relief upon each occasion of his leaving this "hot Siberia" for Moscow or to travel further afield. While here, he wrote two more plays for the Art Theatre, though these were composed with much greater difficulty; he remarked that unlike his youth when "[he] wrote serenely, the way [he eats] pancakes now". These two plays, *Three Sisters* and *The Cherry Orchard* took over a year each.

A quiet marriage to Olga Knipper on 25th May 1901 was performed in keeping with the position of suspicion he had always had towards weddings, with a small ceremony and little outside attention. Knipper was an actress whom he had met at the rehearsals for *The Seagull*, their marriage conformed to his stipulations;

> By all means I will be married if you wish it. But on these conditions: everything must be as it has been hitherto - that is, she must live in Moscow while I live in the country, and I will come and see her ... give me a wife who, like the moon, won't appear in my sky every day.

This proved convenient as Knipper remained in Moscow performing his work and that of contemporary playwrights, and their long-distance correspondence features various treasured pieces of writing, be they shared complaints about Stanislavski's method of direction or advice from Chekhov to Knipper as to her performances in his plays. Prior to the marriage, Chekhov had been considered "Russia's most elusive literary bachelor", preferring brief liaisons and dalliances with unknown women, or brothels, to commitment. Chekhov then wrote one of his most famous stories, *The Lady with the Dog*, depicting a casual encounter between two strangers who, despite their best efforts and risking the security, stability and respectability of their family lives, find themselves irrevocably drawn to one another.

Chekhov's tuberculosis was finally getting the better of him, and by May 1904 it was quite clear that his death was imminent. Despite this, Mikhail recorded that "everyone who saw him secretly thought the end was not far off, but the nearer [he] was to the end, the less he seemed to realise it". He set off for the German town Badenweiler on 3rd June, writing cheerful, witty letters to his sister describing variously the food and the surroundings, while assuring both her and his mother that his health was improving; his last letter contained a sardonic complaint about the German women's fashion. The circumstances of his death have become one of "the greatest set pieces of literary history", and are most accurately recorded in this, Knipper's own account from her diaries, written in 1908:

> Anton sat up unusually straight and said loudly and clearly (although he knew almost no German): *Ich sterbe* ("I'm dying"). The doctor calmed him, took a syringe, gave him an injection of camphor and ordered champagne. Anton took a full glass, examined it, smiled at me and said: 'It's a long time since I drank champagne.' He drained it, lay quietly on his left side, and I just had time to run to him and lean across the bed and call to him, but he had stopped breathing and was sleeping peacefully as a child.

His body, transferred to Moscow in a refrigerated railway car whose purpose was for fresh oysters, was then interred next to his father at Novodevichy Cemetery in Moscow. Although thousands of mourners mistakenly followed the pomp and circumstance of the military funeral procession for the also deceased General Keller, many hundreds of thousands of readers, writers and actors have followed correctly the path he pioneered for the short story and for twentieth century realism.

A Biography of Anton Chekov & List of His Most Famous Quotes

Anton Pavlovich Chekhov was born the third of six surviving children on 29th January 1860 in Taganrog, a port town on the Sea of Azov on the south coast of Russia. During his intense career he would make a name for himself as a playwright and author, though the whole time he practised as a physician. Indeed, he once wrote "medicine is my lawful wife, and literature is my mistress". This affair was an extended and colourful one, begun as a means of bolstering his income but developed as a form of artistic expression, through which he would make several key formal innovations which prevail in the writing of various authors who succeed him such as the method of stream-of-consciousness writing, heavily employed by the Irish novelist and poet James Joyce.

Chekhov's father Pavel Yegorovich, from whose Christian name Chekhov received his patronymic middle name, was the son of a former serf and ran a grocery store in Taganrog. As a devout orthodox Christian and director of the parish church choir in which Chekhov and his brothers sang, the stark contrast between this and his physically abusive attitude at home served as an example for many of Chekhov's portraits of hypocrisy, while also providing Chekhov with a model of how not to conduct himself in public and in private. This proved a valuable life lesson for him, for at every juncture Chekhov would treat those around him with dignity and respect. His mother, Yevgeniya, was a talented and passionate story-teller, and entertained the children with extensive stories about her travels across the entirety of Russia with her cloth merchant father. As his father provided character inspiration, his mother instilled in him a love of stories and a skill for telling them. He would later affirm that "our talents we got from our father, but our soul from our mother". The extent of the influence that this childhood had on him can be seen in his later chastisement of his elder brother Alexander, whose tyrannical treatment of his own wife and children reminded Chekhov all too painfully of their own fraught upbringing; he wrote, tentatively,

Let me ask you to recall that it was despotism and lying that ruined your mother's youth. Despotism and lying so mutilated our childhood that it's sickening and frightening to think about it. Remember the horror and disgust we felt in those times when Father threw a tantrum at dinner over too much salt in the soup and called Mother a fool.

Between the ages of six and eight, he attended a Greek school in Taganrog, run by the Greek Church of Taganrog and funded by wealthy Greek merchants. Among the subjects taught were Greek language, God's law, mathematics, history, calligraphy and singing. Then, from 1868 he attended Taganrog gymnasium, the local grammar school, where he proved a distinctly average pupil. Despite being academically reserved and largely undemonstrative he nonetheless forged himself a reputation as a prankster, for making up humourous nicknames for his teachers and for being a reliable source of witty, satirical remarks. It soon became apparent that his interests lay away from academia for he became involved in amateur dramatics, frequently attending performances at the Taganrog Theatre. The first of these performances was Offenbach's operetta *Elena the Beautiful* which he saw when he was thirteen, and from then on he became an avid theatre attendee and spent much of his savings on visits, despite the theatre being out of bounds for Gymnasium students without special dispensation to visit; permission was rarely given, and mostly on weekends. So regular was he that he had a favourite seat, whose most attractive characteristic was its location; situated in the back gallery it was cheap, and being so far out of sight it proved an effective place to hide from the Gymnasium staff who would routinely check for unauthorised students. To further conceal themselves from these spot-checks, Anton and his schoolmates would disguise themselves with make-up, wigs and props such as spectacles and fake beards. Much of the savings which he spent at the theatre came from the annual 300 ruble grant he received from the Taganrog City Council after a failed assassination attempt on the then Tsar, Alexander II of Russia. Inspired by the drama he witnessed at the theatre, he tried his hand at writing short, amusing 'anecdotes' and stories. Alongside this he is known to have written a long, tragicomic play, entitled *Fatherless*, though he later destroyed it and no manuscript remains, and which his brother Alexander denounced as "an inexcusable though innocent fabrication".

His preoccupation with the theatre had a marked result on his school career, and the greatest blow came when he was fifteen and kept down a year for failing a Greek examination. During this time he sang under his Father's direction in the Greek orthodox ministry choir, a time which he would later recall as one of "suffering". A letter written in 1892 describes how "when my brothers and I used to stand in the middle of the church and sing the trio 'May my prayer be exalted', or 'The Archangel's Voice', everyone looked at us with emotion and envied our parents, but we at that moment felt like little convicts". The family gave an appearance of idyllic happiness and talent, though this contrast between this outward façade and the tyranny and despotism they experienced at home under Pavel's strict rule serves as another example of exactly the source of the picture of hypocrisy Chekhov paints in his work. When Chekhov was sixteen, Pavel mismanaged his own finances quite spectacularly during the process of building a new house which resulted in a declaration of bankruptcy and a subsequent fleeing to Moscow to avoid debtor's prison.

By now Chekhov's elder brothers Alexander and Nikolay were already studying at Moscow University so the majority of the family reunited there, living in poverty, a change of circumstance which left Yevgeniya in a state of emotional and physical infirmity. Chekhov, however, remained in Taganrog living with a man called Selivanov who, like Lopakhin in *The Cherry Orchard*, had bailed out the family for the price of their house, to complete his education. Although his board was free with Selivanov, he was left to pay for his schooling, covering the costs and surviving on a disparate income cobbled together from the selling off of family possessions and bolstered by private tutoring, catching and selling goldfinches, and by writing and selling short sketches to the newspapers. Every ruble he could spare from his education and his now less frequent theatre visits he sent to his family in Moscow, enclosed with humourous letters designed to cheer them up in their poverty and misery. He now began to take a more earnest interest in his education, reading extensively and analytically, including the works of Cervantes, Turgenev, Goncharov and Schopenhauer. Meanwhile he enjoyed a series of closeted love affairs, including one with the wife of one of his teachers. His schooling completed and a scholarship to Moscow University obtained, he moved there in 1879 and rejoined his family.

He now assumed responsibility for the family, supporting them by writing regular satirical sketches and vignettes of contemporary Russian lifestyle under pseudonyms such as 'Antosha Chekhonte' and 'Man Without a Spleen', and his prodigious output earned him first a reputation as a reputable chronicler and then, in 1882, a regular position writing for Oskolki, a journal owned by Nicolai Leykin, the most successful Russian publisher at the time. Although the wit and brevity of his work here prevails through much of his later writing, it was considerably harsher in tone, perhaps a reflection of the stressful position of poverty, study and patriarch in which he found himself. In 1884, he qualified as a physician and, although he earned little from the profession and often treated the poor free of charge, he considered this his principle profession. At this time and for the next two years he would regularly cough up blood, a symptom of tuberculosis with which he was all too familiar as a physician. However, not wishing to "submit himself to be sounded by his colleagues", he kept the condition to himself. The continued success of his periodical writing enabled him to move the family into progressively more comfortable accommodation, and then in 1886 he received an invitation to write for *Novoye Vremya* (*New Times*), owned and edited by the millionaire media magnate Alexey Suvorin. Paying double per line what Anton received from Leykin and being given three times the column inches he took the offer immediately and became close friends with Suvorin, a friendship which would last his lifetime.

His work at these periodicals was not the sole extent of his literary output, for in 1885 he published a short story, *The Huntsman*, which quickly attracted scholarly attention and recognition. The sixty-four year old celebrated writer Grigorovich wrote to him shortly after it first appeared on the shelves, saying "you have *real* talent—a talent which places you in the front rank among writers in the new generation." The letter continues in this effusive manner before resolving to offer Chekhov the practical advice to slow down, write less, and concentrate on literary quality. In reply, Chekhov admitted that he had been struck "like a thunderbolt" on reading the letter, confessing to hitherto writing his stories "the way reporters write up their notes about fires - mechanically, half-consciously, caring nothing about either the reader or myself." In making such an honest admission, Chekhov arguably undersold himself as a serious author, for despite the appearance of a nonchalant and casual approach, later analysis and comparison of early manuscripts reveals a huge extent of careful revision indicating a far more involved, authorial approach than he allows himself in correspondence with Grigorovich. Nonetheless, receiving such warm congratulation and encouragement along with such earnest advice from so respected an author caused Chekhov to sit up straight and approach his writing with far more serious, artistic ambition. Now twenty-six, and with the patronage of such a revered and loved author, his collection of short stories entitled *V Sumerkakh* (*At Dusk*) won him the much coveted Pushkin Prize, awarded "for the best literary production distinguished by high artistic worth".

Following this act of formal recognition and somewhat burnt out by the years of continued literary output his enduring success afforded him the time and the money to take a sabbatical, so he engaged in a journey to the Ukraine in 1887 whereupon he was reminded of the beauty of the Steppe. This excursion inspired the novella *The Steppe* which he started on his return, and which he described in a letter to Grigorovich as "something rather odd and much too original", and which was eventually published in *Severny Vestnik* (*The Northern Herald*). Later that year he was commissioned by a theatre manager to write a play, and a fortnight later Chekhov produced *Ivanov* which, though he considered the process "sickening" and described in a letter to his brother Alexander in the manner of a comic portrait, it was a huge success and was widely regarded as a work of excellent and noteworthy originality. Furthermore this period is considered the source of a literary device noted by Ilia Gurliand, who overheard it in conversation, as Chekhov's Gun; "if in act 1 you have a pistol hanging on the wall, then it must fire in the last act". Then, in 1889, his brother Nikolay died as a result of tuberculosis. Their brother Mikhail, who recorded Anton's depression during the period of mourning after the death, had been researching prisons as part of his studies in law, and Anton too became interested and eventually somewhat obsessed with the idea of prison reform.

This newfound interest in the humanitarian questions surrounding the prison system, combined with a conceivable yet subconscious desire to escape the close environment of mourning surrounding his brother's death, led Chekhov to journey to the penal colony Sakhalin, an island off the far East coast of Russia, where he spent three months interviewing convicts and settlers with the aim of compiling a census of the island. He made several now notorious remarks to his sister about what he witnessed (among others, a relatively lighthearted and blunt description of Tomsk, "a very dull town. To judge from the drunkards whose acquaintance I have made, and from the intellectual people who have come to the hotel to pay their respects to me, the inhabitants are very dull, too." [-the inhabitants of Tomsk later retaliated by erecting a mocking statue of Chekhov]). More seriously, though, many of the things he saw during this trip horrified him, writing that "there were times I felt that I saw before me the extreme limits of man's degradation." Among these was the plight of the children of the island, describing one such incident in his journals:

> On the Amur steamer going to Sakhalin, there was a convict who
> had murdered his wife and wore fetters on his legs. His daughter, a
> little girl of six, was with him. I noticed wherever the convict moved

the little girl scrambled after him, holding on to his fetters. At night
the child slept with the convicts and soldiers all in a heap together.

Concluding that the solution to this inhumanity lay not with charity and philanthropy, but with Government intervention and reform, he wrote *Ostrov Sakhalin* (*The Island of Sakhalin*), a work of social science which was praised, not for its literary brilliance, but for its steady and worthy informativeness, which was serialised and published in 1893-4. Though this initial work which stemmed from the trip was not literary in nature, the extended contact and expansive experience he received found itself expressed in *The Murder*, a story which, though longer than his others, is still considered short in nature.

In 1892 Chekhov had bought Melikhovo, a small country estate forty miles north of Moscow, which was his and his family's home until 1899. He joked about his residence there, quipping to his friend Ivan Leontyev that "it's nice to be a Lord" though this lighthearted remark belies the seriousness with which he undertook his responsibilities as a landlord. Within a few years of his taking residence there he had established his usefulness and sense of duty to the peasants, affording them relief from the 1892 outbreaks of cholera and bouts of famine, and building three schools, a fire station and a clinic, and offering his services as a physician to the peasantry of the surrounding countryside. Often he would find queues of patients lining up outside his door in the morning who had travelled by foot or by cart to receive treatment, and frequently he was called out to visit those too sick to travel. His brother Mikhail who resided with the family at Melikhovo recorded this honourable commitment to his role as estate physician, writing

> from the first day that Chekhov moved to Melikhovo, the sick began flocking to him from twenty miles around. They came on foot or were brought in carts, and often he was fetched to patients at a distance. Sometimes from early in the morning peasant women and children were standing before his door waiting.

Though these demanding hours left him with significantly less time for writing, they enriched his literary output for he was able to write informatively and genuinely about the peasantry and their living conditions, most notably in his short story *Peasants*. He did, however, visit those belonging to the upper-classes as well, though he was not enamoured by them, writing in his journal "Aristocrats? The same ugly bodies and physical uncleanliness, the same toothless old age and disgusting death, as with market-women".

He began to write arguably his most famous work, *The Seagull*, in 1894, in a lodge he had built himself in the orchard on the estate. Its first night on 17th October 1896 at the Alexandrinsky Theatre in Petersburg was something of a fiasco; it was booed by the audience, many of whom left, and this poor reception saw Chekhov fall out of love with the theatre. However, despite its poor reception by the play-going audience, it impressed the theatre director Vladimir Nemirovich-Danchenko so much that he proceeded to convince his colleague Constantin Stanislavski to take the play on and direct it in the innovative, progressive Moscow Art Theatre. This revival, in 1898, for the less-closeted Moscow audience was enormously well-received. Whereas the Petersburg performance had rendered the play literally and played down its more psychoanalytical aspects, Stanislavski payed far closer attention to the play's psychological realism and brought the deeply buried subtleties, lost on the Petersburg boards and on the audience's narrow-mindedness, to the surface. The play was such a success here that the Art Theatre commissioned further work from Chekhov, staging *Uncle Vanya* which he had completed in 1896. Furthermore, the positive critical reception had a restorative effect on Chekhov's interest in stage writing.

However, by now Chekhov's health condition was worsening, having suffered a major haemorrhage of the lungs in 1897 while visiting Moscow. His early reluctance to be seen by doctors prevailed and he protested to the notion of entering a clinic, though he eventually assented whereupon a formal diagnosis of the tuberculosis on the upper part of his lungs was reached, and the doctors ordered various changes in his lifestyle. His father then died in 1898, after which Chekhov bought a plot of land on the outskirts of Yalta and proceeded to build a villa, moving his mother and sister in with him the following year. Even though he pursued the enjoyment of gardening he had developed while at Melikhovo by planting trees and flowers, he kept dogs and tame cranes and regularly received highly regarded company such as Leo Tolstoy and Maxim Gorky, he spoke of a sense of relief upon each occasion of his leaving this "hot Siberia" for Moscow or to travel further afield. While here, he wrote two more plays for the Art Theatre, though these were composed with much greater difficulty; he remarked that unlike his youth when "[he] wrote serenely, the way [he eats] pancakes now". These two plays, *Three Sisters* and *The Cherry Orchard* took over a year each.

A quiet marriage to Olga Knipper on 25th May 1901 was performed in keeping with the position of suspicion he had always had towards weddings, with a small ceremony and little outside attention. Knipper was an actress whom he had met at the rehearsals for *The Seagull*, their marriage conformed to his stipulations;

> By all means I will be married if you wish it. But on these conditions: everything must be as it has been hitherto - that is, she must live in Moscow while I live in the country, and I will come and see her ... give me a wife who, like the moon, won't appear in my sky every day.

This proved convenient as Knipper remained in Moscow performing his work and that of contemporary playwrights, and their long-distance correspondence features various treasured pieces of writing, be they shared complaints about Stanislavski's method of direction or advice from Chekhov to Knipper as to her performances in his plays. Prior to the marriage, Chekhov had been considered "Russia's most elusive literary bachelor", preferring brief liaisons and dalliances with unknown women, or brothels, to commitment. Chekhov then wrote one of his most famous stories, *The Lady with the Dog*, depicting a casual encounter between two strangers who, despite their best efforts and risking the security, stability and respectability of their family lives, find themselves irrevocably drawn to one another.

Chekhov's tuberculosis was finally getting the better of him, and by May 1904 it was quite clear that his death was imminent. Despite this, Mikhail recorded that "everyone who saw him secretly thought the end was not far off, but the nearer [he] was to the end, the less he seemed to realise it". He set off for the German town Badenweiler on

3rd June, writing cheerful, witty letters to his sister describing variously the food and the surroundings, while assuring both her and his mother that his health was improving; his last letter contained a sardonic complaint about the German women's fashion. The circumstances of his death have become one of "the greatest set pieces of literary history", and are most accurately recorded in this, Knipper's own account from her diaries, written in 1908:

> Anton sat up unusually straight and said loudly and clearly (although he knew almost no German): *Ich sterbe* ("I'm dying"). The doctor calmed him, took a syringe, gave him an injection of camphor and ordered champagne. Anton took a full glass, examined it, smiled at me and said: 'It's a long time since I drank champagne.' He drained it, lay quietly on his left side, and I just had time to run to him and lean across the bed and call to him, but he had stopped breathing and was sleeping peacefully as a child.

His body, transferred to Moscow in a refrigerated railway car whose purpose was for fresh oysters, was then interred next to his father at Novodevichy Cemetery in Moscow. Although thousands of mourners mistakenly followed the pomp and circumstance of the military funeral procession for the also deceased General Keller, many hundreds of thousands of readers, writers and actors have followed correctly the path he pioneered for the short story and for twentieth century realism.

Quotes

Any idiot can face a crisis - it's day to day living that wears you out.

Medicine is my lawful wife and literature my mistress; when I get tired of one, I spend the night with the other.

People who lead a lonely existence always have something on their minds that they are eager to talk about.

Doctors are just the same as lawyers; the only difference is that lawyers merely rob you, whereas doctors rob you and kill you too.

If you are afraid of loneliness, do not marry.

Knowledge is of no value unless you put it into practice.

Don't tell me the moon is shining; show me the glint of light on broken glass.

I promise to be an excellent husband, but give me a wife who, like the moon, will not appear every day in my sky.

Let us learn to appreciate there will be times when the trees will be bare, and look forward to the time when we may pick the fruit.

Life does not agree with philosophy: There is no happiness that is not idleness, and only what is useless is pleasurable.

There is nothing new in art except talent.

A good upbringing means not that you won't spill sauce on the tablecloth, but that you won't notice it when someone else does.

Love, friendship and respect do not unite people as much as a common hatred for something.

The world perishes not from bandits and fires, but from hatred, hostility, and all these petty squabbles.

Advertising is the very essence of democracy.

Faith is an aptitude of the spirit. It is, in fact, a talent: you must be born with it.

People don't notice whether it's winter or summer when they're happy.

We shall find peace. We shall hear angels, we shall see the sky sparkling with diamonds.

You must trust and believe in people or life becomes impossible.

If you cry 'forward', you must without fail make plain in what direction to go.

No matter how corrupt and unjust a convict may be, he loves fairness more than anything else. If the people placed over him are unfair, from year to year he lapses into an embittered state characterized by an extreme lack of faith.

When you're thirsty and it seems that you could drink the entire ocean that's faith; when you start to drink and finish only a glass or two that's science.

All of life and human relations have become so incomprehensibly complex that, when you think about it, it becomes terrifying and your heart stands still.

How unbearable at times are people who are happy, people for whom everything works out.

Man is what he believes.

One must be a god to be able to tell successes from failures without making a mistake.

To advise is not to compel.

A fiancee is neither this nor that: he's left one shore, but not yet reached the other.

Money, like vodka, turns a person into an eccentric.

No psychologist should pretend to understand what he does not understand... Only fools and charlatans know everything and understand nothing.

Only entropy comes easy.

The more refined one is, the more unhappy.

The thirst for powerful sensations takes the upper hand both over fear and over compassion for the grief of others.

The University brings out all abilities, including incapability.

To judge between good or bad, between successful and unsuccessful would take the eye of a God.

We learn about life not from plusses alone, but from minuses as well.

When a woman isn't beautiful, people always say, 'You have lovely eyes, you have lovely hair.'

A writer is not a confectioner, a cosmetic dealer, or an entertainer.

Doctors are the same as lawyers; the only difference is that lawyers merely rob you, whereas doctors rob you and kill you too.

It's easier to write about Socrates than about a young woman or a cook.

Reason and justice tell me there's more love for humanity in electricity and steam than in chastity and vegetarianism.

The sea has neither meaning nor pity.

The wealthy are always surrounded by hangers-on; science and art are as well.

When a lot of remedies are suggested for a disease, that means it can't be cured.

When an actor has money he doesn't send letters, he sends telegrams.

About Us

We have many volumes of Chekhov available, together with other short story compilations, novels, essays and poetry from the most celebrated writers of all time. Use the search words 'miniature masterpieces' for other great short story compilations from incredible writers such as Arthur Conan Doyle, Joseph Conrad, Honore De Balzac, Robert Louis Stevenson and Rudyard Kipling among others. Use search words 'portable poetry' to find illuminating compositions by world renowned poets such as Rabindranth Tagore, Walt Whitman, Edgar Allan Poe, Thomas Hardy and Oscar Wilde among others. Use search words 'word to the wise' for some of the greatest novels, plays and essays ever written from history's very best including Jane Austen, Charles Dickens, Wilkie Collins, Elizabeth Gaskell, Anthony Trollope and Anthony Hope. Along with Anton Chekhov we offer many other foreign writers that have been translated to English such as Rumi, Henrik Ibsen, Miguel Cervantes, Dante Alighieri, Leo Tolstoy and Fyodor Dostoyevsky.